SHOOT THE MESSENGER

A REVERSE HAREM SPACE FANTASY
#1 MESSENGER CHRONICLES

PIPPA DaCOSTA

'Shoot the Messenger'

1# Messenger Chronicles

Pippa DaCosta

Urban Fantasy & Science Fiction Author

Subscribe to Pippa's mailing list at pippadacosta.com & get free ebooks.

www.pippadacosta.com

SUMMARY

In the Halow system, one of Earth's sister star systems, tek and magic—humans and the fae—are at war.

Kesh Lasota is a ghost in the machine. Invisible to tek, she's hired by the criminal underworld to carry illegal messages through the Halow system. But when one of those messages kills its recipient, Kesh finds herself on the run with a bounty on her head and a quick-witted marshal on her tail.

Proving her innocence should be straightforward—until a warfae steals the evidence she needs. The fae haven't been seen in Halow in over a thousand years. And this one—a brutally efficient killer able to wield tek—should not exist. But neither should Kesh.

As Kesh's carefully crafted lie of a life crumbles around her, she knows being invisible is no longer an option. To hunt the fae, to stop him from destroying a thousand-year fragile peace, she must resurrect the horrors of her past.

Kesh Lasota was a ghost. Now she's back, and there's only one thing she knows for certain. Nobody shoots the messenger and gets away with it.

～

IMPORTANT NOTE: The Messenger series is a *reverse harem*. The harem elements develop during the series. This is NOT a love triangle.

PART I

"Father, O Father, what do we here,
In this land of unbelief and fear?
The Land of Dreams is better far
Above the light of the Morning Star."

Old Earthen, William Blake

CHAPTER 1

"*You have eighteen seconds to live.*" My hovering drone's voice sounded flat, the words spoken in the same way all secure messages were delivered. He might have equally said the weather outside Calicto's environmental domes had settled today—no ion storms on the horizon—or reminded the recipient to pick up a case of salt on his return journey from the mines.

An awkward silence fell over the restaurant. The recipient—a stocky man of some fifty years with arms and legs the size of ventilation ducts—blinked in disbelief at the drone, and then narrowed those gritty eyes on me.

"Sota?" I asked, professionally formal.

Sota—the drone—wasn't much larger than a soccer ball. He didn't look at all threatening to anyone unfamiliar with military tek. *"Sixteen seconds."*

The recipient dipped his greasy fingers into a small cup of synthetic cleaning fluid and wiped his hands dry on the shirt stretched over his barrel chest. "Is this some kind of joke, Messenger?"

I had delivered some unusual messages—a happy

birthday ditty at a funeral, dates for illegal inter-species rendezvous, packages of cyn, and parcels that squeaked in a decidedly living and illegal way. It wasn't my job to query the messages, just deliver them. But an eighteen-second death threat delivered by a drone and what he saw as a harmless messenger girl? Yeah, some might consider it amusing.

I flicked my fingers against my palm, activating the ocular display and schedule for the day. The recipient's name blinked low in my vision, along with his date and place of birth, occupation and current address. "You are machinist, José Crater of Calicto's Sector C, Level Four, Container Zero Zero Five, born GE thirty fifteen?"

He smirked, fat lips stretching. "That's me. But you'd better check your source. That message is definitely *not* for me." He leaned back in his chair and spread his arms, oozing confidence. *Too much* confidence.

I discreetly scanned the other tables. Seated at all of them were men and women equally smug as Crater. They chatted and laughed and did all those normal things, but several were carefully side-eying us with more than a passing interest. Most wore the typical ragged mineworker overalls. Probably just clocked off the day shift. Crater and his crew weren't just machinists. People like him were the reason I delivered messages armed with a hot pistol and electrotek whip.

I ignored the urge to reach for my whip and tacked a smile on my face that suggested, *"Hey, I'm just the messenger. Let's all just get along."*

Crater grinned back. He was in his territory, surrounded by his people. If this was a joke, it was on me.

Sota buzzed in the air to my left, hovering around seven feet off the ground, patiently waiting for my instructions. SOTA—Secure Observational Tactical Assistant—was seldom quiet.

I pulled a palm-sized signature strip from my coat and tossed it onto the table. "The contents of the message are not my concern, sir. Acknowledge receipt and I'll be out of your hair."

I winced. The guy likely had more hair on his back than on his head. His big grin wobbled. "I'm not acknowledging any*tang*." He grunted, accent slipping into the outer Halow dialect. "Who sent it?" he asked.

"The sender is anonymous," I drawled. Most secure messages were sent anonymously, a safeguard against the messenger getting picked up by the marshals and snitching on the senders. My messages had never been intercepted.

He snorted. "Do you know who I am?"

I considered reciting the information I had in his sizeable file, just to irk him, but the onlookers were losing the humor in their glares. I did know of his reputation. He spearheaded the mineworkers' union on a lovely backwater rock near Calicto's domes. He might have started out honorable, but word in the sinks was that he and his men were itching for a fight with the Halow government.

The mineworkers' creed and their arguments were none of my concern. I'd done my job, delivered the message. It was time to leave. "The contents of a message, the sender, and the recipient are none of my concern," I repeated in a monotone. "I'm just the messenger. Acknowledge receipt and I'll be on my way. A thumbprint will do."

If he didn't acknowledge receipt, I didn't get my cut, which would mean another week of tasteless rations and no water. I couldn't remember the last time I'd tasted real water—the wet kind, not the synthetic syrup.

He picked up the signature strip, pinched it between his chunky fingers, and regarded it with a sneer. "I've got a message for you to send back."

I sighed and rolled my eyes so hard it *hurt*. "Do you know what anonymous means, Mister Crater? It means put your fucking mark on the signature strip and acknowledge receipt before we have ourselves a disagreement." I peeled back my long coat, revealing the coiled metal-linked whip and holstered pistol. Neither weapon was common Halow tek and both would like to rip strips off Crater.

To his credit, the surprise on his face was genuine, if diluted by years of lines and fractures. His cracked lips quivered. Right now, he would be wondering how a girl like me—armed to the collar of my long coat—had walked through the restaurant's security sweeps without setting off a single alarm. Few people took the time to really consider the secure part in *Secure* Messenger, and fewer knew how it was done. I had just shot up in his estimations. Unfortunately, that new respect also meant the death threat suddenly had teeth.

Crater shot to his feet, bumping the table and knocking over his cleaning fluid. I snatched for my whip. Someone nearby let out a bark of alarm. Weapons rattled. Crater opened his mouth, but whatever he was about to yell never left his lips. A precision blast tore off his lower jaw and ripped out much of his cheek. Half his face vanished in a splash of blood and bone, and the big man dropped like a sack of machine parts, dead before he hit the ground.

I blinked, clearing a red blur from my right eye. Shock sank its claws into time, slowing everything around me to a crawl.

Sniper.

The open hatch leading out onto the public catwalk was the only line of sight into the restaurant. Through the hatch, I saw people streaming back and forth, sliding in and out of view. But across the walkway, over the cavernous proportions of the central plaza, a flash of light glinted off a lens. My ocular readout measured the distance as 650 yards over a crowd and through cycling air currents—an impossible shot, even with guided ballistics.

Time slammed back into motion. Crater's associates exploded from their tables. A pistol blast singed my hair. I whirled and ran for the exit. Another shot splattered a burning ball of sparks against the wall. I veered left, darting into the security sweeps. The system let me pass on through without so much as a blip, but when Crater's people rushed inside, guns hot, alarms shrilled and bars slammed down, sealing them inside with their howled curses.

I dashed out of the restaurant and into the milling crowd.

My hand instinctively rested on my whip. Magic buzzed up my arm, eager to be unleashed. A glance back through the crowd and it appeared clear. Crater's people weren't following, but they would as soon as they hacked their own security.

I strode on, keeping my head down. I'd threatened Crater, twice including the original message, and I had been two feet away when his brain matter blew out the side of his face. It would be difficult to argue I wasn't the one who'd killed him. This was bad, but not over yet.

"Sota, what's the quickest route to the source of that shot?"

My drone wouldn't have missed the shot or its source. He captured and recorded everything.

"The quickest route to getting dead, Kesh?" he replied, voice back to his normal, virtually human drawl and dripping with sarcasm. He hovered behind my shoulder, staying low to keep our pursuers from spotting him. "There's a tram arriving in three minutes," he added, unprompted. "If we hurry, we can board, and we'll be back at your container in approximately twenty minutes."

Sota's plan was entirely too predictable and typical of the drone, who rarely thought much beyond his own self-preservation. "Sota, show me the route to where the shooter was holed up. Now."

An arrow blinked in my vision, pointing the way over catwalks, across the plaza and into what looked like a block of habitat containers still under construction. Sota whispered smoothly, *Take the drone home. Spend the night in—*

"Shh. They won't follow us." We crossed the plaza. So far, so good. "They'll think I ran for the trams."

"Oh. Fine," Sota huffed.

A smile lifted my lips. For an ex-military drone, he had a coward's protocols. That's what happened when you spliced the artificial intelligence of a personal assistant with an attack drone's processors. It made for some interesting late-night conversations.

Sota hovered closer to my shoulder, stirring my hair. "Did you see what happened to his face?" he mock-whispered. "I don't want that to happen to my face."

"You don't have a face."

I veered off, out of the crowd, toward the massive stacks of residential containers. Digital security threw a laser net across the site's entrance. Teasing a few magical threads, I sent out a mental push. The laser-like mesh peeled open, inviting me inside. I stepped through, and Sota buzzed in low behind me. The lasers zipped closed behind us.

Sota scanned the yard. With space inside Calicto's environmental domes at a premium, the site entrance immediately funneled into a narrow security scanner. Sota's single large lens of an eye screwed down, reducing its "pupil" to a red dot. That intense red dot of the SOTA drones was often the last thing many soldiers saw right before they had their bones flash-incinerated. But Sota wouldn't—*couldn't* hurt me.

"Down, boy. I'll protect you." I flashed Sota a grin and plucked my whip free. Its crackling magic-charged length uncoiled, spilling blue sparks across the floor and over my boots. "Stay close."

He tucked in close, static energy tickling my neck. Just like at the restaurant security, we walked through the scanners, barely stirring more than a fine layer of dust. As far as the tek was concerned, we didn't exist.

"You are creepy," Sota reported, the words all the more amusing when coming from a tactical drone.

Around us, the habitat containers had been slotted into place, each potential new home stacked on top of another, climbing twenty stories high.

I entered the nearest container and peered out through an open window. Someday soon, it would be someone's single window overlooking the plaza outside. At ground level, we were too low for the shooter to get a clear shot. He or she had to be several levels above.

My boots left shallow impressions in a layer of metal shaving dust as I walked down the single main corridor toward the stairs module. The air tasted metallic and tinged with something organic that tugged on my memory. Something sweet and tempting.

I shook my head, shrugging off the familiar sensation. "Any movement ahead of us?"

"Nothing on this level."

"Anything above?"

His motors whirred. "Maybe."

I rolled my eyes. "Can you be more specific?"

"No, something is blocking my sensors beyond twenty meters."

That was unusual. Sota's sensors were some of the most advanced available. If they were blocked, someone was deliberately hiding something—or themselves—from scanners.

"Activate stealth," I ordered.

"Really?" His motors whined.

"Do we have to go through this every time?"

"It's a terrible drain on my batteri—"

Sota received the look I reserved for assholes and disobedient drones everywhere.

His background buzzing ceased. His matte black, chunky outer shell cracked open and reformed into a conical shape. His coating rippled, turning him almost entirely transparent except for a slight reflective dissonance with his surroundings. He couldn't activate his weapons while stealthed, but he made a great scout.

I nodded at my drone and tracked his rippling distortion in the air until he disappeared up the stairs. A small box in the corner of my vision relayed Sota's point of view. I watched from the bottom of the stairs as he drifted down a corridor exactly like the others in this block. Vacant doorways gaped left and right.

"Stop," I whispered. "Look down." He focused on the

gray patches tracking down the corridor. Footprints. Large, with deep treads, likely male and probably from the mines. Factory workers weren't equipped with heavy work boots.

"Careful," I warned Sota.

He focused his lens down the corridor.

"I don't see anything else..."

He couldn't reply, not while stealthed. Something I'd promised I would rectify once I had the right equipment for his next upgrade.

I climbed the stairs and saw the boot prints leading away. They originated in the first right-hand container. A quick glance inside revealed a gap in the wall where it hadn't yet been sealed to its neighbor. A plastic sheet flapped in the wind. And outside, a crane's boom rested a few meters from the edge. That had been our suspect's point of entry. Whoever he was, he must have had balls the size of boulders to climb that crane. This had been planned, just like the message. *You have eighteen seconds to live.* Whoever orchestrated this had lain in wait, knowing I would arrive with that message. Eighteen seconds. Long enough to line up the target in their crosshairs. That didn't account for the impossible shot through various air currents and a busy crowd. Something *more* did that.

Sota's outline wobbled with dissent. He didn't want to do this. But when I salvaged him, this had been part of the deal. I fixed him, and he worked for me. Besides, leaving wasn't an option. Crater's crew wouldn't forget I'd apparently assassinated their leader right in front of them, unless I found evidence that I hadn't fired the shot. Sota would have recorded the scene, but it wouldn't be enough. Images could be doctored. Plus, Crater's kind were the kill first, ask questions later type. Oh, they may eventually realize I hadn't actually taken my pistol out and a point-blank pistol shot couldn't have made the bloody mess that had been Crater's face, right after tossing my remains into the Calicto wind. What was another dead messenger to them? I'd already lost my commission. But my reputation was still salvageable if I caught the real killer.

The boot prints led me down the corridor. My whip's magically charged tendrils licked at my ankles. Sota was a ripple in the air a few meters ahead. With a brief nod from me, he drifted forward through a doorway. Sota's feed flickered in my vision. He looked down, revealing a sweet piece of kit: a high-powered rifle resting on its stand.

I stepped into the room. "Deactivate stealth."

Sota hovered in close to the rifle while his gears and plating rebuilt his armor, once again cloaking him in matte black. His lens grew, telescopic action letting Sota get an up-close look at the weapon. "Its construction doesn't match any in my databanks."

If a tactical drone didn't recognize it, then the rifle was rare, possibly unique.

"Self-guided projectiles," Sota went on. "Neuro-controlled. This rifle is not human compatible." Sota's voice held a note of awe. "Is it wrong that I'm a little turned on right now?"

I chuckled and crouched on the opposite side of the gun. "You're always turned on." Reaching out a hand, I stopped short of touching the weapon. The last thing I needed was to leave evidence of my being here.

Sota swiveled toward me. "Kesh!"

A hand twisted in my hair, yanking me up and shoving me forward. My cheek hit the wall—rattling my teeth and igniting fiery pain through my jaw. I flicked my whip, or tried to, but a viselike hand twisted my arm behind my back, angling my shoulder on the edge of agony. Another twitch and my attacker would break my arm.

"Retaliate with equal force!" I hissed, knowing Sota would fry this asshole in seconds. I'd lost Sota's view in my vision when he dropped stealth, but I didn't need to see whoever it was. Any second now, Sota's armory would buzz and turn this guy to dust. Any second...

"Sorry, Messenger," a smooth male voice purred, coming in close to deliver his words and brushing them against the curve of my neck like a lover delivering promises. "Your drone is not responding."

I jerked my head back, slamming my skull into bone with a satisfying crunch. He grunted, grip loosening. I bucked free and whirled on him, teeth bared, whip cracking, sparks flying—and froze.

Protofae.

No.

It can't be.

This one didn't look like the willowy wraiths often depicted in history books. Strength radiated from a powerful physique honed over the years for battle. Under his arm, he'd trapped Sota, and where his sleeve rode up, dark, intricate tattoos marked his skin. Those marks told me exactly what he was. A warfae.

A dribble of blood ran from his nose. He ran his tongue over his lip, licking it clean.

Impossible. He couldn't be here. The treaty forbade it.

His lips held a wild snarl, the type issuing a warning. That same warning burned in his long-lashed blue eyes.

Sota was silent. The fae's bicep strained, trapping my drone still.

I blinked, almost expecting him to vanish and for this to be a hallucination. But he hadn't moved, and there, gripped in his hand and pressed against Sota's casing, a slim, silver device blinked a single blue light: a portable EMP. One hit and Sota's personality would be fried. Sota was... unique. Losing him wasn't an option.

Sota's red eye stared through me.

"Don't..." I pushed out an empty hand, showing the fae how I wasn't attacking. If he decided I was too much trouble, my whip wouldn't save me. I scrabbled around my head for the correct protocols, but the shock of seeing him here tripped me up. Should I kneel to him? I would have, once.

His eyes flicked between the drone and me, reading my face, my fear, scrutinizing it all. Sharp, angular features spoke of the cruelty he was capable of. His dark hair was pulled back in a tight, intricate braid and clasped close against his skull, further accentuating his knuckle-breaking bone structure. Black battle tattoos tracked down his neck and disappeared beneath his collar. The more tattoos a fae had, the more enemies they had killed. How many did he have?

I had tattoos like his, but I wasn't fae. I never would be, never could be, despite my sacrifices.

I swallowed. "That drone... Please, don't take hi—it." How could I explain to a fae that I needed Sota—needed tek—like I needed a part of me? "I don't care what you are. I won't tell anyone you were here."

He regarded the whip and pistol and raked his derisive glare over me, making it clear how he looked down on my kind—humankind—with disdain. "No, you won't." He backed out of the door.

No, no, no. My drone was irreplaceable. I'd built him from discarded scraps and fragments of code, given him a new life. To begin with, he had served a purpose, but he had grown into more than a tool. Sota was my friend.

I dashed after the fae and darted down the corridor, following snippets of his shadow. Fae were too fast—one of the many reasons they thought themselves "superior." But I'd learned to be fast too. Learned to run with them, *hunt* with them and to be hunted.

It had been so long, and those memories were so deeply hidden they almost felt as though they belonged to another person. How could he be here?

It didn't matter. I needed to win this.

That damn drone was everything to me, and more. The secrets he held. If they got into the wrong hands...

Seeing him swing around a corner and hammer down the stairs, I dashed ahead, bounced off the wall and leaped down the stairs in one pounce, landing and launching into a run. There, ahead, he sprinted in a blur, dark braid lashing. Maybe I could catch him. Maybe...

He shot through an open segment of a container and launched into the air, apparently at... nothing. He fell— and landed in a perfect roll on a neighboring block of containers. I didn't hesitate. Didn't slow down. My boot hit the edge and I sprang. There was never any doubt I would make it. I hit the container roof and fell into a roll, snapping pain through my shoulder. The momentum carried me onto my feet. He was gone again, darting downward, leaping and vaulting over gaps and barriers— down, down, down. Impossibly fast. I hesitated at the edge of a 160-foot drop. A hovertram pulled away from the tramstop below us.

The jump I needed to make was too far... Recycled air pushed at my face, whispering encouragement. He was already racing toward the edge of another roof, free-running closer and closer toward the moving tram.

It was already too late. I'd never catch him in time.

I plucked my pistol free, lined up my sights—

He dropped off the edge, fell through the air like an arrow, and landed catlike, poised on the tram's roof.

Crosshairs danced across his back. I tugged the trigger. The pistol spat and my heart leaped. The fae feigned left, avoiding the bullet as easily as if I'd thrown a stone.

He has Sota...

The warfae straightened on the tram's roof, rocking with its movement. He turned. The wind tugged at his dark clothing and whipped his braid across his shoulder. A vicious smile slashed across his lips, the kind of smile I'd seen before, heralding the death of so many. Malice flashed in his eyes. His glare bored through me, daring me to chase him down.

I lowered my pistol.

Under his arm, Sota was silent, his lens dark. I reached through the mental link but found it stretched too thin to be of any use. "I'm coming for you, my friend..." I sent. The words had barely left when the link snapped, whipping back against my psyche. There was no way of knowing if Sota had heard.

I pointed at the warfae and mouthed, "I'll find *you*."

With the challenge laid down, his savage smile grew until the tram carried him out of sight between container towers.

Dry air washed over me from a hovercab above. I turned on the spot, suddenly exposed. My message recipient was dead, killed by me—apparently. And a warfae had just stolen the evidence of my innocence.

Sirens squealed in the distance.

I turned away from the edge and dropped onto rickety scaffolding, out of plain sight and into thick shadows where metal clanged and cloying air hung limp.

I had to find Sota. If that fae discovered my secrets, more than just my life would be at stake.

CHAPTER 2

*L*ights blinked on in my habitat container, welcoming me home with warm "tropical sunset" hues. Sota had set the theme, saying he liked to feel the warmth in the light. I'd given up correcting him on the limitations of his *feelings*. He liked his fiction. Now the white and orange halos of color splashed against the wall only reminded me that he wasn't here to argue.

"Lights, default."

The lights lifted to a brighter white, illuminating the small rectangular space I called home.

The one window looked out into a narrow gulley between containers, affording a view consisting of a 5x5 patch of corrugated cladding for the identical rows of containers opposite mine. I pulled the blind down and flicked a switch to turn on the fake rain-on-glass projection. I hadn't felt real rain in a long time. The projection was nothing like the real thing. The fresh, clean smell, the pitter-pattering sound. *Best not to think on it...* I'd already woken too many memories today.

Unhooking my whip and pistol, I set both weapons

down on the kitchen counter and shrugged off my coat. A few dark spots marred the coat's fabric. Any permanent marks would interfere with the garment's ability to enhance my tek-whispering. Hopefully, its self-clean coating would soon break down the blood.

I planted my hands on my hips and scanned my container. How was it possible this space felt *smaller*?

Sota's dock sat empty. Its receiving light blinked, searching for the drone's signal.

I would get him back.

So, the guy was fae... So, he'd killed a mineworker... I had faced much worse.

Tussling with the fae hadn't been on today's to-do list. Get up, go to work, deliver messages, come home again, rattle around my container, maybe drop by The Boot. My days weren't complicated. That's the way I liked it. Easy. No drama. That was the way it *had* to be.

I watched the fake rain stream down the projector screen. *Like a thousand tears.*

How long had it been? Five years? And in all that time I had never once slipped. Here, I was a nobody. Just a messenger. Invisible to people as well as tek. But now...?

This wasn't about me. It couldn't be. The fae had taken Sota because of the footage of the assassination, leaving me to take the fall. That was all.

I combed my fingers through my hair and winced as my nail snagged on a dried clump of something I didn't want to think too hard on. Stripping off, I stepped into the shower tube and braced both hands against the pads. Air mixed with chemicals blasted over me from above. The burn quickly faded to an almost pleasurable numbness. Dark, swirling thorn tattoos marked my skin. Sometimes I thought they looked like vines, other times like shackles.

Reminders. Brands. Memories. I pushed the thoughts away and ignored it all, like always.

At least Crater's death had been quick. The asshole hadn't seen his end coming. That had to be better than having death stalk you for weeks, months, years. A criminal like him, he must have known someone would take him out eventually. But why did the warfae want Crater dead? How was a mineworker embroiled with a fae who shouldn't exist? A fae who used tek, a fae who moved freely on Calicto a thousand years since the treaty. Enough damned time had passed that most common people thought they were a myth, a story told to keep foolish settlers from roaming into the no-go zones at the edges of Halow space.

Doesn't matter.

Sota had the evidence I needed. His footage of the scene was the only definitive proof that I was innocent. I had to get him back. Whatever Crater and the fae were involved in, I didn't need to know the whys or what-fors.

Dry-showered and skin buzzing, I dressed, tossed back a protein bar and flicked on the newsfeed. An image flickered in the air, recoiling from my resonance. I moved away, and the picture cleared.

"...was a prominent figure among the mineworkers' union, having successfully campaigned for a substantial ration increase..." I picked up my coat and brushed the dried blood off. "Authorities have admitted that there appears to be no recorded evidence of the assassination and that the security systems failed to detain the offender, who is still at large. Arcon—the manufacturer of ninety percent of Halo's surveillance and detainment systems—chose not to comment."

Arcon. I snorted a laugh. They had sent someone after

me after learning that an illegal messenger could stroll through their tek as easily as walking through an open door. Of course, they had brought all their ultra-enhanced tek with them. Their conclusion? I didn't exist. Tek-whisperers were a myth. Their security was infallible. That was the day I upped my delivery rates.

Was that how the fae had eluded Calicto's planet-wide scanners? How else might an armed fae move so freely in one of the most monitored societies in the Halow system?

My smile faded.

Everyone left a trail on Calicto, if you knew where to look.

I threw my coat over my shoulders and hitched my weapons. I was getting my drone back—and no mythical warfae would stand in my way.

~

THE AIR in the market gulley smelled like salted meats, sweating spices and the press of too many bodies all funneled into a narrow stretch of street wedged between two rows of tightly packed habitat containers. This was Sage, Calicto's B Sector, and my neighborhood. Vast fans hummed above, drawing air through the gulley and recycling it through various filters, only to push it out again below our feet, drier, and laced with something sweet and sickly. Some bureaucrat a million miles away probably had to tick a box labeled "Calicto Aid," and figured the smell of flowers would put smiles on our faces. Unfortunately, what they couldn't have known unless they'd bothered to take the time to visit, was that artificial fragrance mixed with Calicto's habitat air made a nauseating combination. I'd lived here for enough rotations that it no longer turned

22

my stomach, but it kept home container prices down and the tourists away—just the way Sector Bs like me preferred.

I carved through the crowds alone. Usually, Sota would be providing a running commentary, listing any new imports from around the Halow system. He prattled on about nonsense so often that I filtered him out, but now that I was alone, I missed the constant stream of information and found myself strangely disconnected from the goings-on around me. I also missed his early detection sensors. He could have spotted any of Crater's gang long before me. It was unlikely Crater's crew would track me back to B Sector—like their security sweeps, I'd whispered my way around any nearby monitoring devices, preventing them from capturing my image—but there was always a chance I'd missed a device, especially if any of his crew had ocular implants. Biotek was difficult to whisper around.

I nodded at a few familiar faces. Questions lit up in their eyes when they noticed I didn't have Sota shadowing me. I hurried deeper into the gulley where the lights struggled to penetrate the gloom. Naked cables crisscrossed the space above the gulley, turning the thoroughfare into a tunnel. It's widely known that all the "best" things happened in the sinks—the name given to this end of the gulley. "Best" for B sectors, generally meant rowdy, dirty and probably illegal. Cameras had long ago failed, leaving the authorities blind to the sinks, and none had dared to venture down here to fix them. *Not in sight, not in mind,* as Merry liked to say.

It was Merry I saw as I peeled back the thick, leathery drape and entered her ramshackle hut. Merry wore a high-collared coat, buttoned all the way from her ankles to her chin. I'd never seen her wear anything else, but I'd never seen her outside the hut either.

She muttered to herself, lost in concentration as she lifted storage boxes and shuffled various bits of substation trinkets around the large front desk.

"Merry." I let the drape fall closed behind me, muting the sinks' background hum.

"Yes, yes." Merry waved long fingers at me, either shooing me away or just acknowledging my arrival. She continued to flit about behind the desk, scurrying back and forth.

"Crater is dead."

"Crater, Crater... Should Merry know Crater?" she asked quickly.

"One of today's recipients and the mineworkers' union leader."

She stopped, straightened from her hunched posture, and finally looked over. "Oh." Her nose twitched, a sure sign she was disappointed. "Before or after Kesh get her cut?"

"Before." Her glossy marble-like eyes contracted. There was little Merry hated more than not getting paid. "It gets worse," I said. "Crater's crew think I killed their leader, and the evidence I didn't is on Sota, but he was stolen from me."

"Stolen?" She barked a short, tinny laugh and went back to her searching. "Must be some thief to steal drone from Kesh."

Some thief, indeed. I couldn't tell her about the fae. At best, she would think I was lying. At worst, she would alert the authorities and I'd suddenly be at the center of a planet-wide fae hunt and I did not want that heat. The less attention on me, the easier things were.

"Merry, I need to know who sent that message."

She shook her head. "No, no, no..." And pointed a finger. "Kesh know that information is secure. Merry not paid for snooping. Merry paid for discretion."

"I know that." I reined in the frustration from my voice, but Merry's ears heard everything. Her wiry eyebrows pinched inward. "But this is different," I told her. "He has Sota."

"Pfft, make another drone. Take another message. Innocence easy to prove. Surveillance." She circled her hand above her head, even though we both knew there was no surveillance in the sinks.

For people like Merry, it was easy to forget how the surveillance that monitored them, kept them *safe*, didn't apply to me. Normally, being a tek-whisperer was an advantage, but not today, not when I needed that proof. If there was any footage out there, it probably consisted of me running away from the scene.

"Sota is unique," I said carefully. "And you know there's no surveillance around me... You don't have to tell me who sent the message, just point me in the right direction. That way, your discretion will be intact and I'll leave you alone."

Merry looked at me as though debating if I was worth the trouble. We weren't friends. At best, we were business associates. She was probably wondering how far I would push this.

"Job came from Istvan—unlikely real name." She scratched at her neck. "I get you location code, you track. Then no more."

A code would be enough to narrow down the sender's vicinity. It should be easy enough to track down an *Istvan* from there. Finding the sender would lead me to the fae.

He had to be involved with the message to have known when to shoot Crater.

Merry whipped a datastrip off her desktop and swept her finger across it, leaving behind a six-digit number. "There. Go." I scooped up the strip and memorized the number. "And do your job!" she called as I pushed through the drape.

The assault of hot and spicy smells wrapped around me. Whooping fans, distant clangs of metal on metal, and the chatter from stacked containers accompanied my walk deeper into the sinks. I flicked my collar up, kept my chin tucked in, and moved among the drifters. Anyone down on their luck usually got washed into the sinks. The homeless, the unemployed or the unemployable, or those system-wide drifters who had never had a home to call their own. There were plenty of vultures here too. I passed by brightly lit sex parlors, pawn stores, beggars and bars. One of the most popular bars was The Boot, a mismatch of modified containers stacked together like kids' plastic blocks and arranged over various floors. A lot of business went down in The Boot, most of it illegal. I pushed through the swinging steel doors. Heading toward the bar, I caught sight of my reflection in the dozens of mirrors hanging on one wall. There had to be roughly fifty people in the main bar—where I'd just entered—now fifty-two, including me and the tail I'd picked up after leaving Merry's.

He wasn't the most discreet of tails. The guy had a limp and wore overalls dirtied up with grease from boring machines. I'd turned into The Boot as a final check, and sure enough, there was his reflection in the patina-marred hanging mirrors, pushing through the doors and scanning the crowd for me.

"Hulia." I leaned on the bar and waved over the dark-skinned, bright-eyed woman behind the bar. Double eyelids flickered at the sight of me.

"Kesh!" She finished pouring a customer a drink and then slinked my way, shoulders and hips swaying rhythmically.

"Hey, Hulia... Is Kampa working?"

"Sure, she is." She grinned and poured me a drink. "She's around here somewhere. You lookin' for a little action, Kesh?" She raised an eyebrow and grinned like she'd just won a bet. "Didn't know you swung that way, darling. Ask nicely and I bet she'll do you for free. We've all been wondering what's under that coat of yours."

"You'll find out the day you tell me what you really are, Hulia." She wasn't human, of that I was certain.

She chuckled and leaned in. "What I am would blow your little mind, Kesh Lasota."

"Is that a promise?" It was harmless banter, the same teasing we had tossed both ways all the years I'd been coming to The Boot. I couldn't say Hulia's words didn't draw me in. Curiosity was a weakness of mine, and there was something about Hulia that made her... irresistible.

"For you, darling, you know it." She giggled and, spotting Kampa, waved her over. "Get that drone of yours to film you two in action and I can make you a pretty sum."

I recoiled and pulled a face.

"Too much?" She shrugged. "Can't blame a girl for trying."

"Hey, Kesh." Kampa leaned a hip against the bar and examined her long nails. Nanotek glistened on the tip of each finger, working to finish each nail's polish in a glossy red. She had already had them work on her face, smoothing away lines. "About that... thing," she murmured,

27

averting her gaze, "you did... It worked, so, yah know... thank you."

That *thing* had been a particularly nasty low-life stalker who had figured "no" didn't apply to him. I'd made sure the right kind of evidence—most of it legitimate, some of it fabricated—found its way to the right kind of marshals to get him off her back and put down for a few rotations. That *thing* wouldn't be bothering her or anyone for the next couple of decades.

"You're welcome." I picked up my drink and gulped half of it down. A pleasant warmth filled some of the emptiness Sota's theft had left me with. I would have liked to stay, maybe share a few drinks, but my tail would probably be calling in backup soon. "I need to call in that favor."

Kampa straightened. "Oh?"

"You see the stiff by the table in the corner?"

"The old guy on his own, pretending he can blend in like a whore at a virgin ceremony?"

"Go keep him company while I slip out the back?"

Scarlet lips broadened into a wide smile. "My pleasure," she purred. The tek she wore in her hair and inside the seams of her clothing shimmered into action, simulating long lashes, slightly wider eyes and fuller lips. I watched her sashay her way over to my tail and pour all her alluring self into his lap. He wouldn't be going anywhere anytime soon.

"You in trouble?" Hulia quietly asked.

I shook my head and pushed away from the bar. "Just a little unwanted attention. I'll catch you later."

Crater's men didn't think much of me if they'd sent one guy with a limp to track me down. Hopefully, they would continue to think little of me. Their mistake would sure make my life easier while I searched for the fae.

I stepped out into the narrow alley behind The Boot and blinked into the purplish light, adjusting my eyes to the contrasting shadows and glare. A silhouetted figure lumbered toward me, shoulders almost touching the containers stacked either side of him.

To my right, another figure swaggered forward, his knuckles dressed in steel.

Ah. Not so stupid. Limpy had been the decoy.

I reached inside my coat. "You guys sure you want to do this?" My whip uncoiled, spilling sparks around my boots. Magic tingled across the back of my hand and up my arm, urging me on. The men didn't answer and kept on coming.

Time to get my hands dirty.

"I didn't kill your boss." I stepped forward, placing myself in the middle of the alley. The light from my whip sent my shadow dancing on the metallic walls. The guy on my left peeled his coat back and freed a pistol. His lips pulled back in a snarling smile.

"So who did?" Knuckles grumbled. "The tooth fairy?"

"Some kind of fairy," I muttered. Nobody would joke about the tooth fairy had they met the terrifying origin of that myth.

I eased more magic into the whip. These guys were easily twice my weight and probably strong enough to punch me through a wall—if they could catch me.

I tightened my grip on the whip. "Here's what's about to happen. You surrender, and maybe I don't put you down? How does that sound?"

"Sounds like you've taken too many hits to the head, Messenger." Lefty snickered. While he taunted me, he lowered the pistol. "So why don't you come along nicely with us, eh?" His lips parted, and his stubby tongue darted out to wet his cracked lips. "Maybe you come nicely and we don't have to rough you up some?"

I chuckled dryly. "I hate to disappoint you."

"The night's young. We're just getting started," Knuckles said, picking up on Lefty's lascivious glances.

They stopped within arm's reach, one on either side of me, leaving nowhere left for me to go. Oh, what a fragile little messenger. How would I ever escape the mean and scary thugs?

I stomped on Lefty's foot. He jerked forward, swinging wildly for me. I sidestepped. And Knuckles's glowing fist hit his pal square in the face. Lefty grunted, and blood spurted from his nose. I kicked high, jabbing my heel into Knuckles's gut. While he bowed over, I cracked my whip open and looped it around an iron strut braced across the alley above. Hauling myself out from between them, I planted both boots on the wall, kicked out, and freed the whip from the strut, landing on all fours. I sprang forward, away from Crater's men.

Knuckles snarled something behind me, but I was already out of the alley and darting across the sinks' ramshackle streets into a narrow, shadow-filled gullet. Electric heaters buzzed, slung like streetlamps outside of shanty homes.

None of the homeless cared who I was or why I was running. Few bothered to look up as I dashed past.

"Hey!" Knuckles's shout echoed after me. I'd lose him in the sinks, as long as I kept switching back—

I slammed into a wall that hadn't been there a blink before, and I would have bounced right off if the wall's arms hadn't clamped around me.

"Easy there, lady."

Typical. Some guy wanted to be the hero? I shoved against the man's chest and spotted the golden star of the law pinned to his coat. A marshal. Really? Of all the people I could have run into, it had to be a lawman.

Turning my head away, I checked behind me. Knuckles wasn't there. The law had probably spooked him. Marshals were good for that, at least.

"Get your hands off me," I snapped, probably too harshly.

His grip eased. I pushed out and quickly stepped around him. *No need for a fuss. I'll just be on my way.*

What was a lawman doing in the sinks? They almost never ventured down here.

"Wait a second," he drawled.

With my back to him as I picked up my pace, I discreetly recoiled my whip and tucked it inside my coat.

"Hey, girlie."

What did he just call me?

"Stop!" he barked.

I stopped. Shutters on the nearby containers rattled closed. *Yeah, go on, cowards. Hide from the lawman.*

I heard his boots crunch on gravel, and then I saw that wall-like chest again. The marshal's star winked. He wouldn't drop this. I would have to look him in the eye and have a conversation. Hopefully, words would be enough. I'd already assassinated a terrorist today. I didn't want to add a marshal to that list.

"The sinks are no place for a lady."

I snorted. "Luckily, I've never been one." I flicked my hair out of my eyes and looked up. By cyn, he was way too pretty to be anywhere near the sinks, let alone be wearing a marshal's star. I'd seen tek-shifters pretty themselves up,

31

and they'd still only been half as handsome as this marshal. Hair as black as onyx and green eyes that looked to be laughing even though his mouth held a firm, authoritative line. It wasn't authentic. Nobody was that good-looking without enhancements.

"Do you need an escort?" he asked.

Was he for real? I raked my glare over his pretty-boyness. "Do you?" His long coat reached to his dark boots, keeping the sinks' metallic dust off his clothes. His coat likely hid various weapons. Was he as quick of a draw as I was?

A spark of something ignited in his eyes. I wasn't sure if I'd pissed him off or if he was secretly laughing. Poking him some more would yield interesting results, but every second I wasted was another second Crater's men would use to outflank me.

He studied me, my face, my coat, taking his time, reading every inch. If he liked what he saw, his expression showed no sign of it. He stepped aside, graciously sweeping a hand out. "It seems I misjudged you." His voice —smooth, and warm, and curiously arousing—could have melted steel. And didn't he talk all proper-like. Mr. Marshal was well educated.

The sinks would eat him alive. Good riddance. I strode on by him, ignoring the tiny pang of regret that I likely wouldn't get to admire that face again.

I'd managed a few steps when he raised his voice, asking, "Do you have a license for that whip?"

Oh, he'd spotted my discreet concealment. I walked on without missing a beat. Carrying any weapon in public required all manner of background checks. Checks I had neglected to take. "Do you have a license for all that pretty, Marshal? There must be a law against allowing that sexy out in public."

He didn't reply. My steps slowed. *Don't look. Don't look. He wants you to look. Keep going. Leave right now.*

Just one peek. It would be a crime not to.

I glanced over my shoulder.

Trash tumbled, and the spark of a shorted-out cable hissed beside a dumpster. But the alley was empty. Impossibly, the marshal had given me the slip. My steps faltered. He couldn't have gone far. He'd been there just moments ago... I scanned the narrow alley but found no traces of him, or anyone.

It was probably for the best. If my luck held, that would be the last I ever saw of him.

Striding on, I put the encounter behind me. Whatever he was doing in the sinks, he had better get in and out quickly.

Would I just walk away and leave the pretty boy to get stabbed and left in a gutter?

My pace slowed.

I didn't have time to babysit the suicidal pretty boy.

I checked my ocular map for Merry's location code coordinates. The sender, Istvan's zone, was a few quick tram rides away. I had some time to check that the marshal wasn't about to get stabbed in the back. Shiny stars like his often turned up on the black market, usually tarnished with blood.

I stopped. Looked back. Still nothing.

He'd be fine.

I flicked my collar up and headed out of the sinks. The marshal was on his own.

CHAPTER 3

I stood outside the glittering pyramid made of shimmering metals and translucent plastics, and wondered if the universe had a sense of humor at my expense. First, a death threat via messenger, and then this...

Smartly dressed people milled up and down the entrance steps. Beside the grand entrance, the name of the corporation that owned the building was carved into a shiny slab of stone, proclaiming its permanence.

Arcon.

Istvan had sent the death threat from Arcon headquarters.

Arcon—the same company that had hunted me and, after failing to catch me, deemed I didn't exist. The same company whose state-of-the-art surveillance and security washed off me daily.

Wonderful.

I set myself up in an eatery across the street and browsed the datanet for any Arcon staff members called Istvan. Sure enough, Istvan was on the payroll. But it was worse than I imagined. He wasn't some grunt holed up in the basement. He signed the company's checks. Istvan Larsen was Arcon's CEO.

I fell back in my seat and squinted at the ostentatious pyramid through the window. Why was Arcon's CEO sending illegal death threats via the underground messenger network? And why did he want a mineworker, on the other end of the Calicto demographic spectrum, dead? Men like Istvan Larsen and Crater didn't mix. But something had caused them to cross paths. Did Crater have something on Istvan? Or something on Arcon? If that was the case, surely there had to be a tidier way of assassinating a mineworker than sending a fae after him. How could Arcon's CEO contact a fae, let alone convince him to kill for him?

All the questions set my thoughts spinning. I was missing something. I was missing a lot of things. None of this made any logical sense.

Doesn't matter, I reminded myself. *I'm not here for the whys and what-fors.*

Istvan was my connection to the fae who had Sota. A fae I was going to put down. He wouldn't be smiling when I caught up with him. He'd surprised me. That wouldn't happen again. When we next met, I'd be ready.

Opening my palm, I tapped the contact link for Arcon.

"Good day, this is Arcon Systems. How may I direct your call?" a polite female voice asked.

"Hello." I polished my accent into something more like the marshal's fancy talk. "I'm Lucy Walker with the Calicto News agency. We're running a story on Arcon's failure to detain the criminal behind the Crater assassination. Would Mister Larsen be available to comment?"

Much call holding and transferring ensued, but I eventually secured a meeting with the top man himself. I was to meet him in twenty minutes, leaving little time to smarten my appearance. It was a good thing I'd come prepared. After checking I was alone in the restroom, I shrugged off my coat, turned it inside out and tugged it back on. The rows of mirrors above the sinks reflected my image back at me. Time for a change. Marching into Arcon in my messenger garb would likely get me arrested.

A tap of my palm and my ocular display sent an array of possible appearances across my vision. I selected one and watched the coat go to work. Its length reeled in, pulling up to just above my knee, while wrapping me in the illusion of little shoes, office pants, and a slim-fitting jacket. The illusion wouldn't stand up to physical scrutiny, but I didn't plan on getting too close to Larsen.

I smiled. The girl in the mirror smiled back as her short hair grew out and turned white. I twirled the ponytail around my fingers, plucked a chrome stiletto from a hidden pocket inside my coat and used it to pin my hair up. There, perfectly respectable. Whaddyah know, I was a lady.

~

A GAGGLE of school children was being led around Arcon's foyer when I arrived at the front desk. They giggled, shoes squeaking against Arcon's shiny floors, while their teacher pointed out the sculptural facets of the building's cathedral proportions.

"Mr. Larsen will be right down, Miss Walker." The receptionist beamed. Her nameplate read Caroline Ludo. "While you're waiting, would you please apply your thumbprint to the scanner?"

"Sure." I pressed my thumb to the little scanner on the desk. The light blinked red. I tried again. Another blink. "It doesn't appear to be working."

"Oh, let's take a look." She swiped a few fingers across the scanner. "Try now."

I obliged, with no luck.

"Huh, now isn't that strange," Miss Ludo remarked.

Not really.

"I'll have to... I guess I'll just..." She rifled below her desk and pulled out a tek-pad. "My apologies. I don't know why it's not working. Please place your hand here?"

I pressed my hand to the pad, and predictably, it blipped a negative reading. I wasn't worried. Tek failure was extremely rare, so when it did fail, people often made mistakes, like not logging me in.

"Well, that is really unusual. I've never had two failed readings..."

I shrugged. "I guess Arcon doesn't make 'em like they used to, huh?"

She frowned. "Erm, no." Removing the pad, she squinted at her tactile screens for a few moments and muttered, "I guess I'll just enter you manually."

While she swiped and tapped at her screens, I admired the glittering foyer. Cameras monitored the entrance from all angles. They looked like silver baubles hanging in the corners. Later, when someone high up Arcon's ranks reviewed this footage, they'd be alarmed to find Miss Ludo apparently talking to air. It was almost a shame I wouldn't be around to see them lose their little minds over me.

"Miss Walker?"

The man who thrust his hand out seemed younger in person than in the flat image on the corporation's datanet. His storm-gray suit would have been unremarkable if not for the scarlet tie. Short sandy blond hair held hints of curls. Something the datanet hadn't captured was the intelligent sparkle in his eyes. Ocular implants. Biotek.

I internally scolded myself. Of course the CEO of Arcon would be sporting its latest tek. Depending on his upgrade, he might see right through my illusion. I didn't think he had, or else his security would have been getting up close and personal. Perhaps his implants were for another reason?

I avoided the handshake and replied coolly, "Mister Larsen, you're doing the right thing by speaking with me. For our piece to go live without a comment would be... quite damaging."

He withdrew his hand, only briefly thrown off balance by my cold shoulder. "Indeed. A terrible business..." He buttoned his jacket and nodded to Miss Ludo. "Is the meeting suite available?"

"Yes, Mister Larsen. We had trouble with the sign in process—"

"See to it," he interrupted, and this time his tone held a dangerous edge that belied his charming smile. He turned to me. "I appreciate you meeting with me. Would you like a tour?" All traces of that razor's edge had vanished.

"A tour?"

"Of the building. Most everyone wants the tour. Arcon isn't generally open to the public."

My smile was cutting. "I'm not most everyone, Mister Larsen. Let's find somewhere to talk privately, shall we?"

He hesitated, just a few seconds, but it was enough to dislodge some of his good-natured ambience. "Of course, this way."

I followed his swift pace, wondering if Arcon's staff had underestimated Larsen and later paid the price. From my brief scan of his public persona, I knew he had built Arcon from the ground up. At just twenty-six, that was quite an achievement. His personal records weren't public knowledge, but the gossip on the net said he was of old Earthen blood, which might account for his elevated status in society.

Larsen escorted me into a private elevator where a few minutes of painful silence incubated many, many questions between us. A tiny camera stared down at us. A man with Larsen's resources could easily track someone like Crater and know exactly where he would be. Then all he had to do was send in the fae. I side-eyed Larsen. He didn't look dangerous, but neither did I.

The elevator doors opened into a carpeted hallway dressed in muted reds and wooden panels that must have cost a planetary fortune. I curled my fingers into fists to stop from reaching out and stroking the wood. Just because I hadn't seen wood in forever didn't mean the reporter I was pretending to be hadn't. The privileged clearly had access to enough wood to line their hallways with it. Could it be from Earth? No, that was too much of a stretch.

Larsen opened a frosted glass door and breezed into a meeting room the size of my entire container. "Would you like a drink?"

"No... thank you." The windows beckoned. The view over Halow was... I didn't have the words. And now I did reach out and touch the floor-to-ceiling windows. They sloped gently inward, a quirk of the building's pyramid shape. Beyond, Calicto glittered far into the distance in a rainbow of color, light, movement, and beyond the habitat's curved domes, ion storms fractured purple skies. The only time I'd seen it from so high up, I'd been stowed away on a ship making its final approach. Living in Sage, cruising the sinks, it was easy to forget how beautiful Calicto was from a distance.

"I imagine you must have a view just like it from your apartment in... where is it you live?"

Larsen had crept up beside me. It was the only explanation because I hadn't heard him move. His eyes sparkled, waiting for my answer.

"Oh, sure. Of course. All the time. Really, I get bored of looking at it." He was testing me, scrutinizing me. I waved at the view like it was nothing and moved to the long *wooden* table. "Is this... oak?"

"It is," Larsen said. He crossed the room and opened a drinks cabinet. "You've seen oak before?"

"No," I lied. "I mean, only on the datanet." I brushed my fingers across the glossy surface. "And you actually made a table out of it, like the old days, huh?"

"Call me a traditionalist. Besides, keeping trees behind glass in museums seems like such a waste." He moved to stand beside the ornately carved oak chair at the head of the table.

The table alone was worth more than my entire life's worth of possessions. The chair—carved by hand—was a work of art. I wanted to ask if both were from Earth but wasn't sure whether I was ready for the answer. Maybe those rumors that he was of old world blood had some truth in them.

"So..." I cleared my throat. "Mister Larsen. Crater's assassination. What do you know about it?"

"Very little." He poured himself a syrupy drink and lifted an empty glass, offering to fill it for me. "Are you sure you won't have some?"

"All right, a little." I needed something to stop my

nerves from rattling. I hadn't expected to be met with such extravagance.

Larsen handed my drink over and sipped from his own glass.

I tasted the drink and recognized it as a much smoother, finer example of the wine The Boot served on special occasions. But no water. The man still had limits. I tilted the glass, acknowledging his kindness. "Thank you."

He seemed pleased and leaned against the meeting table. "There was nothing wrong with the equipment Arcon installed at that establishment." He briefly admired his view, watching a local shuttle slide on by—and then turned his gaze on me. "It performed exactly as it should have."

"By detaining the wrong people?"

He lifted his chin. "If you walk into a security scanner with hot weapons, they will react. It's what they do. Crater's men were the obvious threat in that room."

"If that's the case, why did your equipment miss the assassin?"

He smiled, so confident. "The assassin *wasn't* in the room with him."

Did he know that for certain because he was the one who had hired the assassin, or was it an educated guess? I couldn't tell by watching him, and I was usually quick to read people. He should have been simple to read. A suit at the top of his game, thousands of people below him, doing his bidding. And yet, I didn't get that impression from Larsen. His presence seemed almost small, but in a familiar, friendly way.

"Why do you think Crater was assassinated, Mister Larsen?"

He laughed a smooth liquid laughter, the type women

everywhere had no choice but to notice. "I have no idea. I imagine a man like that has many enemies. He was a wanted terrorist, correct?"

"Alleged terrorist."

"Well, then, I doubt the marshals will waste much energy in tracking down his killer."

Larsen looked the part. Spoke the part. There was no denying he was smooth and refined, like the wine we were both drinking, but it didn't add up. Perhaps it was his smile. At a glance, it looked real, sitting prettily on his lips, but upon closer inspection, it seemed shallow, as though that smile was a mask hiding something else behind. But what?

There was one simple way to test the man's involvement. Surprise him.

I set my drink down on the table and looked Larsen in the eye. "What do you know of the protofae, Mister Larsen?"

The sparkle in his eyes sharpened, but as quickly as I'd seen it, the intense effect vanished, leaving me to wonder if I'd simply seen the exact reaction I had wanted to see. "The fae?" he chuckled. "You aren't suggesting they had anything to do with a terrorist mineworker?" He laughed harder.

I let my lips curve at one corner. "You're right, it is ludicrous. Who would believe a fae killed Crater?"

"Who, indeed." His laughter faded as he noticed I wasn't laughing along with him. "You're serious?"

"You tell me."

"The fae?" he almost snarled. "That's absurd. Nobody has seen one in..." He grasped for the timescale. "In what might as well be forever. A fae couldn't get near Calicto, not with all this... *tek*." He definitely snarled that last word.

But wasn't his business built on all this *tek?* Why the sudden disdain?

"What else do you know?"

His eyes narrowed. "What is this? Are you trying to implicate me in that man's death?"

"I don't need to implicate you when you've done a fine job of doing exactly that all by yourself. Do you often circumvent your own security and send illegal messages, Mister Larsen? The next time you do, you might want to use a fake name."

Tension gripped his body, and gone was the easy mannerisms of Arcon's friendly CEO. He straightened and stared through me without blinking. The full weight of his ocular-enhanced glare set my teeth on edge.

"I think it's time you left, Miss Walker."

But I couldn't leave, not without a lead on the fae who had stolen Sota. "I think it's time you dropped the lies, Larsen."

A change came over him, like flicking a switch, and the man stilled. He tilted his head and asked softly, "Who are you?"

I grinned and reached for my concealed whip. "A nobody." The second I touched my whip, magic flared to life, upsetting my disguise. My illusion pixelated and dissolved in front of Larsen's widening eyes. I flicked the whip, freeing its length, lassoed it around and lashed at Larsen in a move I'd performed a thousand times before. The whip would coil around his neck. I'd yank him forward and get my answers. Only, it didn't happen like that. Larsen threw up his forearm, tangling my whip around his wrist, and *he* yanked, pulling me off balance.

Not possible, my thoughts screamed as I toppled toward

Arcon's CEO. *The magic should be burning through him.* Unless he wasn't human...

His fingers clamped around my neck, jolting me to a stop at arm's length. He squeezed, but only enough to hold me. Then he revealed that he too knew how to play the illusion game. Larsen's smart, young businessman appearance fell apart—just like my disguise had. His sandy blonde hair was the first to go, dissolving into dead-straight blackness. The rest of him collapsed like a creature shucking off its shell. What lay beneath turned my heart to ice. The warfae.

"You just sealed your fate, Messenger." A purring sound emanated from the back of his throat. He lifted me off my feet, into the air. I kicked out, hitting his waist, but he only smiled.

Istvan Larsen hadn't sent the assassin. He *was* the assassin.

"Where's... Sota?" I croaked. I couldn't use the whip in close quarters, and it didn't matter anyway. My magic wouldn't hurt the fae. I groped for my pistol with my free hand.

"Now? Likely dismantled."

"No," I gasped. Shock spilled numbness through my veins. I searched the fae's bright eyes for lies, knowing they couldn't lie. He wore the ocular implants to prevent anyone from seeing the truth in his glare. His stare didn't waver, didn't falter. Sota was truly gone.

"It's better for me if the evidence disappears."

He had killed Sota.

He had killed my drone.

I yanked the pistol free and fired, not caring where it hit. The fae howled and slammed me down. Timber snapped and pain crackled up my back, pushing in dark fingers of unconsciousness. I lay stunned, surrounded by fragments of Larsen's oak table.

The warfae appeared in my watery vision, drifting there like a dream. "You're a complication I didn't anticipate."

Hate burned the blur away. I saw him clearly now.

"If word ever escaped that Istvan Larsen was fae..." he began and gestured around him at the huge meeting room. "That *Arcon* was fae... Well, you can imagine how some might perceive it."

A fae oversaw Halow's surveillance and security. The same surveillance and security that watched over hundreds of thousands of people on hundreds of planets. A fae deep in the heart of human territory.

He smiled at the horror on my face.

"I see you understand." He pointed a finger at me, mirroring my earlier threat. "You found me, and for that, you must die."

I plucked the stiletto dagger from my hair and flung it like a dart, straight at his right eye. It should have hit. It *would* have hit had he been human. But the bastard whipped his head aside at the last moment and the dagger sliced across his temple. He recoiled, staggering backward. Where he pressed his hand to his face, blood streamed between his fingers.

I snatched my whip and pushed to my feet. My pistol was gone, but I couldn't fight him anyway, not like this. I needed a plan.

He was too fast, too strong, too fae. There was only one way out of this.

Run!

With my whip uncoiled, I ran at the glass.

A pistol shot barked. Something slammed into my back

and punched through, tearing a hole in muscle and flesh. My last step buckled beneath me, but I had enough momentum to thrash the whip against the glass, igniting a spark. When my shoulder hit the window, glass shattered, and I fell through.

For a few breathless moments, there was nothing around me but air and glittering glass. Then I hit the fifteen-degree building façade with a shuddering *oomph* and started tumbling, over and over. I threw out both arms, stopping the roll. Leather squeaked on glass. My coat had tangled around my legs. I half skidded, half fell. I flicked the whip at passing nodules—the large bolts used to fasten the panels to the building. The whip's coils snagged on one and snapped me to a halt, wrenching agony through my arm.

For a few thudding heartbeats, I stayed pressed against the glass, aware that something cool and wet dribbled down my side but hardly caring. I didn't need to look down to know it was a long way to a sudden end. The circulating breeze fluttered across my face. I couldn't lose consciousness. If that happened, I wouldn't be waking up.

Move.

Giving the whip a jolt, I freed it from the bolt and slid downward, this time more controlled. Down and down and down until my whip snagged another bolt, and then another. Finally, I landed on the ground and immediately pushed off to get out of the open. As I limped into hiding, bloodied and numb, I realized with a sinking sense of dread that this was a long way from over. It might even be just beginning.

CHAPTER 4

*M*y container door hung ajar.

The neighbor in Container 15 had his virtuavision up too loud. Music thudded against the walls and floor, muffling my approach.

Blood dripped from my fingers while I lingered in the hallway, contemplating whether to venture inside or walk away and hope I didn't bleed out. My entire lower right hip fizzed unpleasantly. I'd lost feeling in my side, and tingling needles of pain jabbed their way down my right leg. The longer I left the wound untreated, the more damage I'd do. And right now, I didn't have the luxury of time to heal.

I freed my whip and toed the door open.

A figure loomed at the back, watching my fake rainfall. Broad shoulders carried an ankle-length coat. A mop of dark hair stuck out at unruly angles. I'd seen him before, earlier in the day. The sinks hadn't killed the marshal, and now he was here, poking through my things.

My neighbor's music ended suddenly, and silence fell over my container. My heart thudded too loudly, thumping in place of the beat. If I was going to leave, now would be the time, before he turned around.

"Looks like someone went to town on your place," the marshal said.

He was right. Anything not bolted down had been tossed about and knocked to the floor. Some cupboards hung open, their contents shoved from inside, and one door hung from a single latch.

The fae, or someone connected to him, had been here. He knew where I lived, probably knew my name. It wouldn't be long before he knew *everything*.

I shoved the door open wider and wandered in, toeing through the mess. Had the intruder been looking for me or something else?

"Is anything missing?"

I blinked up at the marshal. Concern tightened his green eyes, and then his gaze skittered down my coat, catching on the bloody patch at my hip or my whip, neither of which I'd bothered to hide.

"I'm fine," I replied automatically as I reached for the lower storage unit and the med-kit still lying inside.

I straightened and spotted the marshal eyeing something behind me. My bloody boot prints led inside, indicating I was not fine.

"I need to call this in." He tapped his palm. "This is Marshal Kellee..." His words petered off.

I pretended not to notice how he struggled to find a signal and instead tore open the med-packs. Luckily, the pistol's bullet had sailed right through; otherwise, I would have needed to dig around my own insides to find its fragments.

"What are you doing here?" I opened my inner jacket and peeled back the bloody and torn upper-garment, revealing a gaping exit wound. A large nodule of dark blood oozed free. Nobody should ever have to see their innards.

"One of your neighbors called in a disturbance. I was already nearby in the gulley..."

I jabbed a staunch pad over the hole just as the marshal moved closer, and dropped my clothes back over the wound before he noticed any incriminating tattoos. Pain exploded up my side. I gritted my teeth, gripped the counter, and rode it out. All things considered, I was lucky to be walking. Most fae weren't sloppy enough to leave their victims breathing, but I doubted the warfae had expected me to leap out of his window.

I couldn't stay here. He would send someone to kill me or come himself. More likely come himself. Twice now he'd surprised me, and both times he'd kicked my ass.

I was off my game.

My lips ticked.

The head of Arcon was fae.

In many ways, it was brilliant. Where better to hide than in plain sight?

The idea was so ludicrous. Even if I told someone like the marshal, they wouldn't believe me. The fae despised tek. And the head of the largest tek company in Halow was a fae disguised as the charming Larsen. I'd been there, he'd thrown me into an oak table and shot me, and I still wasn't sure I believed it.

I frowned at the marshal eying my oozing wound, my thoughts muddied by pain and shock. He was staring like he might tackle me and take me in.

"Earlier, in the sinks, we met," he said.

"Some coincidence that you're here now..." I grabbed another staunch pad, breathed deeply, and lifted the back of my upper-garment to get a look at the entry wound. Crackling sensations danced through me, alternating between pain and numbness.

He saw me wince. "You should have a doc check you out."

"Yeah, I should." I gave him a look that dared him to ask why I wasn't getting medical attention, but the marshal glared back, not taking the bait. All he had to do was look around to know I was in serious trouble.

I shrugged one arm out of my coat and tried again to get the back pad in place, but twisting made me want to throw up my breakfast bar. It didn't help that the marshal wasn't leaving, and I really did not want him or anyone to see the marks on my skin. He probably wouldn't know what they were, but it wasn't worth the risk.

"Will you let me help?" He came forward.

"No." My bloody fingers slid across the pad, leaving tacky trails. This wasn't going well. "Stay there. Don't come near me."

He stopped, my pain mirrored in his eyes. "At least tell me what happened."

"Why?"

"So when you pass out, I'll know what to write in my report."

I snorted a laugh, ditched the wrinkled pad and used my teeth to tear open a fresh pack. *Help get me arrested, more like.* "Like I said, everything is fine, Marshal. I don't need or want your help." This time, I pressed the pad in the right place. It latched onto the good skin and plastered itself into and over the wound, sealing it tight. Pain throbbed deep and low and hot, saliva filled my mouth and my vision blurred, but it passed. It always passed. The fix would have to do until I found somewhere safe to hole up.

The marshal had fallen silent, stewing on me, my words, and the situation. I figured he didn't much like being told no. He scanned the mess, reluctant to dismiss everything his instincts were telling him.

"Do you have a license for that whip?" he asked for a second time, nodding at the whip I'd placed on the counter.

I touched the whip. "What whip?"

He pushed his coat aside and tucked a thumb into his pants pocket, revealing the pistol hitched at his hip. "Because if you don't, I'll need to take you in. You know the law regarding illegal possession." His eyes had turned shrewd while that tightness to his lips had widened into the beginnings of a smile. I wondered if he smiled at all the criminals he was about to apprehend. Maybe he thought his looks might steal their hearts as well as their freedom?

"You do not want to mess with me right now, Marshal," I drawled from the corner of my mouth, hiding a sneer.

"A crime has been reported. It's my duty to do everything in my power to see that any wrongdoer is brought before the law."

"Wow." Wasn't his world so wonderfully black and white. His duty wasn't about helping me; it was about upholding the law, even if that law screwed me over. "You going to arrest me?" I pushed upright, dragging the whip with me.

"Do I have to?"

I took one last look at my home. There wasn't much here. In truth, it had never really felt like a home, just a halfway post between points A and B. And now Sota was gone and there was nothing left here for me.

A glance past the marshal revealed the section of

counter where Sota's dock had waited was empty. The dock was missing. Why would the intruder take the dock if the warfae had dismantled Sota? He wouldn't. Sota was alive.

The marshal still waited for my reply, his hand resting easily on his hip, so close to his pistol. "Go back to upholding your laws and forget what you saw here." I turned my back on him. "At least one of us can..." A blur of cloaked movement shot through the open door. Something small, bright and buzzing sailed over my shoulder and landed at the back of my container.

The crackling ball hissed and spat, arcing out veins of electricity. *Grenade!*

The marshal's outline blurred—too fast to be human. He swooped in, snatched up the fizzing ball, whirled, his coat fanning out, and smashed his elbow into my projector screen and through the window. The grenade sailed through the hole. The blast hit a second later. A wave of noise and heat slammed through the window and exploded through my container. I recoiled, throwing my coat around me, and staggered against the assault on my senses. Alarms shrilled, inside my head or in the building, I wasn't sure.

Fingers dug into my arms, and the marshal was in front of me, mouthing something I couldn't hear through the ringing in my ears. I blinked, seeing something unusual in his mouth. Then he shoved me toward the shattered window, leaving me with no choice. I clambered through and hissed at the sting of jagged metal cutting into my hands. Alarms still wailed, drowning out everything but the thudding of my heart. I twisted to look back through the window for the marshal. A figure cloaked in a shimmering exo-suit had joined us. The intruder fired a two-pronged device, designed to deliver a shock into the marshal's body. The barbed teeth sank into the marshal's arm. Electricity danced down the connecting lines. But the marshal did the impossible. He clamped a hand around the lines and tugged, pulling the intruder toward him. The marshal's fist met the intruder's face and crumpled the metal mask inward. Blood spurted from the mouth grill, and the intruder dropped. But another dashed in, and behind him, another, both wrapped in exo-suits that enhanced their strength and agility. The second stepped over his fallen companion and swung for the marshal. He jerked to the side and threw the intruder back with an uppercut that almost took the guy's head off.

I knew I should have been climbing down to the street below, but I couldn't take my eyes off the marshal's terrible lethality. Was he fae? But he didn't move with the same liquid grace they did. He fought brutally, no holding back, no fancy shit. The third intruder revealed a pistol, but he never got to use it. The marshal moved in a blink, impossibly appearing behind the last assailant. He hooked his arm around the suited figure's throat and twisted. I didn't hear the neck break, not over the shrieking alarms. The last intruder collapsed.

The marshal looked up, and I saw again what I thought I'd seen earlier. Sharp teeth. Our glares locked. He'd killed, and we both knew it. Not very lawman-like. His eyes asked, *What are you going to do with that knowledge?*

I started down the mangled fire escape, avoiding the sharpest pieces of twisted metal. The street below had borne the brunt of the explosion and buckled under its weight, but the containers, although dented, had survived intact. People were emerging from their homes. *Witnesses.* The first responder bots would be here soon, and after that, it would be difficult to escape unseen.

The marshal landed in a crouch beside me on the street and drew up to his full height. My container was too high to safely leap from the window. Yet more evidence he wasn't anything like what he appeared to be. But what *was* he? He tugged his coat straighter and eyed the swelling crowd. A lawman would take control, probably arrest me, take me in for questioning and expose me to the kind of people who had already tried to kill me. But exactly what kind of lawman was he?

I watched him closely, waiting for him to reach for his weapon or his cuffs. That would be the right thing to do, but something told me he followed his own set of laws. If he battled with his morals, none of it showed on his stoic face. All the smiles and all the humor had vanished. He looked down at me for answers I had no intention of giving him. So where did that leave us?

"Go," he said. "You were never here."

I wouldn't hang around and question his attack of generosity, even if it was suspiciously nice of him. Collar up, chin down, I walked away from the crowd and the marshal, and slipped deeper into the gulley. It wouldn't matter soon anyway. After I got myself patched up, I would leave Calicto. Larsen—if that was his real name—had sent those intruders. The fae knew too much. He *saw* too much. I needed space to regroup and plan. And then I would return. The truth hiding in my past demanded it.

CHAPTER 5

*T*itillating music drifted from The Boot as I pushed through the door into the bar. Hulia was on stage, playing hauntingly beautiful music on an electronic violin. She dipped and swayed, dreadlocks swishing over her shoulders. Beneath the flood of colored lights, she almost looked as though she were moving through water. When she played like this, people came from all around to spend all the v-coin they had just to listen to one more piece of music.

I shivered off hot and cold waves and headed upstairs, passing by a homeless man on the stairs and two young women getting personal on the landing like it was their last night alive.

The Boot was the only safe place to hole up for a few hours while I planned how to get off Calicto unnoticed. I helped myself inside Hulia's apartment and clicked the door closed behind me. Blues of all shades assaulted my eyes. Couch cushions, wall color, even the lights rippled a light watery blue. She liked her blues.

A shudder ran through me. The pistol wound needed attention.

I peeled off my coat, revealing the blood-soaked staunch pads sticking to my waist and back. Going to an ER was out of the question. Larsen might be looking for black spots in his Arcon surveillance feeds. Black spots that would indicate how someone like me had fooled his scanners and gotten close enough to share drinks.

Okay, so I had to get myself cleaned up before Hulia got back.

Her music still played its lullaby a floor below.

I was safe here, for a little while.

Stripping off, I took to her dry-shower. The pads dissolved under the chemical assault, leaving the puckered wound exposed. My stomach lurched at the sight. Covering it would make it worse. It needed sealing.

I stepped from the shower, bunched up some towels and pressed them to the freshly weeping wounds, ignoring the sickening roll in my gut. I'd had worse. I'd patched up worse and lived through worse. It had been a few years since I'd spent nights fixing myself up, but that shit didn't just go away.

A quick search through Hulia's bathroom cupboards revealed a well-stocked med-kit. After digging out some drugs to numb the pain, I set about cleaning the wound and stapling its edges together.

I was almost done when Hulia returned. "Giiirrl, what in the three systems are you doing to yahself?"

Hulia sashayed toward me, eyes wide. I was sitting in my underwear in her living area, surrounded by bloody swabs and my filthy clothes.

Her doubled eyelids flickered and focused a little too hard on my chest. It wasn't my physique that interested

58

her, but the dark, swirling marks that painted my skin. She couldn't miss them. They started at my calves, wove their way around my knees, up my thighs, and swept around my waist. From there, the black swirls spread out, flowing across my stomach and over my breasts.

If she knew what they were, if so much as a flicker of fear widened her eyes, I would have no choice but to act.

"That is some serious ink you've got there. Must have taken an age to laser in..."

Only a lifetime, I thought while picking up my discarded clothes. She wasn't afraid. She didn't know. Her ignorance had just saved her life.

"I saw you come in. What I didn't see was how someone had gone to town on you." Her gaze drifted to the array of bloody towels. "Are you okay?"

I shrugged on my upper waistcoat, fastened it tight and pulled on my pants. "I'm sorry about all this."

"Don't be." She waved a hand. "Anything you need. Always. You know that. You've helped me and mine out enough times. I owe you." She approached and looked at me as though she might be holding herself back from wrapping me in a hug. "You got yourself some trouble, eh?"

"A little," I admitted. "I'm handling it."

She grabbed two glasses from her kitchen area and filled them with something colorful and sparkly. When she handed mine over, I gulped it down so quickly it barely touched my throat. The warm tingling it left me with helped soothe my nerves. Part of me wanted more, wanted to drink so much that it numbed my thoughts and chased all of this away. Five years I'd been on Calicto, carving out a new life. But the fae being here...? Yeah, I was in a world of trouble. The kind that meant my life as Kesh Lasota was about to end, if it hadn't already.

I handed the glass back. "Do you mind if I rest up here? Just for a few hours."

"Course, Kesh." She finished her drink and returned to the kitchen to pour another. "But you... you might wanna sit back down for what I'm about to tell you."

More bad news. I followed her to the kitchen area and handed over my glass. She refilled it and handed it back. I gulped down a few more mouthfuls. I would need it. "Go on..."

"Word on the feed is there's a hit out on you. Fifty million."

The drink threatened to come back up again. "What?!" I spluttered. Fifty million v-coin was more than I'd make in a lifetime. A fortune for most folks on Calicto.

"I figure it's you. There's no name, but they got the description right down to your coat and boots. That whip of yours is a big giveaway. The entire sinks will be looking for you."

"Who's bankrolling it?"

"Crater's gang."

Where had they gotten their hands on so much v?

"You're safe here," she said, her eyes weary. "But I can't vouch for anyone else... If someone saw you downstairs..."

Would Hulia give me up? I looked at my friend with fresh eyes. She hardly knew me. I'd helped her out over the years and she'd made sure her door was always open, but she didn't *know* me. I'd deliberately kept it that way. For that much cash, I would think twice about handing me over. I wouldn't even blame her for it.

"Nobody saw," I whispered. "They were all watching you." Fifty million. That amount was beyond Crater's reach. They had help. The kind of help Arcon might have offered them?

I dragged a hand down my face, trying to wipe away my numb shock. I had to get off Calicto tonight. That kind of bounty would follow me into all the corners of Halow. The more folks looking for me, the more my past would get stirred up. I couldn't afford for the law or bounty hunters to pick me up.

It was all coming undone.

But what had I expected? Someone like me couldn't hide forever. The Halow system suddenly felt like too small a place.

"Can I do anything?" Hulia asked, reading the grimness on my face.

I shook my head.

"Rest up here," Hulia said in a tone that left no room for argument. "I'll keep an eye out downstairs."

After she left to watch the bar, I fell back into the couch cushions, rested my head against the wall, and closed my eyes. I would have to whisper my way off Calicto and onto a ship. That was easier said than done. It's one thing to avoid security footage, quite another to disappear in front of real people. Once off Calicto, I'd buy myself some time to figure all this out.

I hadn't planned on this. In truth, I'd stopped planning altogether and started living a life that didn't belong to me. This was my fault.

The fae were always going to come back.

It had only been a matter of time.

~

"YOU THERE, SARU. STAND."

I eyed the fae through the curved bone-like bars. He held a prod with two nasty spikes in the end. Ghosts of old wounds

61

throbbed down my back. His stony glare wasn't fixed on me, but on the boy in the cell next to mine, the boy with the elegantly sloped eyes and summerlands skin. Older than me, by a few years, he had started growing into his body, filling out muscles, broadening into a well-bred male saru specimen, and his fae master had sent him here for training. I knew him as Aeon, but his slave name—his real name—he had refused to tell me. I couldn't blame him. I hadn't shared my real name either. Some things were sacred, even to saru.

The fae smacked the prod into the bars, sending a spray of sparks flying. "You will stand!" A vein pulsed at his temple, and his eyes glowed a sharp green. I knew his name: Dagnu. It meant 'bad blood'.

Aeon slowly rose to his feet. His fingers twitched at his side.

He lifted his head, tilting his chin up, and presented Dagnu with a defiant snarl. Defiance strummed through Aeon's body, pride quivered through his muscles. All things saru couldn't own for long.

Don't. I didn't speak the warning. There was little point. He wasn't the first to occupy that cell, and he wouldn't be the last.

The fae's lips twitched knowingly.

I turned my face away.

Aeon would return broken—if he came back at all.

A sudden sound jolted me awake. I blinked, clearing the fog of ancient memories or dreams or both. Why was everything blue? Blue walls, blue cushions. Hulia's. I must have fallen asleep on her couch. I leaned forward and wished I'd stayed that way, stayed dreaming. Aches radiated through my battered body. That's what happened when you narrowly survived a warfae's attack—three times.

The apartment door flung open and Hulia burst in. "You have to go. Now!"

I was on my feet, my hand on my whip, all dregs of sleep vanished. *They've found me.* I flung a glance at her window.

"Not out the window, they'll be watching it." She scooped up my coat and shoved it into my arms. "Do the illusion thing you do with the coat and go out the front. It's the only way."

"Who's here?"

"The law." Her eyes saddened. "Merry's dead."

"Merry?" How had they found my source? Merry was careful. But surveillance watched her like it watched everyone. And now Larsen knew me. Nobody was safe.

Hulia frowned and worry pulled at her mouth. "Someone... someone wanted to send a message, Kesh. It wasn't pretty."

A crashing noise erupted outside the door. I threw on my coat and searched the inventory for a disguise while Hulia lingered by the doorway. "Quickly, Kesh."

A disguise they wouldn't look twice at. Something they would expect to see in The Boot. I jabbed at the scantily clad version of something one of Hulia's ladies might wear and let my coat spill the illusion over me.

"Marshals..." Hulia drawled. Her door sprung open, and in stomped four heavily armed marshals. Three men, one woman.

I leaned against Hulia's counter, fighting down panic, and arched an eyebrow. "Looking for something?" They ignored me and set about opening storage units, hoping to find the elusive messenger stuffed in a cupboard. The search didn't take long. Hulia's place wasn't much bigger than mine.

The marshals filed past me, heading for Hulia.

"Like I told yah, she's not here." Hulia rolled her eyes. "Probably halfway to Nyron by now."

"You left downstairs in a hurry. Why?" The lead marshal drew up face to face with Hulia. He was taller, broader and likely felt he had every right to be here.

Hulia shrugged. "Needed to pee."

The backhand came out of nowhere and hit Hulia's cheek with a vicious crack. She stumbled against the wall.

I'd crossed the floor in three strides before realizing that getting involved would risk my illusion failing.

The female marshal stepped in front of me. "Are you going to make this difficult?" she asked, eyes cold.

Another crack sounded. Rage fizzed in my veins and warmed my chest. My heart thudded hard. I glared back at the woman, knowing exactly what she saw looking back at me. Hulia and I were two nobodies living in the unmonitored sinks where nobody gave a damn what happened, and the law would do whatever they wanted, claiming the reprobates had attacked them first.

My disguise would hold so long as I didn't touch anyone and didn't charge the whip with magic. The second I did, the illusion would fall away just like it had in Larsen's suite.

"We know she came in here," the marshal beating on Hulia growled.

I couldn't see past the woman sizing me up for a fight, but the smell of rich, coppery blood told me all I needed to know. The two remaining marshals stood somewhere close behind me. I was outnumbered. Outgunned.

"You're going to tell us exactly where she went." The bully hoisted Hulia off the floor by her hair. Her right eye had already swollen shut, and blood marked her chin.

"Don't," Hulia muttered, but it wasn't meant for the marshal. And the dream was so close that I heard myself say the same word to someone else, so very long ago. *Don't.* But he had anyway, and no good had come from it. But that wasn't me.

I punched Miss Marshal in the face, snapping her head back, and whirled, freeing my whip in a blur of movement. The illusion collapsed. Magic tingled up my arm, burning hot and free. I flicked the whip, charging it up, and cracked it across the face of one marshal. He screamed as his skin unzipped and magic cauterized the wound. The other marshal fumbled for his pistol. I kicked him in the chest, lassoed the whip around his neck and yanked. Spluttering, he fell to his knees and clawed at the whip's coils.

An arm hooked around my neck and pulled me backward against an armored chest. "There you are," the bully purred in my ear. "I knew if I rattled the cage you'd fall out."

I slammed my head back, hitting something hard with enough force for his grip to weaken. I'd lost my stiletto trying to blind Larsen, but I wasn't without other weapons. Reaching into one of my coat's many pockets, I pulled out a handful of silver balls and threw them into the air. The balls hung suspended there, frozen in a blink—reading the scene, assessing for threats—and then turning into tiny airborne razors, they struck, zipping past my face to sink into the marshal's. He howled, shoved free from me and waved at the air, trying to shoo off the metal menaces.

I grabbed Hulia's arm and pulled her out the door. "Is there another way out?"

She nodded, wiped the blood from her lips and darted down the hallway ahead of me. We jumped down the steps and ran around narrow corners until Hulia stopped at a hatch. She flung it open and a waft of dry, metal-tasting air billowed upward.

The chute would take me beneath the sinks' streets, where all the waste from the gulley went.

I touched her face. "I'm sorry."

Her smile was fragile and wet with blood, but it held. "What are friends for if not beating up lawmen every now and then?"

Friends. I hadn't had one in so long. And now I was leaving her in a whole heap of trouble. "Tell them I forced you to hide me."

She nodded. "Make it worth it."

Shouts rattled down the hallway.

I stepped into the hole and fell.

CHAPTER 6

Shuttles came and went from Calicto at regular intervals, ferrying mineworkers to and from the planet's nine moons, rich in silica and tungsten. I boarded a cramped and noisy shuttle that looked as though it had been bouncing between planets for a few hundred years. Stains dirtied the seats, and a fine layer of machine dust came away on my hands as I grabbed the rails and made my way to the back.

All I had to do was hitch a ride on a freighter heading for outer Halow. Away from Calicto, the fae probably wouldn't follow and I'd have space to breathe, heal and figure out how to get Sota back.

Sinking into a tiny window seat, I rested my forehead against the dirty glass and watched as the shuttle pulled away from its dock and maneuvered through Calicto's environmental locks. Twenty minutes later, the little shuttle was accelerating into Calicto's abrasive atmosphere. The walls and floor rumbled, rattling every loose bolt and its passengers. I gritted my teeth until the shuttle eventually leveled out. Calicto's vast environmental domes glittered below like a collection of bubbles on rocks. From the outer atmosphere, those domes sparkled and shone, looking idyllic. I remembered thinking the same thing when I'd first arrived five years ago. The fae painted all humans as animals. I'd been expecting hideous living conditions and a brutal existence. What I'd gotten was something between the two.

"Is this seat taken?" The marshal gripped the pole and swung himself into the seat beside mine, filling the cramped space with his coat, his wry smile and all his pretty manliness. Shimmying past his knees was out of the question; there was nowhere to go. The shuttle wouldn't dock for another few hours. I was stuck with the lawman, and his lopsided grin told me he knew it.

"What are the chances of me meeting you here, huh?" His dark green eyes sparkled at some secret joke only he knew.

I ignored him, or tried to. Clearly, he was going to be a problem.

He still wore his long coat. It didn't appear to have any enhancing abilities but as an expert at deception, I knew there were other ways to hide the truth. He would be armed. And I knew he was a killer. "You just happened to be traveling to the colonies, Marshal?" I asked, making small talk.

"Something like that."

He'd been tailing me. There was little point in avoiding the obvious. "How did you find me?"

"You're not as invisible as you think you are."

I shot him a pinched, tight smile. I had gone to great lengths to whisper my way across Calicto and onto the shuttle, so the marshal was either full of karushit or he was very, very good at hunting people down. "Do enlighten me."

He leaned back in the seat, getting comfortable, and why not, neither of us was getting out of this conversation anytime soon. "Once I had a feel for what you are, I looked for surveillance black spots. Dead space. Tek glitches. Followed you right here." He let that sink in for a few moments, appearing to absently watch the people around us, and then added, "You were at the Crater assassination."

My smile vanished. I checked the faces of those nearby. Burly men, haggard women. Some might be Crater's people. Most were lost in their personal entertainment devices, but if any heard the marshal and suspected me, it wouldn't take much to fire off a message and organize the kind of welcoming party I wouldn't wake up from.

I narrowed my eyes at the marshal. He was dangerously close to getting in my way.

"You going to arrest me, Marshal?"

He twisted in his seat and looked me square in the eye, issuing a challenge. "You keep asking me that. Do you want me to?"

The shift in his position had bumped his knee against mine. He didn't appear to notice, but I did. He had hemmed me in. "Isn't arresting people what you do?"

"Guilty people," he corrected. "It's an important distinction."

Important distinction. Damn, his tight accent slew me. It wasn't a Calicto dialect. Maybe he originally came from one of the farming colonies where dynasties dealt in crops. *Focus. It doesn't matter where he comes from.* "Ah, so you're an honorable marshal. Well, aren't you cute."

His lips twitched. "Sarcasm doesn't suit you."

I touched my chest and gasped, eyes wide. "Really?! I can't imagine why." Turning my face away, I pretended to stare out of the window at the star-speckled blackness but instead studied the marshal's reflection. His smile faded before vanishing completely, leaving his expression somewhere between concerned and curious. I might have imagined the pointed teeth I'd seen when he killed the intruders. They weren't there now. Perhaps those lethal weapons only came out to play when things got rough. As an expert at illusion myself, I wondered if the marshal's pretty was camouflage and beneath all that alluring male plumage lurked a shrewd and dangerous lawman who had me firmly locked in his sights. He had followed me this far, but now that I knew I had a tail, I would ditch him at the next port. All I had to do was survive the next few hours without giving anything away. And if I was right about the marshal, he was about to try everything in his little black book of charm to get me to talk.

"If you're not here to arrest me, why are you here? What do you want?"

"Call me curious."

I'd call him something, all right.

The shuttle's engines whined, signaling it was slowing down, but out of the window, we weren't anywhere near atmosphere.

The marshal leaned out to peer around the standing passengers and narrowed his eyes. He caught me watching him closely and pressed his lips together, apparently annoyed. Whatever was happening, it wasn't good.

The shuttle jolted, and the pilot announced over the comms, *"Please stand by for inspection by the port authority."*

"Just when I think it's safe to talk, someone tries to kill you." The marshal slipped a hand inside his coat.

Wait. What? I reached for my whip.

He removed his hand and dangled wrist-cuffs between his fingers.

I jolted away, pressing my back against the window to force some space between us, but there was no room to swing the whip.

He snatched my wrist and ratcheted the cuffs on with a click. He gripped his cuff with his fingers, not latching it on. "Hold still."

"Hold still?" I hissed and yanked on the cuffs. "You said you weren't arresting me!"

Nearby passengers glanced our way.

The marshal yanked me forward and leaned in, bringing me nose to nose with him. There was no laughter in his eyes now. His glare captured mine and held me still. "I'm not arresting you. I'm helping you. Like I've been trying to since the beginning. Now sit still and shut the hell up."

Who in Halow did he think he was? I balled up my fist and swung, anticipating the satisfying crunch when I broke his pretty nose. He caught my knuckles in his palm, close enough to his face to ruffle his messy bangs. Green eyes glared, their startling intensity another reminder of how the marshal wasn't entirely human. His gaze warned that, should I try anything, he would retaliate, screw our audience, screw the authority about to board. He would throw down right here, and only one of us would walk away. I'd seen what he was capable of. A cramped interplanetary shuttle was not the place to test him, but once we got outside, all bets would be off.

"Marshal," an authority official nodded down at us. "Who do you have there?" Beady-eyed and pointy-chinned, he looked like he hadn't laughed once in the last decade. I almost felt sorry for him.

"Cattle rustler."

Seriously? He was going with that lie? I looked about as likely to be a cattle rustler as he looked like a miner. I rolled my eyes. At least he was terrible at something.

"I'm taking her in for processing."

"Destination?"

"Catacoon."

The authority man raised an eyebrow, probably because we were heading completely the wrong way to be docking anywhere near Catacoon. As ruthless as my marshal was, his lies needed work.

"Name?" the authority guy asked.

"Marshal Kellee."

Authority man jerked a thumb at me. "*Her* name."

The marshal sighed. "Yah know," he said to me, "this isn't working." He pulled a pistol from his coat and—*swish, click, boom*—shot the man in the chest. The authority guy sprawled backward, spilling into onlookers. Screams rang out and the crowd surged.

I froze. Did he just kill that man?

"It's set to stun," Marshal Kellee explained, dragging me off the seat by the cuffs and into the heaving crowd. He shoved and elbowed his way through, pulling me behind him. At the door, where the other marshals fought to keep the masses back, Marshal Kellee lifted his gun into the air and fired off an energy round. Sparks exploded overhead. The crowd dropped, and the authority men went for their weapons.

"I'll be needing your shuttle," the marshal told them.

"W-what?" one stammered. His gaze fell to the star on the marshal's chest.

"Your shuttle is now mine," Kellee said without a shred of doubt. "Step aside."

Nobody moved.

Kellee wet his lips. "I have a very dangerous criminal in custody, and I am commandeering your ship so I can safely escort her to the processing facility on Calicto." Blinks all round. "See this." He tapped the star pinned to his coat. "This means what's yours is mine." He pointed the pistol at the nearest guard's face. "Do I have to get personal?"

Violence. The universal language. The authority cops stepped aside, and Kellee pulled me through the airlock doors, swiftly locking them behind us. Pressurized air hissed. He let go of my cuffs and dropped himself into the pilot's seat. The shuttle was tiny compared to the ferry we'd spent the last hour in. Big enough for a two-man crew, but little else.

"You'd better sit down." He flicked a bunch of switches on the control panel. "I don't plan on hanging around while they realize I just bluffed my way into stealing their ride."

I eased into the co-pilot's chair and watched his hands sweep across the controls with efficient ease. "You don't have the jurisdiction to commandeer this ship?"

He snorted and nodded at the front-facing screen curved around us. "You see that?"

I saw a whole lot of black nothingness outside.

"Out here, Messenger, jurisdiction is just a word like any other. It all comes down to the delivery." He strapped himself in and hit a button that disconnected our shuttle. A mechanical jolt trembled through the floor. "And who's holding the biggest gun."

I strapped into the co-pilot's seat.

The marshal entered what I assumed were coordinates

back to Calicto. I watched his hands closely, committing each button push and entry to memory.

"You're some hot property, Kesh Lasota."

I side-eyed him. I didn't recall telling him my name.

"Those weren't real port authority officials." He pushed a button, and the shuttle bolted into the black, rattling the cabin. "My guess is they were Crater's men and your shuttle ride was doomed from the beginning. Like I said, you're not as invisible as you think." He glanced over. "Have I done enough to prove I'm not out to get you?"

"That depends on where we're going." *And what you want from me.*

"To a rock in the middle of nowhere." He flicked his screen and sent our destination onto my screen. He was right. We were heading out into deep space. Not much out there but rocks, criminals and pirates. Which one was he?

"Are you going to tell me what's going on?" he asked.

I shifted in the chair, sinking deeper into its embrace, and eyed the cuffs still locked around one wrist. *If only I could, Marshal...*

CHAPTER 7

Marshal Kellee removed the cuffs as soon as the shuttle was locked on course. We traveled the rest of the way in silence, until a tiny shining mass took shape beyond the shuttle's screen, growing like snowflakes on the glass.

I peered closer. "What is that?"

The marshal glanced sideways and must have seen the anxiety I was working hard to hide. "You don't travel much, huh?"

"No, not much," I admitted, trying not to let on how this was only the second time I'd been space-bound in my entire life. I gripped the seat's arms, digging in my fingernails. During my first space-faring trip, the ship had been huge. So vast, in fact, that it had felt as though the planets moved around it. This little shuttle felt more like a ration can.

The marshal nodded at the growing station, its branches spinning lazily. "That's Point Juno. We're in Halow's outer system. That station is about all that's around here unless you want to travel a few days farther toward the debris zone. There's a few unregistered points out that way, built by scavengers mostly."

Closer and closer we drew, pulled as if by some magnetic force, until the station filled the screen. Specks of dust fluttered between Juno's jutting branches, buzzing back and forth. Ships. I pushed to my feet and leaned over the shuttle controls. So many ships.

I caught the marshal watching me and settled back in the seat, shrugging off the sight like I saw enormous space stations every day.

He chuckled, sparking a filament of annoyance inside me. Not at him, but at myself. I was better at hiding my thoughts than this. I *had* to be better.

The marshal swept the shuttle under one of the station's arms, threading it through buzzing traffic. Colored lights blinked, painting the scene in neon greens and pinks. Our little shuttle seemed to speed up now that we were close to the station's superstructure, but the marshal's hands deftly maneuvered us around, up, over and through.

My gut lurched as the shuttle dipped. My nails bit into the seat. Was all this *whooshing* normal? The marshal's gaze was glued ahead, switching from the controls to the window. He didn't seem concerned.

By the time the marshal spun the shuttle around and locked it in a dock, sweat dampened the back of my neck.

He turned and paused after seeing my face. "Are you okay?"

I stared at a static point ahead. Some kind of antenna array. Whatever it was, it helped anchor me and stop my head from spinning. "I'm absolutely fine." I would be fine once my head stopped spinning and the motion sickness passed.

He unbuckled himself from his seat, keeping his face turned away, and headed to the rear of the shuttle.

"It takes some getting used to." His deep voice rumbled with repressed laughter.

I couldn't summon enough energy to care. Pressure seals hissed, and a welcome blast of cool air swept into the shuttle. Peeling my trembling body out of the seat, I breathed in, filling my lungs with fresh air, and touched my whip. The weapon's coiled energy skipped into my palm, and my magic threaded warm fingers across my skin. The combination of pleasure and pain distracted me enough to put one boot in front of the other until I had passed through the depressurizing locks into a single-level apartment. Low couches grouped in one corner, a table and two chairs occupied a spot by a window and, outside, glittering metal funneled to a patch of black space. We were in what I assumed was the marshal's home, inside the station's belly.

He shrugged off his coat, draped it over the back of a couch and crossed the apartment, rolling up his shirt sleeves past the elbows, revealing well-defined bronze-skinned forearms. He had the physique of a manual laborer, something used to physical exertion, not a paper-pushing street-marshal.

He stepped behind a counter, hands working across some flat panels with the same familiarity as when he'd piloted the shuttle. A soft sound rang out, and two drinks containers rose out of the countertop.

He scooped one up and took a long drink. I watched his throat move and trailed that movement down to the gaping neckline.

He set his glass down and finally noticed me at the door. "You can come in. I don't bite." His gaze lingered on me, and mine on him. There was a challenge in the way he looked at me. It had been there from the first moment we'd met in the sinks. But what kind of challenge, I wasn't yet sure. Was he daring me to contradict him, waiting for me to figure him out?

I took another step inside, and the pressured door automatically hissed closed with a comforting weightiness behind it. The vacuum of space was right outside, way too close for my liking. It occurred to me that I was a million miles from my home, on an unfamiliar waypoint, in an unfamiliar part of space, with no knowledge of how to pilot a shuttle, and my only company was that of a lawman who I knew could be lethal.

I shrugged off my coat and laid it over the couch, next to the marshal's. He wasn't so tough. He was just one male, albeit his species was unknown. My whip was safely stowed inside my coat. If the marshal was as innocent as he claimed to be, then I wouldn't need it. But if he tried anything, he'd soon learn that my whip wasn't my only weapon.

The apartment was functional. Clean, tidy. Minimalist. And about five times the size of my box. As I roamed, I found nothing personal. Unless a small fish bowl with one lonely fish bobbing inside could be categorized as personal. It and its fish, however, were worth a fortune in water. I snorted at the extravagance. What kind of archaic fool keeps a fish in a bowl filled with priceless water?

The space looked like a show apartment or a hotel room. He didn't spend much time here. Or perhaps this was where he brought all his women before... whatever guys like him did out in the blackness of space. No, that wasn't fair. Was the marshal dangerous? Yes. I'd seen how dangerous he could be. But, so far, he had only shown me kindness. He clearly wanted something from me. How would he react when he didn't get it?

I reached the counter after giving myself the tour and picked up the drink. "Nice place. Must have cost a pretty amount?"

He leaned a hip against his side of the counter and didn't reply.

"Not bad, for a marshal." The drink tasted like water with a touch of lime. It wasn't water, but it was damn close. How could a Calicto lawman afford all this?

"I wasn't always a marshal," he admitted. "That's a... new career." He picked up his drink and headed toward the couches. Without his coat hiding his outline, I studied the confident way he moved. Broad shoulders carried a man who didn't know how to hesitate. No wasted gestures. No wrong step. It helped that he had an easy stride and a tight ass I would have liked to admire for a lot longer than the minute he gave me as he reached into a panel in the wall and revealed a slim personal interface screen.

A seat emerged from the wall. He settled into it. "There's a shower out back and a private bedroom. Make yourself comfortable. I have reports to file, then I'll ask you some questions and you're going to answer them."

He didn't look up, just sipped his drink and tapped away on the PI screen. If he believed it would be that easy, he had the wrong girl. But I'd take advantage of his hospitality. After downing my drink, I headed for the back rooms.

"Kesh?" My name on his lips pulled on an invisible string, bringing me up short. When I looked back, the marshal rubbed a hand across his chin, carefully measuring his next words. "You're safe here."

Safe.

Safe was an interesting concept. In this place, in this system, I wasn't safe. Safe was a refuge inside my mind. Safety wasn't something anyone could give me, but it was a nice idea. "Whatever you say, Marshal."

I left the room and heard him say, "Call me Kellee. Can you at least do that?"

~

BLOOD DRIPPED *from my fingers and pattered against the dusty ground. Falling like the rain. Pitter-patter, pitter-patter. Dampness on glistening leaves and on my tongue too. Wetness and blood. But not my blood.*

A fluttering sounded to my right, buzzing in my ear. The curious pixie hissed close, stirring my matted strings of hair. I bared my teeth at its twinkling light and the creature darted off. Like the pixie, but from somewhere far away, I was observed by curious fae. They looked down on me, untouchable, like gods.

Other pulsing lights danced in the dark. I ignored them and listened hard. Listened to the rapid beat of my heart, to my blood pumping through my veins, filling me up, making me something more.

Movement shifted to my right. I didn't hear it so much as feel it. Inside—in what they called the animal *part of me—I knew I was no longer alone. My slick fingers curled tighter around my knife's oak handle.*

I imagined I heard those watching, imagined they chanted my name. They knew what was coming. They loved me for it. And somewhere inside, deeper than the hate, deeper than the injustice, I loved them too.

Eyes glistened in the dark. Human eyes, gently sloped. Aeon. And in his hand, an oak-handled knife shone. Just like mine.

I blinked awake. There one moment, here the next.

My heart hammered against my ribs, trying to break free. The dream would leave me soon, but while it had its claws in me, I couldn't move. Didn't dare. The pitter-patter of rain on thick, fat leaves beat against my thoughts. The wetness still hung in the air. So much water it fell from the sky. As did the blood.

And Aeon.

I shoved from the bed too fast, almost staggering over my own feet. *Whose bed is this? Where in the three systems am I?*

The walls, the floor, the bed, the smell—like warm, spicy male cologne. *Where the...* I pressed a hand to my head, squeezing out the past, making room for the present. The shuttle, the authorities, the marshal, the station, the assassination, the fae.

I am Kesh Lasota.

Messenger.

Tek-whisperer.

I am invisible.

Kesh Lasota. Right. And this room... This was the marshal's place. I'd lain down, just for a few minutes to rest my eyes. How long had I slept? A weary weight had settled in my bones, now replaced by stiffness. I'd slept for hours, not minutes. Dammit. Sota may not have hours.

I headed for the door and paused, realizing I was barely dressed. Tossing on my outer garments—self-cleaned and patched up while I'd rested—I strode out into the living area, expecting to find Kellee where I'd left him, monitoring his screen. The ambient light had softened, indicating resting hours, but there was no sign of the marshal. My coat lay on the back of the couch. The marshal's was missing.

Throwing my coat on, I turned, considered heading for

the main door and spotted the glimmer of Kellee's personal entertainment screen extended from the wall. Leaving it open and unattended? He wasn't used to having company. As I sat behind it and swept my hands across the semi-transparent interface, it also became clear that the marshal hadn't set up his console for someone of my *talents*. My fingertips tingled, and at my hip, my whip warmed, sensing my latent magic coming to life.

I sidestepped the marshal's woefully inadequate security measures. His PI opened like a flower, revealing everything the marshal had been working on while I'd been sleeping, which was apparently me.

A blurry image flicked across the screen. A figure caught in motion crossing a plaza. Around the person, people were frozen statues, their images encased in electronic ice. The figure was a ghost. But to anyone who knew exactly what they were looking for: the gait, the coat, the hair. The figure was clearly me. The next slide showed a bounty issued on behalf of Crater's organization. The v-coin payout had enough zeros to make coordinates jealous.

I looked up, over the screen, at the plush apartment with all its luxuries.

Of course.

I was another notch in Kellee's bounty-hunting belt.

Crater's men would likely descend at any second. Worse, Arcon might be about to latch a shuttle to the private dock.

Kellee had set me up. He wanted all the v-coin.

I shoved from the seat. I had to get out of the apartment and off the station.

The apartment door swung open, and the marshal sauntered in, white bag in hand. "Good, you're up." He dumped the bag on the counter. "I didn't want to wake you."

He was at ease, comfortable in his own home and his deception. I'd seen him fight. He was fast, brutal, and efficient, but only when he saw the strike coming. Right now, he was vulnerable.

My whip hummed gently against my thigh.

"I brought you lunch," he chattered. "When did you last eat? Must have been a while ago..."

I sauntered toward the counter, catching a whiff of something sweet and spicy. My mouth watered. There would be time to eat once I had the marshal subdued and piloting the shuttle away from here. "Suteran food?" I asked.

"It is." He seemed surprised and distracted as he collected a couple of plates. "You've eaten Suteran before? It's rare around these parts. I hear they can't give it away near the debris zone. I've often thought about flying out there just to see if it's true."

I eased my hand inside my coat.

"Why haven't you?" I asked, keeping up the easy conversation.

His eyes flicked up. He reached for the bag.

Power surged up my arm, licking over the whip's tek and charging it with lethal force. The length of the whip flew upward, aglow with magic.

The marshal was gone.

The cool kiss of a blade touched my neck, biting just below my ear. He hadn't pulled me back, but he didn't need to. His breath tickled the hair over my ear. The knife did all the talking for him. "If you don't like Suteran, all you had to do was say so." He'd angled himself to the side, knowing not to stand directly behind me to

83

avoid any backward head-butt I may have been considering.

My whip collapsed into a coil of metal chain on the countertop. And my magic fell away with it.

"That's one fancy whip. Almost like it has a mind of its own."

"Maybe it does," I replied softly. If he was going to hurt me, he would have already.

He shifted slightly. The gritty edge of the knife dug in. I didn't feel it cut, the edge was too sharp, but I felt the trickle of blood slide down my skin and inside my collar. He leaned his hip into my lower back, careful to keep the pressure on without hurting me.

"Do you have anything else inside that coat you're considering flinging at me?" he asked.

"Wouldn't you like to know." He had probably already rummaged through the dozen pockets. He wouldn't have found anything. The coat knew when to keep its secrets.

"I know it's not the food. Suteran is damn good. So why the sudden hostility?"

His tone held an edge. It wasn't as sharp as his knife, but it still cut open old wounds. The blade nicked over old scars. Gooseflesh scattered down my neck and farther. It had been a long time since someone had gotten the best of me—warfae excluded.

"How'd you afford this place?" I asked.

"I told you. Previous work. Now why don't you answer my questions, seeing as I'm the one with the knife?"

"What does it matter? You're just going to hand me over to Crater's men anyway."

Quiet swelled, softened only by the humming of the circulation filters. "You hacked into my PI?"

"Hacking is so... clumsy."

"All right. You *whispered* your way in." He shifted against my back. "Do you think you know me, Kesh Lasota?"

I knew no human could outmaneuver my whip. I knew Marshal Kellee liked to bend the rules to suit him. And I knew he had no reason to keep me alive, or keep me safe, if not for the bounty.

"I had nothing to do with Crater's death," I told him. "The miners will kill me and ask questions later."

"I believe you."

I smiled. "But it doesn't matter what you believe, right? You're just in it for the v?"

The knife vanished, along with Kellee's weight against my back. I dabbed at the blood on my neck and turned, catching a glimpse of sharp incisors behind his slightly parted lips. I'd expected to see anger on his face, maybe some resignation. The heat in his glare burned away any snide remarks. He breathed too hard for someone under control, and for the first time, an icy finger of fear traced down my spine. I hadn't believed he would kill me, but something had changed.

He turned his face away and swallowed. The bloody knife trembled in his hand.

"I'm not about to sell you out." He ground out the words, still looking to the side.

No, I see that now. You're about to kill me.

"Whatever you say, Kellee."

He flinched at the sound of his name and drew in a deep breath. It seemed to center him enough for him to look me in the eye without snarling. But something slithered behind his skin, something he kept so well hidden that I only now began to understand just how dangerous Kellee might be.

What are you?

"You have a hard time trusting people," he remarked, moving around the counter to resume emptying his Suteran takeout. He moved differently. Gone were the smooth, confident gestures of a man in control. Now he moved as though with every grab at the food cartons and every snatch at the cutlery he was teetering on the verge of snapping. "But you need to trust me."

Was he joking? I'd be a fool to trust the thing I'd seen lurking beneath his skin. He was wound so tight he almost charged the surrounding air.

He dumped a plate in front of me. "Eat the damn food."

The spread looked delicious, fruity with something like noodles and brightly colored vegetable slices tossed in. Was it drugged? My stomach growled.

He growled deep and low at my hesitation. "I won't harm you. But you're testing my patience, Lasota." He stalked off and disappeared toward the back of the apartment. I heard a door close.

If Marshal Kellee didn't want the bounty, what did he want from me?

I eyed the door—my escape route—knowing what I had to do, but running wouldn't solve this. He would find me again. I picked up a green shoot covered in syrup and bit down. He was right. The food was good. I was halfway through the dish when I realized the marshal had taken his bloody knife with him.

CHAPTER 8

Whatever lurked beneath the marshal's skin didn't appear to be there now. He'd emerged from the back of the apartment without the knife, served up his takeout, carried it to the table by the window and tucked in as though I wasn't in the room.

I leaned back against the counter and watched him eat, the silence pulling thin between us. The next person who spoke would set the tone. If I threatened him again, he'd likely kick my ass again. He wasn't fae fast. He was faster. Almost a blur. I didn't sense any magic on him, but then, the magic I knew about was fae-based. And everything I'd seen of him so far indicated he wasn't fae. So what was he?

He finally finished his food and leaned back in his seat, in no hurry to talk. Behind him, through the window, the station's framework glittered, illuminated by the blink of passing shuttle lights.

"What are you?" he asked.

I wanted so badly to ask him the same. "What do you mean?"

"It's a simple enough question."

"I'm human. Obviously."

He pressed his lips together. He didn't like the way I sidestepped his questions. He was probably used to suspects spilling their secrets every time he flashed his badge.

After taking his time to consider my answer, he angled himself in the chair to face me. "All right, here's what I don't understand. You wield tek, and that weird glow you sometimes summon is magic. Somehow, you can combine both. That shouldn't be possible. Tek and magic repel each other. Always have. We both know you're not fae. But you're not human either. What you do... it defies everything we know about human capabilities. Humans can't wield magic. So, what are you hiding, Kesh Lasota?"

He was closer than he knew. "It's not magic you're seeing. It's just enhanced tek."

He wasn't buying it. "You interfere with any complicated tek in your immediate surroundings. I can't imagine it's a conscious skill. It's something built into you, a latent ability. Were you born with it?"

It had been trained into me, the tek-repelling. Plant-based secretions had been poured under my skin until it became part of who I was. But I wasn't about to tell him that. The truth of me? It was out of bounds. The marshal didn't need to get involved.

He had asked enough questions. Now it was my turn. "Why are you keeping me here?"

"I'm not." He stretched out a leg and leaned back against the window, folding his arms across his chest. "You can walk out that door and hitch a ride off Juno anytime you want." He appeared to be relaxed, but he could spring from that position with the barest physical tells. I'd hunted hundreds of killers. Fought hundreds more. The marshal moved like them, but in a way that hid what he was capable of. Most killers wore their brutality like a badge, but not him. The image of himself he presented was a mask, hiding the truth inside. We had that in common, at least.

"So, if I ask you to take me back to Calicto, you will?" I tested.

"Do you want to go back?"

"I have to," I replied. Would it be so wrong to let the marshal have a little information? He had connections in law enforcement. He might be able to use those connections to help me get inside Arcon. I'd always worked alone. It was safer that way. But the situation with Arcon and Crater's faction? Those walls were closing in. I was good at what I did, the marks painting my skin proved it, but the warfae was better than me. They always had been in the end. "I have a friend," I explained, mirroring Kellee's crossed arms. "He's in trouble."

"Oh, you do have friends. Do you attack them with your whip too?"

I gave him a dry look. Kellee was a long way from being a friend. "He was taken."

"Is that why you're running?"

"I'm running so I can regroup off Calicto and hit back twice as hard."

He scanned my expression with a hard one of his own. "Figured as much. You have half the Halow system out to kill or capture you, and you're going to charge back in to save a friend?" He scratched his chin and briefly averted his gaze. "He must be some friend."

"He is." He couldn't know Sota was an AI, and it didn't matter anyway. To me, Sota was real enough.

"You're going to get yourself killed."

I offered him a slice of a smile. "You don't know me. You have no idea what I can do."

"I have an idea, all right." His gaze slid to the whip.

I huffed a laugh. Whatever. This man couldn't know me. Some days, I didn't even know myself. "So, why am I here, Marshal? What do you want from me? You aren't helping me because you're a nice guy. You want something, and apparently, it's not the money."

"Do I look like I need the v?" He spread his hands.

He didn't, but the rich always wanted more. "Then why?"

He chewed on his words before replying. "You're right. I'm not a nice guy. Not even close. And I do want something from you." He tilted his head and appraised me from head to toe. Beneath the weight of his unblinking gaze, my heart picked up its pace and an unexpected flickering shortened my breath. He was quick, and intelligent, and a mystery. And I'd always had a weakness for anyone with enough skills to outmaneuver me. It didn't happen often.

Apparently done with his visual inspection, he stood and strode across the room toward me. Instincts warned me to back off and put space between us to swing the whip if I needed to, but I stood my ground. At the last step, he veered to my right to lean against the counter beside me. "Crater was assassinated, but not by you. Do you know how I know that?"

"No, but you can help by telling Crater's men to back off. If they rescind the bounty, that would give me room to breathe." He stood too close. He wasn't armed, although I hadn't seen him replace the knife, but it didn't matter. He radiated *threat*.

"They don't listen to the law so they won't listen to me. Besides, Crater's death isn't the real problem here."

"Isn't it?"

"Don't play coy, Lasota. It doesn't suit you."

My little smile died. "So tell me what really happened, smart ass."

"Witness reports claim the entire left-hand side of Crater's face exploded. The autopsy confirmed those reports. A high-powered projectile struck Crater behind his right ear, entering his skull from behind. Hence why half his face was missing. You stood in front of Crater the whole time you were delivering a message. You didn't kill him." Kellee toed open a hidden storage unit concealed beneath the counter and picked up a black bag from inside. He dumped it on the countertop and opened it, revealing the smooth metallic sheen of the warfae's rifle. It had to be the same gun.

Why was it in a bag in Kellee's cupboard and not some secure police HQ somewhere? "Isn't that evidence?" I asked.

"You recognize it?"

"Yes," I admitted. Kellee already knew I would. My attempt to lie my way around the curious marshal wasn't working. I would need another angle of attack.

"Are you going to explain how?"

I lifted my gaze and looked him in the eye. "Is this an interrogation?"

That earned me a snarl. "Right here, right now, I'm not a lawman. I stopped being a lawman when I stole an authority shuttle and brought you to my home. I don't know you, but I brought you here to keep the small army of bounty hunters and assassins from finding you. As thanks, you attack and threaten me right after I bought you lunch. So, how about you try trusting me? Just for a little while? You can go back to trying to kill me once we're done."

He made a good argument. Damn him. "I found the rifle in the construction site across the plaza from Crater's restaurant."

"Did you see the shooter?"

"No." The lie twisted inside me.

"That's not surprising."

Wasn't it? "Why?"

"Does anything strike you as odd about this weapon?"

I scanned it again, remembering Sota's words. It was a highly modified rifle, likely charged with fae magic when in use. If I told the marshal that, he'd think I was insane. Unless he was testing the waters for information he'd already assumed.

"Guns aren't really my thing. I much prefer whips."

He ran his hand along the barrel, fingers trembling. "Its design is unusual. Heavily modified from the original in a way that doesn't make sense, unless there's an element missing."

"What element?" *Magic*, of course.

"I'm not sure." He again scratched his chin, the gesture a nervous tell. "Tek and magic combined, like your whip, perhaps?"

Good call. My whip was exactly like the rifle and equally rare. "Do you think the shooter left it there to further implicate me?" I asked, thoughts spiraling. If I told him the truth—not all of it, just enough to stop the questions—he could help. He already suspected something, hence all the questions. Marshal Kellee would make a useful ally.

"I think someone disturbed him before he could

dismantle it. He needed a quick getaway. This rifle would have slowed him down."

Yes, it would have. And perhaps then I might have caught the fae. Larsen—unlikely his real name—had left the rifle behind, thinking nobody would know what it was. They certainly wouldn't suspect it was fae-crafted.

"Maybe I disturbed him..." My voice sounded distant, lost behind the history crowding my head.

He turned, sharp eyes scouring my face for clues, for lies, for all the things he knew I was hiding. "If we track down the killer, you're off the hook."

I'd moved closer while looking in Kellee's bag, and now, when I looked up, flecks of hazel darkened the marshal's green eyes, and the hint of something more lurked behind his gaze. Oh, I knew exactly where the shooter was. Right in the heart of Calicto, sitting on his oak throne as the head of Arcon. Was this the right time to tell Kellee? If he didn't believe me, he might laugh me off. But if he did... Unfortunately, if he believed me, that knowledge would likely get him killed. Kellee was a lawman. He would be obliged to investigate. The warfae would kill him. I didn't know Kellee well, but I didn't want to see him tortured and killed just because I didn't think I could get Sota back alone. And I needed help.

"Tell me why you're helping me and I'll tell you everything," I said.

"Everything?"

"All of it."

"Tell me everything first, and I'll tell you why I'm helping you." His lips twitched and humor brightened his eyes.

The itch to punch him twitched my fingers. "This isn't funny, Marshal. There are more lives at stake than you can

93

imagine. This goes way beyond one man's assassination. What I'm about to tell you could change the way you see the worlds, change everything you know."

He arched an eyebrow. "Do I need to sit down?"

My glare darkened. "If you won't take this seriously, then take me back to Calicto."

"Where you'll be shot dead before you leave the dock." He closed the bag and hid it beneath the counter again. "You've been alone a long time, Kesh Lasota. You don't need to be alone any longer. Tell me what you're running from. Let me help you."

What was I running from? Another life, another girl, just like me. She lived in my memories and in Sota's databanks. She was a slave, a killer, a hero to a people that weren't hers. She was everything Kesh Lasota was not.

I swallowed and touched the ghost of an old scar on my neck, long ago surgically removed. "The fae aren't gone." Just saying the words felt like laying land mines. Like any second, the truth would explode, killing me, the past, and the marshal too.

The marshal was no longer laughing. The beast behind his glare stirred, lifting the fine hairs on the back of my neck. A flicker of fear darted through my chest, tightening old instincts. My whip was close, but so was Kellee.

"I know," he said, grinding out the words. "That's why I'm helping you."

CHAPTER 9

I told Kellee about the message, about Sota's eighteen seconds, about the fae I'd failed to chase down. He listened without interrupting. I told him about Larson, about Arcon, and about Merry. The more I told him, the more I wanted to spill all my secrets to this man I hardly knew. But some secrets were too dangerous to spill.

When I was done, hours had passed and my voice had grown hoarse. Marshal Kellee now knew everything there was to know about the messenger, Kesh Lasota.

He poured two drinks and set them down on the table between us. The apartment lights were still dimmed, and from outside, the occasional flare of light would wash across us both, highlighting Kellee's thoughtful expression.

I picked up my glass, folded my legs under me on the couch opposite the marshal's and waited for him to say something. I didn't even care about the silence. I liked it, in fact. Air filters hummed. There was no clanging or groaning from stacked containers. No shouts from too-close neighbors. For the first time in a long time, I almost felt safe. Almost. But a very real and obvious threat existed here. The marshal. I'd told him what he'd wanted to know. Now all I had to do was wait and see what he did with that information, what he did with me.

He leaned forward and picked up his drink, but he saw me watching and lowered the glass. "Crater met with a marshal from my station. A day later, Crater's dead." Now he took a drink, downing the contents in one. "The marshal he met with is missing."

"You think Crater implicated Arcon in something?"

He swallowed. "There have been other... events during the past year. Marshals quitting for no reason. Some out of character incidents... I don't know who to trust."

I knew exactly how he felt. "But what made you think any of this was fae related?"

"You mean besides the rifle, which is clearly modified for fae use?" He leaned back and stared into the middle distance, perhaps seeing the past in the room with us. "I told you I wasn't always a marshal. I did some mercenary work. And before that..." The corner of his mouth twitched. "Let's just say you and I have more in common than you would believe."

I doubted that. If he knew who/what I was, he'd probably kill me without blinking—or try to.

"There's someone who can help us. I think... Well, he's..." Kellee winced. Something in those memories was obviously unpleasant. "He's a fae expert. If we tell him what we know, he'll tell us whether it's possible. Might even help us..."

"Help us do what exactly?"

"Stop them."

"I... I just want Sota back." I took a drink to moisten my suddenly dry mouth. Stop the fae? No. One messenger and a marshal wouldn't be enough to stop them—if they planned on returning.

"I figured you were many things, but not a coward." He smiled, testing me.

If he meant his accusation to hurt, he had me all wrong. "I'm just a messenger. What can I do? If you want to get yourself killed, go right ahead."

"Just a messenger?" He stood, set his drink down and retrieved his coat. "Right. Of course you are. A messenger who escaped a warfae and carries a magic-enhanced whip. That's not all you are, is it...?" He collected my coat and stood over me, holding the coat out. "But sure, I'll play along with your little fantasy—for now."

Fantasy? I snatched my coat and tugged it on. "Where are we going?"

"To get answers."

~

A BLACK ROCK loomed in the shuttle window, growing larger by the second, until it swamped the screen, blotting out everything else. Up close, it glittered with antennae and surveillance masts. We approached a beam jutting from the surface—the dock.

"What is that place?" I asked.

Kellee adjusted the shuttle, keeping us level with a line of green indicator buoys.

"A prison."

The rock had to be at least fifty miles across and just as deep. Kellee had told me this place didn't appear on any official chart. Looking at the barren, isolated rock, I asked myself what crimes someone would have to commit to be sent here. "How many people do they keep in there?"

"One."

One?! "All that prison for one prisoner?"

"Yeah…" Kellee adjusted the shuttle's flight, bringing us closer to the dock's mouth.

"And this one prisoner is your source?" I tried and failed to keep the alarm out of my voice.

"I didn't say it would be easy to get answers."

Once we had docked, Kellee flashed his badge and guards waved us into the narrow rock-lined tunnels. The marshal asked that we not walk through the scanners, and reluctantly, after a few v-coins changed hands, he got his wish. He chatted with them, all small talk and easy smiles. Everyone recognized Marshal Kellee.

Finally, after our confusing parade of small talk between chamber after chamber, we were escorted into an enormous space. The heavy door clanged shut, sealing us inside a chamber so big the glow from the lights didn't touch the walls. Every boot scuff or rustle of clothing was eaten by the emptiness.

At the cavern's center, lit from all corners by powerful floodlights, stood a container-sized, metal-lined glass cage. And inside, head bowed, long, fine silvery hair spilling over one shoulder, stood a male fae. I froze, boots glued to the floor. A thousand memories came crashing in. He looked exactly the way I remembered the fae to be. He even wore the tan leather garments of most scouts, cladding his body from neck to toe. They didn't wear armor, relying instead on speed and agility to outmaneuver their enemies. It made them vulnerable up close—but only if you survived getting within melee range. But this one didn't look vulnerable.

Kellee approached the glass and metal-framed wall.

It's not enough. The cage, this prison… not enough.

The security, the isolation, the whole damn rock—it wasn't enough to hold him. And yet there he was. Trapped.

Slowly, he lifted his head. Violet eyes shone from behind his silvery bangs. "Hello, Marshal."

The voice was everything I loathed. Honey and silk, a sweetness so seductive it hurt to hear it. Instincts clawed at me to run. To run and keep on running to the far corners of the three systems. But another part of me, a stronger, defiant part, wanted to move closer, to hear that voice again, to let his luscious tone wash over me, through me. I measured my breathing—slowly in, slowly out—and calmed my thoughts. This was his prison. Not mine.

"Talen," Kellee greeted. He stopped a foot from the glass and tucked both hands casually into his pockets, his demeanor that of someone who had dropped by to visit an old friend.

"It has been a long time since your last visit," Talen commented, hiding an accusation beneath those words.

"Has it? I hadn't noticed."

The fae's right eyebrow twitched. The movement was tiny. Most would have missed it completely. But I knew what I was looking for. The marshal's words had hurt him. This fae *cared*.

Talen leaned outward and peered around the marshal's shoulder. His intense gaze pierced the shadows, spearing into me. "You have brought me a guest."

Kellee turned, surprised to see me rooted to the floor only a few steps inside the room. "Kesh?"

No, no, don't tell him any more. Not my name, not any of it. If I had known Kellee's source was a fae, I wouldn't have come. The second I stepped into the light, I'd be exposed. Would he know? The marks painting my skin itched. Would he recognize me? I didn't recall him or his name, but there had been so many fae and my name was notorious among them. Not Kesh's name. My *other* name.

But I wouldn't run. Not from him. I briefly touched my neck, feeling the ghost of cool metal. He was caged. I was free.

I willed my feet to move forward and plastered a blank expression on my face.

"Ah," the fae said. The smooth sound unwound me. "Marshal Kellee, would you be so kind as to leave us alone?"

Kellee chuckled. "That's not happening, Talen."

The fae cut him a look so deadly I was surprised it didn't slice through the cage.

Unfazed, Kellee rapped his knuckles on the glass. "Remember who put you here."

"How could I forget?"

Had Kellee captured this fae? I swallowed a hard knot in my throat and stopped beside Kellee. The fae's eyes bored into mine, burrowing deep into my soul and digging up all the gems of my past. Had he once seen me painted with the blood? Had he roared along with the thousands of others who had reveled in their entertainment? He didn't look the type to lose his mind over bloodlust, but they never did.

The fae's smile held secrets. He glanced at Kellee but didn't seem inclined to speak what was on his mind. *He knows. He knows. He knows.* My heart beat out the fear.

Talen dragged his gaze over me, slow and steady. "Thief."

"I am no thief." But I understood why he would think so. He likely sensed the low magical throb I carried with me.

His eyes narrowed, gaze piercing deeper. "What do you want?" he asked, looking directly at me.

I was here. It was done. And if there were consequences, I would deal with them. But right now, I needed answers. "What do you know about fae adopting tek?"

He waited a few beats, his thoughts probably lingering on how I carried fae magic. "We're averse to using tek," he said. "It pains us, as you know. But in extreme circumstances, we'll adopt it, briefly, if we must."

"Is it possible for a fae to live in a tek-advanced society?"

He flicked a hand, dismissing the suggestion. "Unlikely. For a day or two, perhaps. No more."

I looked again at his surroundings. His cell—crisscrossed with metal. The tek observing from hidden corners. The array of tek I had seen on the way in. The prison was encased in tek. How was this fae even coherent?

Intelligence sparkled in his eyes. "You're wondering how I have survived?" Talen asked. "I have been here a very, very long time. Besides living, my only other option is death, and I am not ready to meet the Hunt just yet."

He must be in agony. Every breath, every movement, must hurt. "Then, isn't it correct that a fae exposed to tek over a long period of time could live in a tek-advanced society? Like you are here."

"Live? No. Survive?" He smiled at my question, almost as though it pleased him to have me ask it. "This..." He stepped back from the glass, the movement silent. "Was not voluntary."

"But if he or she were exposed to tek slowly, over many years, they might build up a resistance?"

The fae blinked, possibly for the first time since we

had entered. "It is possible but unheard of. It would take many years of voluntary exposure to human tek and a great deal of pain."

So, Larsen had slipped under the radar over years. Centuries? "How long have *you* been here?" I asked.

"It has been three hundred and forty-two years since the marshal detained me."

Kellee stiffened. Talen had revealed too much, and the fae's smile proved it.

I blinked, careful to school my features. The marshal was *how* old? I stared ahead, refusing to glance at Kellee despite needing to see his reaction.

Talen's soft smile had probably lured hundreds of humans to their deaths over the years. Here, he was using it against Kellee. He knew he'd given something away. From my time behind bars, I knew such slights against a jailor—small as they were—amounted to huge victories.

"You endure pain daily?" I asked, quieter now.

"I do." To survive, he had built up an immunity to tek. If he'd done it, others might have as well. Others like Larsen. It would have taken time. Time during which the fae had fallen into myth and legend. Human generations. But the fae were nothing if not patient. Long-lived, what was a few hundred years of pain?

"Why do you ask, *Kesh?*"

A shudder tracked its way down my spine. "There's—"

"No reason," Kellee interrupted.

The fae studied us. His silvery hair moved beneath the light like liquid mercury. For someone caged for over three hundred years, he looked remarkably well. We studied each other. What family was he from, I wondered. Was he a social fae, a worker, or was he in service to the court? None of the answers mattered, but a fae locked away so far from home was a sight I'd never expected to see. It was like catching a mythical creature in a jar. It shouldn't have been possible.

He moved closer to the glass and tilted his head. His violet eyes darted as he studied me. "What are you?"

I glanced at Kellee and saw the marshal raise an eyebrow. He had asked me the same.

"A messenger," I replied.

"No," Talen said. "You have the magic of my kind. I sensed it the moment you entered. You've spent time with us. A long time." He touched his neck, and before I could stop myself, I had mirrored the gesture. I dropped my hand, but the flash of recognition in his eyes told me he understood.

"I see." His smile grew predatory, and this time, when he looked at Kellee, there was a knowing brightness in his eyes and a smirk tugging at his lips. "Do you trust your companion, Marshal?"

"We're done here." Kellee strode toward the door, leaving me alone, facing the fae.

"I know you." Talen pressed a hand against the glass. His flesh bubbled and sizzled, but he leaned in closer, ignoring the burn. "You have the power to free me from this prison. Do it, do it now and I will forever be in your debt."

My heart raced too hard, tightening my chest. "I can't."

"You can." Closer still. His beautiful eyes shone alarmingly with tears. In all the years I had spent with them, I had never once seen a fae cry. A single clear droplet skipped down his pale cheek. "Do this one thing and I will be yours."

There was magic in those words. A promise, a curse. And my human heart ached for it.

"Kesh!" Kellee snapped. "Get away from him."

I had loved them once, loved them like I was one of them. And this one, lost to his people, lost to his world, captured for centuries. Like me, he had been caged. I pressed my hand to the glass, over where the metal-infused screen scorched his palm.

"I know you, saru. Free me and I will be yours." He dropped to one knee, closed his burnt hand into a fist, pressed it against his heart and bowed his head. "Allow me to serve you."

Kellee grabbed my arm and dragged me toward the door. The fae stayed bowed, his words circling inside my head. *Allow me to serve you.*

"Don't listen to him," Kellee hissed. "Words are the only weapons he has left."

Talen's tear-filled offer haunted me long after the prison door had slammed shut.

CHAPTER 10

Marshal Kellee jabbed at the flight controls, disengaging the shuttle from the prison dock. If he exerted any more force, he'd push his fingers through the console.

I gripped the back of the adjacent flight chair. I couldn't bring myself to sit down and strap in, not with Talen's offer still ringing in my ears. *Allow me to serve you.* If I hadn't dug my fingers into the chair, Kellee would have noticed them trembling. The dangerous kind of anger burned like acid in my veins. It was a trick. No fae would ever serve a saru. They didn't know how to bow to anyone but their sovereign, and even then, it was begrudgingly.

"Are you going to demand I take you back to Calicto?" Kellee asked gruffly, his attention on piloting.

He had said he wasn't keeping me against my will. But walking back into Calicto without a plan would get me killed. One fae at the head of Arcon and another in prison? A day ago, I would have laughed at the thought. If there were two fae in Halow, there might be more. I couldn't tackle more alone.

My knuckles had bleached white. I loosened my grip on the chair. "You took me to a *fae*," I said, training my voice to hide everything boiling inside me.

"You wouldn't have gone had I warned you."

Why? Why had he done this? All we had learned from Talen was that a fae may deliberately build up a resistance to tek. I already knew it was possible, and now so did Kellee. But that meeting had been about more than that.

An ache throbbed through my jaw, radiating from my clenched teeth. "You wanted to see how he would react to me. You didn't just want answers about Larsen, you wanted answers about me."

Kellee maneuvered the shuttle backward, away from the dock. The engines grumbled, vibrating through the floor. The marshal didn't reply. Heated tension simmered around him. It didn't matter. He'd shown his true colors and used me.

"Sit down," he ordered.

I ignored him.

"Sit the fuck down," he growled. The sound raised the fine hairs on my arms. Warring instincts spiked my veins with adrenaline. He turned his head to finally look at me. Whatever he saw on my face eased some of his fury.

He sighed and faced ahead, rolling his shoulders to work out the frustration. "Would you please sit while we maneuver away from the dock? It's safer."

I didn't move. "It wasn't about getting help at all. It was about you trying to figure me out."

"Can you blame me? You're not fae, but you wield their magic. What am I supposed to think?"

"You were going to take me in..."

"I was," he admitted, still working the shuttle's controls. "Until those intruders attacked you. They would have killed us both. That's when things got interesting. Talen's reaction to you confirmed it."

"Confirmed what?"

"You're someone important to them."

A dry, humorless laugh barked free. "No, that's definitely not the case."

He flinched. "Whatever he told you, don't listen. It's misdirection. The first prison they had him in, he turned the entire staff against one another in three weeks. Now he's isolated—for everyone's safety. But I guess you know exactly how to handle a fae, right?"

So do you, Marshal.

I stared ahead at the blackness we cruised through. "*I know you.*" Talen couldn't know me. He had been in prison too long to know me. Maybe he hadn't meant it literally. He knew I had his people's magic. He knew I was saru. In his lofty fae mind, that was probably all he needed to know.

I touched my neck, expecting to find the cool touch of iron, but only found my skin, soft and warm.

"You have the power to free me from this prison.

Allow me to serve you."

Their word bound them, and Talen's words had been explicit. He couldn't know me, he couldn't know what I'd done, but he could be *mine,* and that was no small thing. The thought alone set my pulse racing. The times I'd dreamed of being equal among them, being loved for the right reasons, not the wrong ones. Talen couldn't make me fae, but having him beholden to me... his power as my own, his strength coursing through my veins. To a saru, there was nothing more seductive, not even freedom.

Better to push it aside for now. Larsen was the priority.

"Did you get your answers about me, Marshal?"

He glanced over. I expected to see a triumphant smile on his face but didn't get that at all. If anything, the lines around his mouth made him appear tired. "Some. And a whole lot more questions."

I kept my eyes on the nothingness ahead of us. I had questions too, like how the marshal had captured a fae some three hundred years ago. "You once hunted the fae?"

"No." His quiet dragged on for so long after his denial that when he next spoke, his soft words bore the terrible weight of their meaning. "They hunted my kind. To extinction."

~

THE RIDE back to Juno passed in silence. I left Kellee to stew in his apartment on everything he'd learned from my encounter with his prisoner and ventured into Juno proper. Curved glass revealed the station's spine and the catwalks wrapped around it, each one like ribs around the central cavity. Walking to the edge and pressing my hands against the glass, I peered down into the station's cavernous middle until a hot wash of vertigo forced me back.

So much glass and metal. Dots of color streamed along the transparent ribs—corridors. People. Hundreds of them. Like ants in a hill. I looked up, following the central cavity to a black dome pricked by starlight. *Not ants, more like goldfish in a bowl.* Juno was so vast and beautiful, typical of human tek, but so fragile. Juno was exactly the kind of place the fae despised.

Doesn't matter. None of this matters.

Using my coat's cloaking abilities, I spun myself an illusion to blend in, exploiting the drab colors and altering my facial features enough to fool any surveillance that got lucky and noticed me among the crowds. Arcon may not be watching this far away from Calicto, but their tek was here.

I entered an elevator and rode it down a few levels alongside fifty or so others. All were well dressed and wealthy. They chatted about nonsense. Family, work, travel. All the mundane things people shared when they came together. I listened, absorbing their accents so that when I needed to speak, I would blend in.

Kellee had told me where to find the parts I needed. He hadn't asked what they were for, although I'd seen in his eyes that he'd wanted to. He had wanted to ask about many things. I had no intention of telling him anything he didn't need to know. Once Larsen was dealt with, I would disappear from the marshal's life. Better for him to always wonder about the girl with her illusions. If he knew what those illusions covered, his sense of honor would force him to act. So, I would slip away, never to be seen again, and leave the marshal to his crusade against the fae. It was the only way we would both survive.

The store Kellee had directed me to glittered with electronic components. I dulled my magic and stepped inside. Many items on display cost more than what I earned as a messenger and some also appeared to be illegally modified, but like the marshal had said, there was no law this far outside Halow's main systems.

I collected a few items I needed and some I didn't. Sota would appreciate a few upgrades. It's always best to keep a drone capable of microwaving your bones to ash inside your own skin happy.

After purchasing the components, I left the store and spotted the marshal rising from a bench. How had he seen through my illusion? I ignored him and slipped into the crowd. Sure enough, his reflection in the store windows confirmed he had fallen into step behind me. I had planned to return to his place, but now I wanted to know how far the marshal's tracking abilities went. Playing cat and mouse would have been easier with Sota, but I hadn't always had the drone. Dusting off old skills, I picked up my pace, weaving faster through the shoppers. Once I had a good distance between us, I veered into a restaurant, asked after the washroom, and slipped inside. In seconds, I'd switched my appearance, this time draping myself in male attire. The illusion would hold as long as nobody touched me. The marshal wouldn't spot the change without biotek.

I left the restaurant and eased into a swaggering pace —nothing like Kesh Lasota's purposeful stride. Juno's smooth, shiny surfaces highlighted the reflections of those around me, and so far, the marshal wasn't among them. Good. Knowing how to give him the slip may come in useful.

When I returned to his apartment, he was sprawled on his couch, reading from his personal palm-sized screen as though he'd been there all along.

"Did you get everything you need?" The little smile he wore held a smug edge.

I smiled back. "I did." I set my box of components down on the floor—the easiest place to spread all the tiny circuitry—and set to work.

I hadn't been born to tek like most humans outside of Faerie. So, when I first encountered the strange metal devices with little electronic minds of their own, I'd been fascinated by their construction. Fascinated enough to strip down stolen components and rebuild them into something new. I'd been punished time and time again, but the lashings didn't matter. What was more pain to a creature like me, surrounded by pain and bloodshed? But tek, that was something else. In my cell, my world so small I counted it in steps, the wonder of tek had been the real magic. Not the intangible fae magic. Tek was a whole other world filled with possibility. I'd created new machines, new tek. Those tek trinkets had saved my life a hundred times over—and condemned it.

"Here." I held out a black device no larger than a thumbnail. "It's the best I can do with what I have here."

The marshal had joined me on the floor some time ago to watch me dismantle the circuitry from the pieces I'd purchased and solder them into something else entirely.

He held out his hand. I dropped the comms into his palm and picked up its twin. "What is it?" he asked, studying it closely.

"Put it behind your ear, under your hair and against your skin."

He frowned like I'd told him to eat it, reluctantly picked it up and eyed it between his finger and thumb. "Where's the power source?"

"That's you."

"Me?"

"A human body can generate anywhere between one hundred and two thousand watts. You aren't human, but your physique suggests you have a high-energy output."

The humor in his eyes told me he liked that I'd noticed his physique. "Will it burrow into my brain and hide behind my eyes?" he asked, not entirely joking.

"What?" There was military tek capable of exactly that, but I certainly wouldn't force such a thing on someone—he was smiling again like he knew he'd had me —even someone as annoying as Kellee. The spark of annoyance quickly faded, replaced by an even more infuriating urge to laugh with him. "Just put it on."

Sitting up, he pressed the comms behind his ear.

I did the same with mine and rolled my jaw to activate it. "Now you can hear me—"

He winced and plucked it off. "Can you do something about the volume?"

The marshal had acute hearing. *Interesting.* I took it off him, made some adjustments and handed it back. "That should be more bearable. It's low-tek, so Arcon's scanners shouldn't pick it up. They don't scan for basic systems like this. If they did, they'd pick up all manner of electronic devices people carry with them. Arcon is looking for weapons, not hearing aids."

"What's the distance?" he asked. His voice doubled up as a whisper behind my ear.

"A few miles, but that will depend on Arcon's systems. There are likely sections of the building where the comms won't work at all, but you'll see signs marking those restricted areas as communications dead zones."

I showed him how to roll his jaw to turn the comms on and off. The devices were only temporary, unlike my link to Sota, but it would allow Kellee and me to communicate inside Arcon.

Kellee helped tidy away the spare parts, collecting them into a pile on his kitchen countertop.

"You just have to get me inside," I said. "Tell them you're there to investigate the recent disturbance. Just doing your job. Once in, make your way to any of the rear windows or doors and I'll find you. You can open them from the inside. I'll scramble the surveillance and locks."

He nodded and picked up a cylinder around the size of

his little finger and teased it between his fingers. "What else can you make?"

"Anything, given enough time and the right equipment."

I offered him my hand, palm up. Kellee dropped the cylinder into it and watched as I collected a few more items, worked them together and finally lifted the electronic stickman to my lips and blew a little fae magic into it. I set the little electronic "toy" down on the counter and watched him climb onto wobbly metallic legs.

Kellee tilted his head and watched the toy man wobble about, then poked him. The toy staggered but stayed upright, and then he turned toward Kellee and lifted his wiry arm. Kellee pushed the toy again. Sparks jumped to Kellee, eliciting a hiss from the marshal's lips. He shook his hand out. "What was that?"

"I guess he doesn't much like you."

"It... he's... alive?" he asked carefully, aware of how absurd it sounded.

"He is."

"But you just... you just made it, right there. How is that possible?" He paused, realizing I'd used magic to bring the tek to life. The same as my whip. The same as the fae assassin's gun. The same as Sota, though the marshal didn't know that. All my tek was alive with fae magic, some more than others.

As the marshal understood, the toy electronic man slumped forward and stopped moving. His magic, what little I'd given him, had burned out.

"It's fleeting, especially so far from Faerie." I pressed my lips together, wishing I hadn't said the name, wishing I hadn't made the little man and seen the delight in the marshal's eyes. It was too late. I had said too much.

I lifted my head and caught Kellee's odd expression. The marshal knew. He knew exactly why I didn't behave like a human. He knew where I came from, knew why the imprisoned fae had talked to me the way he had, knew how I could animate soulless objects.

"You lived among them," he said.

I swallowed. "If you mean people in the sinks, sure I did." My attempt to cover up the truth sounded pathetic and desperate.

"You're not part of the sinks"—his voice quickened, his thoughts solidifying—"you just hide out there... hiding from the protofae. You were *born* on Faerie."

I turned away and crossed the room, collecting my coat. All my lies had begun to unravel. "No." More lies. He was too close to the truth. Why couldn't he stop asking questions? In five years, nobody had cared enough to ask me anything, and here he was, relentlessly digging.

"How did you escape? How did you get here? Defense drones beyond the debris zone would have shot down any ship." He came around the kitchen counter, strides driving his questions home. "What are you?"

"I don't know what you're talking about. Now let's get back to Calicto..." Tugging my coat on, I stopped by the airlock doors, ignoring my pounding heart. He wouldn't drop this. Someone like Kellee never did. He would poke and push until the truth pushed back. I would have to *deal* with him. Dammit, I didn't want that.

I watched him bear down on me. I didn't want to hurt him.

"Nobody leaves Faerie. Certainly no human—" He stopped, too close. His words burned like accusations. I lifted my chin and faced him. The marshal's keen mind worked. His questions rallied, and his answers jostled. And there, that moment on his face when he knew it all—or suspected. His eyes widened, and his lips parted. "You're *her*."

My knuckles met his face with a sickening crunch. Pain bloomed up my arm, and Marshal Kellee collapsed into a heap, adding a nasty-sounding crack to the skull. I stepped over his motionless body and pressed my fingers to his neck—assuming he had a pulse where most humans did. His blood beat hot and fast beneath my touch.

His eyelashes fluttered, but his eyes stayed closed.

Stay down, Marshal.

I sighed and rested my palm against his warm cheek. "In all this time nobody cared enough to ask the right questions. And yet, you figured it out in two days." I brushed my thumb against his lips, finding them tempt-ingly soft. To keep my secret, I should kill him, close my hand around his neck and squeeze. I lowered my hand, brushing across his jaw and down under his chin. It wasn't as though I hadn't killed before. But this lonely man with all his questions... This man who had saved me twice already... I didn't *want* to kill him.

Nobody will believe him anyway.

Bunching up his coat, I ran my fingers through his hair, checking for any serious damage, and tucked the coat under his head. His marshal's star winked accusingly. I unclipped it and shoved it into one of my coat's many pockets. "Sorry, Kellee. This way you get to live."

The first airlock door whooshed open under my touch, and within minutes, I was seated behind the shuttle's controls with only the most basic of notions for how to pilot it. I'd watched the marshal closely. All I had to do was uncouple and pull away from the dock. The shuttle's autopilot would do much of it. How hard could it be?

CHAPTER 11

*A*s it turned out, piloting a shuttle was as difficult as you'd imagine, but they were built like colossus tek, so a few knocks here and there at slow speed did little damage. Thankfully. Anyway, I was out of options. Taking the shuttle would keep Kellee off my back. By the time he came to, got himself another ride and tried to catch up, I'd be back on Calicto, walking into Arcon, with his marshal's badge giving me an all-access pass. Hopefully, he'd drop any heroic notions of stopping me and shrug the entire encounter off as a lucky escape. *Right.*

Calicto's port authority guided the shuttle into its dock, and after a few scrapes and bumps, I got the vessel coupled to the airlock. With my male illusion spun and the marshal's badge opening doors as though it were a magical key, immigration was a breeze, and within an hour of landing on Calicto, I was approaching Arcon's main entrance. This time I knew exactly what I was walking into. My whip was coiled warm and snug against my leg, well within the aura of invisibility I naturally threw off.

With the marshal's badge, I should be able to get into the depths of Arcon without raising suspicion.

"I should be grateful you didn't kill me when you had the chance," Kellee whispered into my ear.

I stopped and turned on the spot, and then I remembered the comms device behind my ear. *Dammit.* Reaching the top of Arcon's steps, I veered to the side of the entrance and leaned against the wall, keeping my head bowed. My ocular map showed the web of streets wrapped around Arcon's HQ. Kellee could be minutes away. The lawman was proving to be an enormous pain in my ass.

"How's your head?" I asked, keeping my voice low. People came and went from Arcon's steps. None of them wore the marshal's long coat. If he was watching the entrance, he would probably scan right over my male appearance, not realizing who was inside.

"How many did you kill?" his voice whispered through the comm-link, losing none of its menace.

I smiled to myself. It wasn't a pleasant smile, and I wasn't even sure why I wore it, but it seemed fitting. He thought he knew me. All he knew, if he had guessed right, was my reputation. It might even help me.

"I now understand why you won't fight this fae. He doesn't know who you are. What would happen if he did?"

The smile fell from my lips. "You won't tell him," I replied, sounding more confident than I felt. "You hate the fae as much as I do."

"Do you hate them?" Quiet crackled. *"Or do you love them?"*

Damn him. Damn him to the debris zone and back again. "Your questions will get you killed, Marshal."

"Questions are my job, **Wraithmaker**.*"*

I tore the comms device off and dropped it into my

coat pocket. I was done with the marshal and his stupid questions. The man was a distraction and a dangerous one.

Arcon's foyer hadn't changed in the time I'd been away. Staff bustled about. This was just another day working for the Halow system's largest surveillance firm and the charming Istvan Larsen. And as far as anyone was concerned, today was just another day for the marshal I was pretending to be.

Kellee carved through the people to my right, his gaze locked on me, leaving no doubt he knew exactly who I was despite the illusion. I sucked in a breath, careful to keep my composure. There was no point in running. It would just draw more attention to us, and I wasn't leaving without Sota. How had he found me?

Kellee held out his hand. "You have something of mine."

Dammit. Why did he have to be so damn good at his job? How did he even track me? Unless he didn't use visual clues. One of his other senses? Smell, perhaps?

I pulled his badge from my pocket and dumped it into his hand. He appeared fully healed. I should have hit him harder.

"What now?" I asked.

He blinked, probably because my voice was still female while the rest of me looked male. "Now we carry on with the plan. I get you inside, but I'm coming with you to find your so-called friend."

Because he didn't trust I even had a friend worth saving. Fine, if he wanted to get himself killed, it would save me the trouble.

We walked to one of the reception desks, and Marshal Kellee did his lawman thing, flashing his badge and saying all the right things to get us inside, just like we'd planned. That got us through the front line, but where we wanted to go, a row of security scanners waited—the ones my original plan had me avoiding. I had no idea how Arcon's scanners would react to my presence—or if they would react at all. If they were anything like Crater's, they'd let me pass right on through.

Down a long, narrow corridor, the veil of scanners appeared to be automated. Others ahead of us walked through as though merely passing through a doorway.

I didn't slow, didn't hesitate, and stepped into the invisible net of scanners, passing through unnoticed. *I am a ghost...* Arcon was still so confident that someone like me was a myth. I puffed out a sigh. This would be simple, just so long as—

An alarm barked. "Please wait. Personnel will arrive shortly," a synthesized voice announced.

I turned, already several strides ahead.

The scanners had flagged Kellee as a possible threat.

He waved me on and hung back, looking bored as though this was all routine. A door to my left opened as I strode by. An armed guard emerged. I heard him tell Kellee to present his identification. Once I was out of earshot, I reapplied the comms device and listened in to Kellee being questioned about his reasons for visiting.

Still hidden inside my illusion, I continued with all the confidence of someone who had every right to be wandering Arcon's corridors. I passed by staff unnoticed and kept going. It seemed unlikely that Arcon's scanners would miss me. Sure, I usually passed through these types of security systems unnoticed, but Larsen knew my tricks. If he had any sense, he would have recalibrated those scanners to look for anything unusual—like the vacant space I occupied.

Wraithmaker.

I winced, shook off the name Kellee had dredged up from my past, and walked with renewed vigor.

I didn't know much about where Arcon's labs were, but I knew the warfae had wanted Sota alive. He'd stolen Sota's docking station. My drone had to be here... somewhere.

The next set of scanners let me pass through unchecked. I entered an elevator, hit the button for Research and Development and felt the scanners run their electronic lasers through me.

"Sota..." I opened the mental link between us and called down it. If he was close and powered up, he should hear me.

"Kesh, where are you?" Kellee's thin whisper sounded through my comms, distracting me.

"On my way to Research and Development."

A few seconds passed, and this time, when Kellee spoke, interference crackled. *"Larsen is... the move. Told me to wait... There's a delay. He might know—"* The link cut off.

I was too deep to pull out.

"I'm coming after you," Kellee announced.

"Don't be a fool," I whispered back. "Get out of here." The elevator doors opened, revealing a hive of activity inside a maze of glass corridors. Every office was exposed, with everyone visible at their workstations. All anyone had to do was look up to spot me. I strode on, projecting a 100-percent-absolutely-definitely-supposed-to-be-here attitude.

A sweetness, floral and tempting, circulated in the air. I knew it well, having grown up surrounded by the intoxicating lure of Faerie magic. My power tingled across my skin and hummed through the coiled whip. I couldn't see any obvious source of the sensation, but a fae was here or nearby. Hardly surprising. Whatever Larsen was doing inside Arcon wasn't my problem. Get the job done and get out. I'd be invisible again soon.

"Sota..." I mentally called through our link. *"Help me find you."* The link buzzed with life signs, and my breath hitched. My drone was close.

My ocular map blinked into my vision, seemingly of its own accord. My stride tripped. I pushed forward, heartbeat thudding too loudly in my ears. A single red dot blinked in my vision, over the floor plan of the building. Sota. It had to be. He was down another level, deeper still inside Arcon, but so close.

"K—sh." Kellee's voice crackled through the comms. *"Wa—... Don't..."*

"I'm sorry, Marshal. Sorry for a lot of things." Perhaps the apology would mean more once all this was over.

Kellee said something too softly for me to hear. The deeper into Arcon I went, the more the connection failed. Hopefully, he would heed my advice and leave. Our original plan had us meeting up later. Knowing who I was, he probably wouldn't come, but at least he'd be safe from me, from this world I'd pulled him into.

I rode another elevator down, stepped out on the basement level and blinked into the darkness. The red light on my ocular display throbbed slow and steady just ahead. Why was it so dark?

The elevator door hissed closed behind me, and for a few seconds, I thought I'd be plunged into complete darkness. And then, down a long glass-lined corridor, a single light blinked on, highlighting the startling beauty of the dark-haired male warfae seated regally in his ornately carved oak chair. Long fingers held a wine glass aloft, its contents as blue as his hard, turquoise eyes. His slash of a smile said the words he didn't need to.

I spun, reaching for the elevator, but the doorway and elevator were gone. Only blackness extended ahead of me, like the blackness of space but without the stars.

The red light on my ocular map blinked out, and then the map went out too, leaving me blind to any escape. There was nothing here, just a blackness that swallowed everything.

The ease of walking through the scanners, Sota's helpful guidance into the depths of Arcon... it had all been an illusion. The warfae had dangled the bait, and I'd taken it like the gullible creature I was.

"The Wraithmaker," the fae drawled. His voice sailed into the endless space and crawled across my skin, sinking inside, luring old fears and desires out of the cages I kept them in.

The shift of leather on leather coupled with the soft swish of his hair told me he had stood, but I didn't want to turn to see. There were no windows here. No doors. I had my whip, but attacking him would be pointless. He already had me. There's a time to fight and a time to run. But there's also a time to bow low and live. I had fought him, and I had run from him. I knew what came next.

I swallowed excess saliva, tasting acid—swallowed the bitter anger, despair and shame. After so long, I hadn't believed the shame would still burn.

Cool fingers slid over the back of my neck, curved around, and clamped tight like the iron collar I'd once worn. My heart raced too hard, thumped too fast.

"You're a long way from home," he purred, his voice achingly smooth.

Crater's death, the bounty on my head, Hulia, The Boot, Marshal Kellee. Even Sota. They were frivolous things. Kesh Lasota's trinkets and toys. And beneath the warfae's touch, Kesh's life fell away like one of the many illusions I wore. The truth of me was so very different from that ghost of a girl. I was the slave-raised gladiator stolen away from my home with only a name to call my own. I was the Wraithmaker, killer of thousands in the starlit, blood-soaked arena. I had been Queen Mab's most-trusted personal guard. And I had loved her—until I'd killed her.

The warfae moved around me, keeping his grip clamped around my neck, until he stood in front of me, drilling his gaze deep into mine. "Were you planning on running forever?"

"Only a lifetime." Mine.

His lips twitched. He liked that. He also liked the fact he had caught me. Before, when I chased him down and leapt from his window, he hadn't known who I was. But there was no doubt on his face now. Something had revealed me to him. Sota. The truth I'd hidden inside the drone, told to him on lonely nights when I needed to speak the secrets eating me up inside, had condemned me. Larsen had probably only wanted the footage of Crater's murder, but what he'd found was a priceless prize. And I'd told him everything through Sota. Told him all my fears and all the horrors, told him how I'd loved, hated, raged and lost it all. The warfae pretending to be the human CEO of Arcon, Istvan Larsen, believed he knew me better than anyone left alive. Only one question remained. What did he plan to do with me?

He closed his hand, sealing off my windpipe. My racing heart throbbed hot blood through my body and beat over and over inside my head. Tightness clamped around my chest, squeezing the consciousness right out of me. The darkness all around rushed in until the jewel-like glitter of his eyes was all I could see in an ocean of nothingness.

CHAPTER 12

Cool iron encircled my neck. I remembered it
being lighter, or more likely it had felt that way
because I hadn't known a time without it. The iron dampened my magic, as it did all fae magic. My whip was gone,
as was my coat. He'd stripped me of them and I knew it
wouldn't be the worst of what was to come.

He wouldn't kill me. Not for a long time. The fae made
their victims beg first.

"Stand."

The order reminded me of another time, so long ago,
when I'd been a small girl trapped behind bars. I'd survived
that. I'd thrived. I'd lived to kill for them. I'd loved them
for it, and they'd loved me in return. Loved me enough for
Mab to pick me out of the saru and make me hers.

Fingers dug into my hair. The warfae yanked me to my
feet, hooked his hand into my clothing and tore my shirt
open. It wasn't my human nakedness he wanted to see.
Hypnotic dark swirls marked my pale skin. The marks of a
killer. Awards. Just like his.

"It's true..." he whispered, eyes wide.

I grinned. "Now show me yours."

He threw me down. The backhanded strike cracked against my jaw, whipping my head back and exploding coppery blood across my tongue. I reeled, clutching onto consciousness, and spat the mouthful of blood in his general direction, hoping to dirty up his leather attire.

He lifted a hand to strike me again, and then he caught himself and stepped back, shaking out his aching, bloody fingers. *"I will not kill you."* He'd figured out my little game. A quick death would be a mercy. "You are worth too much."

"Cow-ard," I slurred. He sneered down at me, and I beamed up at him. They were all so painfully beautiful, and he was no exception. I hated him, hated him so much it hurt more than any physical wound, but a horrible, treacherous part of me loved him too, and that made all this so much worse. "I preferred you as Larsen. At least that man had balls. Where are yours, little warfae?" I eyed his crotch, ignoring the bulge of his obvious endowment. "Been living with humans too long? You even smell like them—"

His hand was at my throat again, a little awkwardly this time as he had to fight with the collar. "Your queen isn't here to save you. Why did you do it? Was it really just because you're so stupid that even after everything my kind did for you—raised you up among us—you still can't help but bite those you love like all wild beasts?"

Tears squeezed from the corners of my eyes. My heart pounded too hard, beating itself into a panic. I couldn't breathe, and a part of me hoped it would end here, just to spite him. Then his grip loosened, and my body sucked in air, desperate to keep me alive.

I fell to my hands and concentrated on filling my lungs.

So slowly, the world stopped spinning. The room I'd woken in was barren and lined in steel, probably a storage room. No windows and no doors. Nothing. Just him and me. I would have preferred the darkness.

"What's your real name?" I asked.

He ignored me and leaned back against the wall, staring. Unblinking. His gaze traced my marks. I felt that slow visual exploration as if his fingers were skimming across my skin, or his tongue. Heat flushed my face, neck and chest. The heat of anger and twisted desire.

"What are you doing with Arcon?" I asked, not expecting an answer. I didn't get one. He just stared down his nose at me.

Resting back, I flicked my hair out of my eyes and lifted my gaze. What must it be like to have captured the Wraithmaker, a criminal sought by the entire Fae system? Would he hand me over to his kin or keep me for himself? If he took me home, getting in and out of Faerie unseen would be no easy thing. Istvan Larsen was a watched man. If he decided to take a trip to outer Halow and happened to sneak through the defensive net...

I stopped my thoughts in their tracks. Arcon maintained the defensive net. The barrier between the Fae system and Halow. The first and last line of defense against the fae. Larsen held the key to the door and might let the fae in at any time. And the humans of Halow had no idea how exposed they were.

I rolled my lips and bowed my head, not wanting him to see the new fear on my face. He stepped forward and crouched, resting his wrists on his knees, long, nimble fingers loose.

"Did you dismantle my drone?" I blinked dry eyes, letting the dread sink into my gut.

"The drone..." His eyes narrowed with uncertainty. "Oh, *your* drone. Can you imagine my surprise when my workers cracked it open, revealing not only footage of the assassination, but also a full confession by a wanted murderer? I had wondered why a nobody messenger was so determined to retrieve that drone. You'll be pleased to know any footage of Crater's death was deleted. As for your murder confession..." He touched my cheek and delicately ran his fingertips across my skin. I fought my instinct to lean into the touch. It had been so long since their kind had touched me. So long since I'd tasted their magic and willingly embraced it. "Only you and I know the truth of that. It can be our secret." Every word he spoke sounded like an illicit promise. It didn't matter what those words meant, his tone was sweet seduction wrapped around the hard, ugly stone. He would use my weak human desires against me.

I gazed into his eyes, confused to find something akin to my own longing reflected there. Then it occurred to me that he was likely alone. He had spent years building up a resistance to tek. I might be the only fae-like creature he had seen in a long time. I could use that and the fae's social desires to my advantage.

I touched his hand, the one covering my cheek and tilted my head up. "I had to tell someone the truth. Nobody likes to be alone."

His eyes instantly hardened. He snatched his hand back and straightened. He paused at the door, head slightly turned, words unspoken on his lips, and then he was gone, the door closing behind him, accompanied by the chunky *snick* of a lock.

I still didn't know if Sota was alive. But I was, for now. I had one advantage over Larsen. He would think me

130

human. He would think he was irresistible. That he held all the power. He was wrong.

~

TIME PASSED TOO SLOWLY. Nothing of the world outside breached the room, as though my four walls were all that existed.

My stomach cramped with hunger pangs, and my lips had cracked. I'd been missing two days, at least. Only, nobody missed me. Hulia would likely think I was a long way from Calicto, and the marshal...

Would Kellee miss me?

If he had listened to my warnings, he would have left and not looked back. He *should* have left. But while I didn't know him well, I did know he wasn't the quitting type. Twice he had tracked me down, asking his damn questions. I had faith he would locate me again—if he wanted to. *Wraithmaker.* The fae had killed his people. All of them. And in his eyes, I was fae too. Still, he knew enough about Istvan Larsen to watch the pretend CEO closely. Maybe if I got a message to Kellee, he could alert the authorities to the vulnerabilities in the defense net.

If anything, I was in the best place to act. Nobody could get closer to Larsen. No human, certainly. Luck had put me right where I needed to be to stop him. *Not luck... It was always meant to be this way.*

The door rattled, and Larsen entered. He threw a robe to the floor. "Put that on and follow me."

I rose on unsteady legs and tugged on the toweling robe. My first steps outside the room revealed more steel-lined walls. Larsen opened another door, to a simple, functional bathroom.

"You have fifteen minutes." He closed the door, leaving me alone. I waited for the lock to slide into place but didn't hear it. After a few beats, I tried the door, cracking it open.

Larsen's voice sailed down the corridor. "There's nowhere to go."

I would soon test that for myself, after I'd cleaned up.

The mirror above the basin reflected a dapple of yellow and purplish bruises spreading across my cheek. I'd repay him for that once I had control of the situation.

The dry-shower felt as though it stripped off a layer of skin. Clean, I stepped out and threw my pants back on. I discarded my torn shirt and pulled the robe on over my shoulders, tying it tightly.

The corridor outside was empty. I didn't believe for a second Larsen had left me unguarded. Light-footed, I dashed away from where I believed he was. The few doors I found opened into empty rooms. No windows. Were we underground? Every door, every curve, took me to another artificially lit empty space, until I entered the largest room of all. At least here there was a table and a single chair. And Larsen.

He stood on the opposite side of the table, hands clasped behind his back, eyes sparkling.

Several packets of dried food lay on the table between us. My hollow insides ached. This wasn't Faerie. If I accepted his reward of food, it didn't mean I was indebted to him, but I hesitated. Old habits still had their claws in me.

"Eat freely." He gestured at the table. "Unfettered."

There would come a time to fight, and when the opportunity presented itself, I needed to be ready. I sat and opened the packets, devouring the contents under his watchful gaze. The food was nothing spectacular, but it filled me out and stopped the cramps.

When he placed a tall glass of clear liquid on the table, I stopped eating and eyed it side-on. Surely not...

"I can afford some luxuries," he explained, sensing my hesitation.

Real water?

I lifted the glass and sniffed. Slightly metallic. How had he come by it? Had he imported it? Just the single glass was worth thousands of v, and he was giving it to me? I set it down and pushed it across the table toward him. "I'll pass."

If I had offended him, he didn't show it. If anything, he appeared amused. "There's no debt."

"Still, I don't think I want anything of yours."

"You obviously do. You're dehydrated—"

"What do *you* want? What is all this?" I waved a hand at the empty packets. "Am I a prisoner or a guest? If I'm a guest, I'd appreciate it if you removed this." I tugged the collar forward, digging it into the back of my neck.

He watched, so calm, so measured. "It is just a glass of water."

But it wasn't. Real water was rarer than gold, rarer than wood. This *gift* didn't make any sense. If he was going to send me home, then why hadn't he? If he was going to kill me, then why waste time with this charade?

"Do you miss the rain?" he asked.

I stared at him. *Did I miss the fucking rain?*

And then it clicked. I hadn't been back to Faerie in five years. But he had been away from his home much longer. As fae, he needed the earth beneath his feet like I needed air to breathe. He needed that grounding, living, breathing presence that flooded every single inch of Faerie. In comparison, Calicto, with all its tek and manufactured domes, might as well have been a barren desert. He was starved of home.

A chip of compassion broke from my hate. Oh, I still despised him, but I understood why he stared the way he did, why he had watched me eat, why his gaze lingered as though he were hungry.

I lifted my chin. "Take off this collar and I'll tell you."

The corner of his lips ticked. Nothing like a smile, just an acknowledgment that he knew what I was thinking and he wouldn't barter with me.

"What's your name?" I asked again. "Your human one doesn't suit you."

He closed the distance between us in a few strides, picked up the glass, raised it to his lips and drank long, deep and hard. I watched the smooth line of his neck gently undulate and imagined the cool liquid passing over my tongue. A small drop escaped the corner of his lips and dribbled down his chin. What might it be like to lick that droplet off? What might it be like to taste him? I recognized the tight flutter of anticipation coiling low inside for the lust it was and let it happen. Some things were too good to resist, even if they were wrong. Too quickly, the show was over. He lowered the glass and used his thumb to wipe the drop from his chin. He smiled that same knowing, smug-ass smile as when he'd stolen Sota from me. Bastard. When I smiled back, my lips cracked.

"What's *your* name, Kesh Lasota?" he asked.

"You know it." *Wraithmaker*. Because I'd killed so many, turning their lives to dust, their spirits to ghosts. And in the end, I'd killed the one they had all loved above any other.

"No." He set the glass down, spread his hands on the

tabletop and leaned in so close I could almost count each delicate eyelash framing his brilliant fae eyes. "Your real name. Your *slave* name. That is what you are. Risen out of the slums to serve my people. Trained in the art of slaughter for our entertainment."

I licked a drop of blood from my split lip, relishing the coppery taste. I'd tasted fae blood like his, and I would taste it again soon. "I've never told a single fae soul. What makes you think I'll tell you?"

He laughed softly. "I should give you up," he whispered as though this was our little secret. "But I think I'll keep you for my personal entertainment. After the sacrifices I've made, it's only fair."

It took every ounce of restraint I had not to grab him by his long braided hair and smack his face into the table. He *wanted* me to. That was the only reason he'd moved in so close. He wanted me to react, to make him retaliate twice as hard. But this was not the place to fight. I had no way out. Attacking now would only free me for a few moments, like a bird fluttering inside its cage. No, I needed a plan, an exit, before I made my move.

A moment passed between us, one of mutual understanding. I was his bird, caught in his cage, my wings clipped for his entertainment. But this bird had talons, and I wouldn't hesitate to use them.

With a throwaway laugh, he left the room. I listened to his light footfalls fade into silence and waited for the sound of a door closing. It eventually came, sounding a long distance away. The curved steel corridors had likely bent the sound. I would find the right door, and I would escape him.

I scooped up his glass and clenched it in a fist, ready to throw it against the nearest wall and watch it shatter into a million pieces. But a few drops had gathered at the bottom. Condensation, probably. I touched the glass to my lips, tasted his sweetness, and threw my head back. Real wetness, real water moistened my tongue, and with it came the intoxicating taste of fae. I swallowed the dregs, drank the taste of him down. He had known I couldn't resist for long.

CHAPTER 13

"*P*ut these on." Larsen threw a bundle of clothes at my feet and dangled my coat in front of him like a lure. "And this."

I stood from the cot—one I'd found in one of the other rooms—and approached. It had been a few days since he had caught me. He had returned with food and synthesized liquid. No water. I'd blown my chance at getting more. And no conversation either. But he liked to linger. To watch. All fae liked to watch.

I took the coat and turned my back on him to shrug the robe off my shoulders.

"I took the liberty of emptying the pockets," he said. "*All* of them."

Some pockets could only be found with the magic at my fingertips, but with the collar on, they were shut away anyway. As I dressed, his gaze warmed my marks, stirring them to life with a not unpleasant tingling. Did I have more than him? The more marks I had, the higher my status among the fae. As the queen's guard, few outranked me.

I caught him looking. His eyes lifted, questions burning there. Had he ever seen me fight? Most fae had. Some had been lucky enough to watch the spectacular performance live at the arena.

"An interesting garment," he commented, nodding at the coat.

He would think so. The coat was fae-made. I fastened it closed, something I almost never did, and wore the collar high to hide the iron one resting on my collarbone.

"Can I can get my whip back?"

He merely smiled.

"Afraid I might strangle you with it?"

"You are the least frightening thing in this forsaken system." And with a gesture for me to follow, he turned and strode off, assuming I'd trail behind him.

I counted the doors we passed, looking for distinguishing marks. Initially, they had all looked the same, but in the many hours I'd spent roaming the corridors, I'd found scuff marks and handprints. He moved quickly, long legs breezing down the corridor until he stopped outside a door like any other. A flick of the handle and the door opened, revealing a flight of stairs. I soaked it up, committing the layout to memory so that when he inevitably brought me back, I would know which way was out. An elevator carried us to Floor G2. He flicked his fingers at himself, weaving an illusion. A bitter citrus smell filled the elevator, and his outline blurred and then sharpened. In the fae's place stood an unassuming, drab human male, in comparison. He straightened his scarlet tie, human fingers fumbling a little. Damn, he was good at this. His act was in place moments before the elevator doors opened, and off he strode out. As a human, his stride was heavier, and when he spoke, his voice had deepened with a gravelly undertone. His illusion was perfect in its imperfections. If I wasn't walking next to him, if I hadn't seen his transformation myself, I wouldn't believe he was fae.

We walked down the glass halls, Larsen attracting glances from Arcon staff, and paused outside a clear-walled office. Inside, Sota sat silent on his dock. I tried the door, but it didn't budge.

"Nobody goes in or out without my authorization," Larsen explained.

I pressed my hand to the glass wall. Sota's red eye was a constant glow. His charge light blinked. My friend. My *only* friend in the three systems.

"You will do everything I ask," Larsen spoke softly. "While in public, you will act as though we are acquaintances. If you try to alert the authorities or contact anyone, I will punish him."

Sota? I mentally called. Silence came back. "Is he mentally intact?" I asked, looking up to find Larsen's hideous smile firmly on his lips.

"Yes. He fought our every attempt to crack him open. He has a filthy vocabulary for a tactical drone."

Sota had picked up some of the more colorful language from the sinks and delighted in shocking message recipients with oddly placed swear words in the middle of their messages. I smiled at the memory. He had fought. Good for him.

If I had come sooner, if I had stopped Larsen in his meeting room instead of running...

"You gave him life. Obey me, and your gift will continue."

Obey me. Everything about that order made my skin crawl. I'd spent my entire life obeying them. I had obeyed them until it almost cost me my life, and it had certainly cost the queen hers. "For how long am I supposed to pretend?"

"When your usefulness has expired, I will let you know."

I arched an eyebrow. He didn't want to kill me. All I had to do was pretend to know him as the human Istvan Larsen while I plotted the best way to kill him. In the meantime, I'd garner as much information about his operation and motives for being here and pass that information on to someone who could do something about it. Someone like Kellee. Inside, I smiled. "Agreed."

He nodded. "Now follow me."

We walked through Arcon, floor after floor after floor. Miles of corridors, through a sprawling mass of glass laboratories, weapons development and the day-to-day administration of such a vast company. Wherever he went, people showered Larsen with attention. Staff would fall into step beside him and debrief him on the latest profit margins. Others would stop Larsen and chat like they were the best of friends. The more I watched, the more my insides clenched in anxiety at the depth of his deception. His act went beyond a charade. He lived this role, breathed it, became it. There was danger in illusion. It was too easy to fall into the trappings of another life. Hadn't I done the same as Kesh Lasota?

The glass pyramid façade was just Arcon's frontage. Its collection of buildings spread outward, into neighboring locations, like a university campus scattered across miles of land, and much of Arcon lay buried beneath street level in areas Larsen avoided.

He barely said a word to me the entire time I walked at his side, and without an introduction, his people also ignored me. But they were curious, casting me keen glances as we passed by. I figured the young CEO rarely had company.

Any questions I asked, he ignored.

Several times I lingered near clearly marked exits, instincts plucking on my determination, urging me to flee. But running would solve nothing. I was exactly where I needed to be.

Finally, the tour ended in the long meeting room where I'd leaped through a window. That section of glass had been repaired with a metal plate. From the outside, it must have looked like a blemish on Arcon's perfect façade.

Larsen moved around his oak chair, running his hand along the carved back. The oak wasn't from Earth, I realized. It had been carved as a single piece from the vast oaks—the original trees—found on Faerie. Seeing it there, I could almost smell the accompanying rain and hear its sweet symphony as it fell on the lush undergrowth, lifting delicate puffs of magic into the air. The oak chair would have lost its ingrained fae magic a long time ago, but that didn't stop his touch from lingering, perhaps imagining the same as me.

He looked my way, unblinking, daring me to ask all the questions clamoring in my head. I wanted to know what he was doing here, what the point was in all of this, and I wanted to ask if he missed Faerie like I did. But more than anything else, I wanted to know his name. As much as he pretended to be Larsen, he wasn't human and never would be. The same as I would never be fae. I *needed* to know his name.

He came around the front of the chair and lowered himself into it. When he looked away, I caught the flicker of pain crossing his face. Dropping his head back, he closed his eyes. He still wore the human illusion, but this young human male had suddenly aged.

"A long time ago," he began, keeping his eyes closed, "we would pluck humans from their lives and have them live among us on Faerie. We replaced them with one of our own, a changeling adept at pretending to be human so no one would miss them. In those times, their tek hadn't advanced to the levels of today..." He opened his eyes and blinked, refocusing on the room and me. "It was harmless."

"I know the tales." And it was a long way from harmless if you were one of the humans the fae had taken.

"We would make them dance and sing. And the foolish creatures always fell in love with us, with Faerie."

I turned my attention to the windows and Calicto sparkling outside. Some aspects of Faerie hadn't changed at all in thousands of years. They still lured humans into their games and killed them with their so-called kindness.

"When we grew bored, in days or years, we would send them back to their world, back to Earth."

Where they would die, I thought. They all died, wilted like flowers cut at the stem. The cruelty didn't come from taking the people. The game was all about sending them home again and watching the human rant and scream and demand to return to the world they had come to love. A world that to anyone else, didn't exist. To love the fae was a madness. And the fae knew it.

When he didn't continue his tale, I looked back and found his face turned to the glass, his sharp features in profile. He knew what those tragic humans had gone through because, cut from Faerie, he felt it too.

"How long have you been here?" I asked.

He hesitated and then lifted a hand, tossing away time

as though it meant nothing. Did he even know how long? Something the imprisoned fae, Talen, had said came back to me: no fae would willingly put themselves through this agony. Not only was Larsen severed from everything he knew and loved, but he also endured day after day surrounded by human tek. He had built up a resistance, but it must have still pained him. Was it a punishment? I'd assumed he was doing all of this deliberately, but what if I'd been wrong? What if his act was a prison?

I smiled, realizing the trap I'd fallen into. Sympathizing with my jailor. A novice mistake, and one I knew to avoid. It seemed I had forgotten much in five years.

"Strange, how I stumble upon the Wraithmaker, of all creatures," he mused, still gazing out of the window. "In all the three systems, on all the countless planets, you are the messenger I hired to take the blame for a murder." His gaze cut to me. "What brought you to Calicto?"

"It was the destination of the first ship I boarded after escaping Faerie. Why did you kill Crater?"

He ignored my question and frowned. "How did you escape?"

I smiled instead of answering. I wasn't about to tell him, considering I may have to escape again soon.

"I'm not sure I believe you," he said, candidly. "The odds are impossible. You found me here, of all places, by chance? No, I don't think that's what happened." He pushed from his chair, his movements hardening. "Humans lie as easily as they breathe. You have no honor, no integrity. That's why they sent you." He approached, intent punctuating each stride.

I stood my ground, even when he stopped too close, filling everything with his pretend Istvan Larsen with his sharp suit and the charming glint in his eye. Who was the greater liar here? He may not lie with his words—those were the only part of him that couldn't lie—but the rest of him wove lies as easily as he wove illusions.

Whatever he had planned to do fizzled away under my glare. Instead, he touched my coat shoulder and ran his fingers down a seam. He pined so for home that he sought out its touch anywhere and everywhere.

His head tilted and his eyes narrowed, losing some of their shallow human sheen. He wore biotek lenses to hide their true radiance, but now that I knew what I was looking for, I saw through it to the reality hidden inside. And what lurked in there wasn't entirely whole. This fae—whoever he was—was broken.

CHAPTER 14

Over the next few days, Larsen continued to lead me around Arcon like his new pet. Any questions about me were met with vague dismissals. I let it happen, absorbing the layout of the building and all the information. As far as captivity went, I'd endured worse.

His lingering gazes and unspoken questions indicated he didn't trust me. His paranoid mind had concocted some conspiracy with me at its center. When we were above the basement—the name I'd given my underground prison— he didn't leave my side. I'd slipped away a few times while he'd been distracted, but he always knew where I'd be before I did. The one time I had tried to break into Sota's room, he'd appeared at my side minutes after I thought I had given him the slip. It was uncanny. But then, he *was* fae. Albeit a lonely, insane, underpowered one. But he did have magic. I felt it in his gaze and in the rare times his fingers brushed mine. Either he knew how to preserve it, or he had a source to draw from hidden somewhere. All fae carried their own magical reserve, but it was reduced when away from Faerie. The longer they spent away from their home, the more wraith-like they became. It was why the fae—with their superior power—didn't inhabit all three star systems. That and the fact humans insisted on creating more and more tek, poisoning the fae's backyard.

The latest outing Larsen insisted I join him on involved a party-like gathering. One of Arcon's training auditoriums had been transformed with enormous ribbon bows and spiraling decorations. Apparently, it was Arcon's thirty-year anniversary. Tek surveillance had obviously existed before Arcon, but they'd taken it and now owned the industry. Or rather, Larsen owned it. He was the star of the show. Everyone wanted a piece of the young, dynamic CEO.

I did my part, shadowing Larsen until he allowed me to break away and sample some of the exotic food spread across several tables.

"Hi." A woman thrust her hand at me and beamed a bright smile. "I'm Sindy. I work for Istvan. He keeps you so close. Everyone's been dying to meet you."

I finished the mouthful of rice and some kind of vegetable that had tasted divine after my dull diet of packet food. "Hey." I took her hand and gave it a friendly shake. "Kesh."

She had referred to Larsen by his first name. Few of his staff did that. That either put her in his inner circle or she was lying to make it appear as though they were friends. I couldn't recall ever seeing her, but then, Larsen appeared to cut several of Arcon's departments out of my regular tours.

I picked up another rice parcel and devoured it. I'd eat the whole damn spread given enough time, then I imagined Larsen watching me hoard food and equally imagined the bastard's thrill at seeing his control over me. Suddenly, the food didn't look so tempting.

"So, what do you do for Istvan?" Sindy asked, flicking her razor-straight bangs back. "Karlo in accounting thinks you're an investor, but I... well..." She raked her gaze over me. "Some of us think you're an apprentice. Yah know, someone he's training for a high end executive role."

Her thinly veiled skepticism and jealousy might as well have been a luminescent sign blinking over her head. I glanced across the room in time to catch Larsen's eye. He saw who I was standing with and promptly excused himself from his little gaggle of groupies. I had about eight seconds of fun before he ruined it.

I smiled at Sindy and beckoned her closer. "I'll tell you, if you can keep a secret."

"Oh." Her eyes lit up. She stepped closer in her needle-point heels. "Do tell."

"He keeps me in the basement."

She laughed. I didn't.

I picked up a tiny parcel of sweet pastry, my mouth watering. "He's not who you think he is."

"Kesh." Larsen stood rigidly behind Sindy's shoulder.

He said my name like he was lashing a whip. I grinned back at the fake man and popped the pastry parcel into my mouth, crunching down. Sindy—pale-faced and confused—teetered off. Foolish human.

Larsen stepped to my side, easing his hand around my arm and holding me firmly at his side. His magic tingled, his illusion active. He pretended to admire the food while the party continued behind him. "I warned you."

"Hmm," I mumbled. All these smiling, happy people. What would they say if I yelled out the truth? Larsen would probably cover it up with a laugh and a joke. No one would believe me.

My gaze snagged on a familiar face standing still in the crowd. Artfully tousled hair, keen eyes reading the scene, but no smile. This was the last place Marshal Kellee wanted to be. My heart stuttered at the sight of him. Larsen had no use for the lawman. If Kellee got in his way, Larsen would kill him.

He saw me. People filtered back and forth between us, but his gaze locked on me and then skipped to the man at my side. I knew how it looked. Larsen stood too close, his hand on my arm. Here I was, apparently enjoying the party next to the camouflaged fae. Betrayal hardened Kellee's frown. I wanted to shout to him, that it wasn't what it looked like.

"What part of your drone's beloved character shall I delete for this indiscretion?" Larsen asked, amusement dancing in his voice.

Kellee began to turn. I clenched my teeth together. *Wait!* He was so close, just across the room, and he was leaving because his fears had been realized. I'd lied to him. I was fae. He'd come to check, and now he had seen what he thought was confirmation of all his suspicions.

I had to stop him. I had to reach him without Larsen knowing.

I yanked down my coat collar. Fabric tore. I didn't care. Kellee hesitated. Confusion crossed his face.

"What are you doing?" Larsen demanded. He saw the glimmer of iron resting around my neck and twisted to face the crowd, seeking the source of my fixation.

So many witnesses, but Kellee had gone. There one second, vanished the next. He was good at that.

I grinned at Larsen.

Larsen's human appearance flickered. He towered over me, sneering, his grip on my arm turning to iron like the collar around my neck. He pulled me off the floor and through a doorway, not caring that his staff all watched it happen. I would pay for this. Either by way of Sota or imprisonment. I'd pushed him too far.

I twisted in his grip and bucked, but his fingers dug harder into my arm. I brought my arm up, over his, and slammed it down, breaking his hold. He reached for me again, but I lunged away, almost free. He snatched my coat, yanking me off balance, but instead of falling into him, I dipped my weight sideways, dropped to my hands and elbowed his weight-bearing knee out from under him. He tumbled to the floor on his side. In a whirl, I slipped free of my coat, kicked the garment over his face and pinned it down, digging my knee into his chest. My hands fit neatly around his throat, holding the coat over his face. He flailed, blindly grabbing for my head.

Figures blurred in the corners of my vision. More witnesses. I didn't care. It would solve a lot of problems if I killed Larsen here and now.

Someone shouted at me to stop. Someone else barked to call the law. *Will they send Kellee?*

"Kesh..." Larsen hissed, accusing or begging.

Yes, beg. Beg like all the others did while your kin's cheering filled my head. The scent of citrus spiked the air. His power leached out of him. His illusions wouldn't save him. I squeezed tighter.

The lights went out.

Darkness flooded the corridor, and with it came a rush of citrusy magic.

"*Kesh...*" Queen Mab whispered in my ear.

Larsen bucked. My grip slipped. He twisted. Fingers

149

snatched my arm, yanking me toward him. I searched the dark for *her*, already knowing it was a trick, a terrible hope used against me. But if there was a chance she was here...

Larsen hauled me to my feet and pinned me against a wall. The solid weight of him smothered me, hemming me in. Darkness blinded me while a wall of male fae blocked my escape. People shouted. Movement stirred the shadows. I stilled. My thoughts slowed. Larsen's racing heart beat so close to mine.

Larsen's short breaths tickled my ear. "Very good, Wraithmaker. Now let the entertainment begin."

~

LARSEN WASN'T WEAK. The trick he had pulled in Arcon's corridors, the darkness, the voices. *Her* voice. That took substantial magic. He had a source—somewhere. But it was impossible outside of Faerie. Wasn't it?

After my failed attempt to kill him and his odd enjoyment of the whole incident, he shut me in the basement. I immediately tried the door he closed behind me, only to find it opened into yet another empty room. I tried all the doors. All empty rooms. I wondered if the basement was an illusion too. One I was trapped in.

I jogged the corridors, and then ran them until sweat glued my clothes to my skin. When the food and water stopped coming, I stopped exercising, needing to conserve my strength.

He hadn't left me this long before.

I smashed his glass—the same glass he had left for me in the beginning—against the wall and instantly regretted it—knowing he had left it there for exactly that reason. I counted the pieces where they lay and waited for the anger to wane.

At least Kellee knew I wasn't here by choice. He must have seen the collar. But what if he acted on it? What if he confronted Larsen? The fae had already killed Kellee's people. Larsen would finish the job.

I paced back and forth in my room.

Think. I knew how to push Larsen's buttons. He didn't want to hand me over to the Fae Courts. He said he was keeping me for entertainment, but he'd also said he suspected me of working for them. Handing me over would expose him, and he didn't appear to want that either. I had to figure out a way to use what I knew. Attacking him in the hallway had been foolish, but I'd learned a few things. I knew he had a reserve of power. I also knew he wanted me to fight him, either because of my reputation or to get revenge for the death of his queen. The fae loved to draw out their vendettas. Courtly families warred for years behind closed smiles and veiled threats. Mab had liked that about me. She had told me I was simple, meaning it as a compliment.

So, he wanted to play a game.

I was good at games.

My coat, draped over the back of the chair, caught my eye. I picked it up and rummaged through its pockets, finding nothing. Turning it inside out, I did the same again. Nothing.

With a frustrated growl, I walked the corridors. The walls, the floor, the ceiling, all were smooth. The motion-sensing tek that controlled the lights were locked away behind immovable panels. If I had access to them, I could strip the units down and remake them into useful tek.

I threw my coat on, ignoring the torn flap, and slid

down a wall to tuck myself in a corner. The table was still there, bolted to the floor, surrounded by broken glass.

Not so long ago, I'd stood behind Queen Mab's right-hand side. If she could see me now, she would laugh. The Wraithmaker could easily endure a few days in isolation. This was nothing. But I wasn't the Wraithmaker anymore. I'd seen to that when I killed her. I wasn't Kesh either. And I'd been taken from my home too young to know who I'd been before the fae. I had a saru name from before. That was all. No memories of my home, no memories of my parents. Just a name. It was all I had that was completely me before the fae corrupted me.

I buried my hands in my coat pockets and rested my head back against the wall. I would find out what Larsen wanted from me and I'd give it to him. I'd make him think he controlled me, owned me like the fae owned all saru, and then he would talk. He would tell me his name and his reason for being here. And he would tell me what Arcon was hiding. When I knew all his secrets, I would break them open the way he had broken Sota open. I would reveal the fae to the humans, and he would pay. Nobody would come to save him. Not this far from Faerie.

My fingers touched a small tile of cool metal. I picked it out of my pocket. My home-built comms. Larsen had missed it. Would it work? Quickly, I pressed it to the skin behind my ear. "Kellee?"

The silence dragged alongside the hopeful race of my heart.

"Kellee?" I asked more softly, realizing any chance of the signal reaching me here, below Arcon, was remote. *Please answer. I don't want to be alone.*

"...Kesh."

The signal was so weak I wasn't sure if I'd imagined

hearing my name. I pressed the comms harder into my skin. "Kellee?" *Please...*

And waited.

A heartbeat. Another.

I didn't hear the voice again.

"Kellee," I sighed. "If you can hear me... you can help me now."

CHAPTER 15

I waited, listening to Larsen's soft footsteps coming down the corridor behind the closed door. The door to my room opened inward. He would have to reach in, his forearm exposed. I'd waited a long time, stewing down here. But now was the time to test him.

The fragment of glass dug into my palm, seated firmly. Its triangular point glinted.

The sound of his approach fell silent right outside the door. I held my breath.

The handle dipped.

The door swung open. I swept in, stabbed the point into his arm and slashed upward, splitting dark tattoos and tearing open a vein. Bright fae blood, as scarlet as his favorite human tie, splattered his clothes. Speckles splattered my face. He roared and lashed out, intent on back-handing me against the wall, but I ducked the swing and jabbed the stubby glass blade into his side.

"Is this what you want?" I hissed, pressing in close. I drew the weapon back to strike again, but he slammed his forehead down onto mine in a very un-fae-like move and shoved me backward. He didn't pursue but stood in the corridor, a stream of blood running down the jagged cut on his arm, spilling from his fingertips.

I wiped the blood from my cheek, tasted it on my lips and beckoned him forward with my finger. "Should have worn bracers." The fae often did back home. Bracers protected their forearms and hid weapons. He'd forgotten that. What else had he forgotten?

He looked down as though noticing the gash in his arm for the first time. "Are you done playing games?"

When he faced ahead, he smiled, telling me I had him pegged. He wanted this. Fuck knew why, but I'd give it to him.

He stepped into the room. "You can do better." The flesh on his forearm pulled closed, self-sealing the wound. Only the blood remained. His perfect skin hadn't even scarred, unlike mine.

"Come closer and we'll find out."

One more step, bringing him within arm's reach. He watched me closely, waiting for tells, for any sign of what my next move might be. Wild predators watched their prey with that same patient glare.

I tossed the bloody piece of glass at his feet. "Take me to Sota."

Irritation briefly tightened his smile, twisting it downward.

"I want to know my drone is functioning before *this*"— I gestured at the blood splattered on the shiny floor —"whatever this is, continues."

Wordlessly, fully healed and wrapped once again in illusion, he took me to Sota. Subdued lighting implied it was resting hours on Calicto, and we only passed a couple of Arcon's late-night employees on the walk to Sota's room.

My drone woke the second I touched his outer shell.

"Sota?" I peered into his single red eye. He didn't answer, but the lens moved, contracting and then shifting to the side. "It's okay." I attempted to reach him through our neural link but met a wall of silence.

"What have you done to him?" I snapped at Larsen. "You said you wouldn't harm him."

"I modified a few things." He lifted a hand, stopping my objections. "Nothing untoward. I may even have improved him."

He had *modified* my drone? *Improved* him? I turned my back on Larsen and pressed my palm to Sota's outer shell. "Talk to me."

"I..." Sota stammered like broken code. "I am s-sorry, Kesh."

None of this is your fault. He couldn't hear my thoughts. Larsen had done something to our link, probably severed it for good. He might even have replaced it with his own. "Sota, look at me." The drone's eye swiveled to fix on me. He didn't have many expressions, but sadness rolled off him in static waves. "Whatever he did to you, I'll fix it." *I'm the one who's sorry.*

Larsen loomed to my right, encroaching on my personal space. "Ask him if he wants to be fixed?" the smug-ass fae inside a human disguise asked. He crossed his arms and nodded, already knowing the answer.

I bared my teeth in a snarl. "So, you rewrote his code." Larsen shouldn't even know how to write code. Fae didn't know such human things. Tek things. "I don't care. I'll write it back again."

Sota's single red eye buzzed brighter. Hotter. He was

arming his weapons. I straightened and backed away, alarmed to see his shell crack open, revealing two firing ports.

I swallowed and lifted my hands. "Sota?"

Larsen patted the drone's top panel. "It's okay," he said, echoing me. "She can't touch you without my consent."

He'd stolen my drone. He hadn't just taken him away, he had *reprogrammed* Sota. A hard, stupid knot tightened in my throat, and my vision blurred. I had created Sota from nothing. I had given him life. He was mine. He was all I had. And Larsen had taken the first and last thing I owned away.

Sota's motors whirred. The drone rose into the air. *"Cease all aggressive action, Kesh Lasota,"* he ordered, sounding like the tactical drone he had originally been. There was a threat to his *master* in this room: me.

"Kesh..." Larsen warned, glancing between me and the drone. "Tell the drone you don't want to hurt me."

I didn't want to hurt him. My thoughts weren't nearly as neat as that. I wanted to *destroy* him. I turned from the room and strode away, hearing Larsen telling Sota to power down. The fae followed, his fake-heavy human footfalls racing with the sound of my heartbeat.

I whirled, grabbed Larsen by the neck and slammed him into a glass wall. Cracks sparked behind his head and shoulder. Indignation flared in his eyes. He gripped my arm but stilled when I leaned in. "I'll kill you for this." Tears wet my cheeks. Useless tears. "You turned him against me. I don't care who you are or what you're doing here. I will cut you open and spill that fae blood and magic all over Arcon. I will ruin you and this fantasy of yours, you crazy, fucked-up Faerie reject—"

Larsen brought his elbow down on my hold, buckling

me under him, and in a blur, I was the one with my back against the glass and my feet dangling off the floor. He cocked his head, the fae-like movement odd when coupled with his human face. Parting his lips, he ran his tongue across his pearly teeth. "You've been a ghost for so long I wondered if the Wraithmaker was even in there. I see her now." He drew closer, so close his lemony scent filled my head and his fae-gaze burned through his illusion. "And I see the fire our queen so admired."

More tears fell. I hated them. I hated him. I hated everything. I hated that just the mention of the queen twisted my insides into knots.

"K-Kesh..." The marshal's voice broke through my thoughts. "Kesh, can you hear me?" The comms tickled.

Larsen's gaze shifted from intrigue to suspicion. He moved in closer, his cheek against mine. Had he heard Kellee too?

I couldn't let Larsen discover the marshal. I needed Kellee on the outside of all this. I needed his help.

Larsen's cool breath brushed my cheek. I turned my head toward him, my lips brushing the corner of his mouth. "I will ruin you," I promised, and then swept my tongue across his lower lip, tasting where I'd wanted to since I'd seen him drink the water. His entire body tensed, but his grip on my neck softened, lowering me to my feet. His mouth followed mine, wanting more, but not daring to commit. What he was doing—desiring a saru—went against his upbringing, his life, his rules. He likely hated me too.

I teased my mouth over his, tentatively asking, seeking. I imagined it was Kellee's smart mouth I provoked. Imagined it was the marshal's firm hand resting on my hip and easing higher. Larsen released my throat and drove his hand into my hair, holding me rigid as his mouth smothered mine. The kiss turned brutal and hungry, as though Larsen were starving. I dragged my hand down his waist and around his back, finding the corded tension there. I pulled him close, feeling every stuttering breath, every tight shift, every hard inch of him. I hated him, hated everything about this, hated how I arched closer and how every inch of my skin sparked alive where his hand rode up under my top, hated how I sounded, snatching at breaths the same way my hands snatched at his clothes. I ran my palm up his waist, watching his human illusion spin apart and the fae become real. He shouldn't feel so good. I shouldn't want to touch every ripple of muscle and explore the rest of him with my mouth. But it had been so long since I'd tasted them, so long since I'd loved them, so long since I'd lain with them.

"Kesh... did he hurt you?"

The scorching lust faltered at the sound of Kellee's voice. The madness waned. I pulled my hands back, closing them into fists, and turned my head to the side, shutting Larsen down.

A woman stood at the end of the hallway, stacks of used cups in her arms. She gaped at the glorious black-haired fae from thousand-year-old legends pressing me up against the wall. Larsen's hand brushed my thigh. Just a small, hapless touch, but it ignited an aching desire. A groan escaped me as I imagined that hand roaming inward. I didn't want to want this. He didn't want to want this.

"Oh," the woman squeaked.

Larsen's touch vanished. He stepped back and threw out a hand. His magic flared and the poor woman's entire body fell limp, her eyes glassy like a doll propped up by an invisible hand. She dropped her cups. They exploded across the floor into hundreds of jagged pieces.

He frowned at the interruption. It was a lazy look, the kind of dismissive expression I had seen on countless fae as they regarded their saru slaves, considering their fate.

"Don't kill her." She didn't need to die. Nobody would believe what she had seen. "Glamor her. Make her dream. Spin an illusion. You have the power. She doesn't need to die."

An otherworldly heat burned in his eyes. The same heat I'd seen in so many of them. He had the power to make the woman dance, make her love, or make her die.

I stepped in front of him and heard the woman collapse behind me—his hold on her snapped. His gaze dropped to mine and that heat set me ablaze. "Spare her," I whispered. Whoever this fae was, whatever his past held, there was one way I could placate him. I closed my right hand into a fist as generations upon generations of saru had done, touched it to my chest over my heart and dropped to one knee. "*Please*."

His head tipped, eyes narrowing. He leaned closer, seeking something deeper inside my gaze. The intensity of his glare reminded me that, in his world, I was a lesser thing. I was human, a creature made for the fae and their whims. Long ago, long before legends, they had given us the gift of life. Without the fae, my species wouldn't exist.

I bowed my head, exposing my neck. Traditionally, the pose invited a blade to end my life, but it meant more than that now. I was bowing to him, subjugating myself, acknowledging his status above me. After every battle, trembling and covered in blood, I had bowed to them. Again and again and again. That woman's life was my battle now.

He moved around me. I snuck a glance and saw him crouch beside the fallen woman. At his touch, she stirred but didn't wake. He turned his head and caught me watching. What he was doing was no minor illusion. Whoever he was, he wasn't just another fae. He had the power to make people and worlds bend to his will.

I touched the comms tucked safely in my pocket.

I had to tell Kellee everything.

CHAPTER 16

My basement was wrapped in illusion. I'd suspected as much, but now that I knew what he was capable of, I also knew he could make me see and believe almost anything. Bizarrely, the collar nullified both my magic and the worst of his. He could manipulate what I saw and heard, but not my thoughts. Suddenly, I was in no hurry for him to remove the collar.

After he'd set the woman at her desk and given her dreams of fantastical things, Larsen had escorted me back to the basement, his stern fae face rigid, his body perfectly controlled. He shut me inside without meeting my eye and left. I waited a few minutes and then reapplied the comms and set about walking the corridors, speaking Kellee's name, hoping there was one spot where the signal would get through. I had assumed I was below Arcon, but I could have been on the top floor. I might not even have been in Arcon. That worked in my favor. I'd assumed the comms would never work and given up trying. Now I had hope.

"Kesh!" Kellee said. The signal crackled, but I'd heard him.

I pressed my hands to the walls of one of the nonde-script rooms and bowed my head, hoping the signal held. "Kellee?" *Please hold. Please be there.*

"Yes, Kesh..."

Relief flooded through me. I hadn't realized how much I'd needed this to work. An odd exhaustion rolled over me, tiredness like that of a thousand lifetimes. I wasn't alone.

"Finally," Kellee grumbled, audibly relieved. His voice sounded gravelly and monumentally pissed off. With no other distractions, I heard all the tiny nuances, including the touch of a growl. "Where have you been?"

I smiled. "I've been busy."

"I saw. Sharing canapés with Larsen." The comment was meant to sound light, but he didn't quite pull it off.

I'd missed him. How long had I been stuck in Arcon? Hearing him now, it seemed like forever. I wanted to see his secret smile when he believed I wasn't looking or he thought he knew something I didn't. I wanted to rouse that beast in him and study its movements. It was irra-tional—this want—but I needed it to cling on to. Like hope. Hope was always irrational, wasn't it?

"Kesh?"

"Yes, I'm still here. I was just thinking..."

"It's about time you started."

I closed my eyes and imagined the marshal here with me. In my head, he stood behind me, half smiling like he knew I would come around to his thinking eventually. I'd been so alone. I hated how I ached for company—a fault left over from Faerie.

"This is so much worse than we thought," I said, softly. What if Larsen knew I was talking with Kellee? It didn't matter. I needed this or else I would lose my mind in this maze of illusions. "He's insane but in a way that makes him dangerous. And he knows, Kellee. He knows who I am."

A pause. "Has he hurt you?"

Something in my chest hurt. Not my heart. Guilt? "No. Not really. Not like he's capable of." I swallowed, moistening my throat so the words didn't choke me. "He's been away from Faerie too long. He sees something of his home in me... I think he knows what he should do, but he's torn. I think he's hiding here like I was. But he's been here a lot longer than me. He knows things the fae shouldn't know. He knows about tek. He knows... He did something to my friend. He's different from the fae back... back home." Admitting where I'd come from was easier than I'd expected. If anything, it was a relief to say it.

The signal crackled. I straightened. "Kellee?!"

His voice faded.

"Kellee...!"

"I'm here... I was testing the limits of the signal. I'm in a building across from Arcon. Any farther and I lose you."

I fell back against the wall and closed my eyes. "You have to find out who he is." My voice shook. He would hear the trembling and know how much this was killing me. "He has power, a lot of it. So far from home for so long, he shouldn't have any at all. Ask Talen."

"Talen?" Kellee balked.

"He might know who he is or suspect. I need a name to know who I'm dealing with. As I am now, I'm stumbling around in the dark, trying to pick a fight with something that could be harmless or might kill me with a flick of his fingers." Or worse. I already suspected Larsen was the latter kind. But a name would seal it.

"All right," he reluctantly agreed. "But give me more to go on. I don't even know what he looks like as fae."

"He has warfae markings. The generals were marked in the wars. Those with more marks killed m—"

"I know what they mean." His frustration and anger simmered through the signal. "Aren't most older fae marked that way? I need something unique to him. Something Talen might recognize."

What would Kellee think of my marks? The death of his people was likely long before my time, but the marks— rewards for slaughter—had remained the same for countless centuries, perhaps millennia. I could never let Kellee see mine. "All right, I'll get something for you to take to Talen."

We fell silent, but the signal still held. The suffocating quiet closed in, waiting to smother me when he was gone. "Kellee?"

"Yes, Kesh."

"Can you... can you just talk?"

"—what?"

"Please." *I don't want to be alone.*

"No, I said... *about what?* What do you want me to say?"

"Anything." The single word came out in a rush.

"All right." He cleared his throat. "Do you know how hard it was to get invited to the Arcon party? I had to track down a guest and steal his ID. The guy never saw what hit him. He woke up hungover, with no memory of attending the party."

I smiled. "You stole his ID. That's not very marshal-like."

"The law doesn't seem to apply around you."

"Kellee..." I wanted to ask him to stay, wanted to ask him if he hated me for who I was, wanted to ask if he thought we would both walk away from this unscathed.

But I couldn't speak the words. I didn't know him. He didn't really know me. I was desperate, I knew that. At some point, Larsen would decide what to do with me, and it would all be over, one way or another.

"You keep saying my name." He chuckled. "I'm not going anywhere. What do you want to know?"

Do you hate me like I hate him? I couldn't ask him, so I said instead, "How was your day marshaling?"

He told me how he had helped subdue a protest against water rations outside one of the Halow embassies. A few days ago, he'd caught an armed thief in the sinks and brought him in before the guy could sell his stolen goods. He'd returned the items to their rightful owners. He talked about his work, about others in his department, friends he had, the normal life he led. I crouched against the wall and listened to the sound of his voice. It was nice—too nice. Larsen would return, and I had to get him to talk.

"Marshal?" I asked, interrupting his story about someone who had tried to pickpocket him in the sinks. "Don't come to Arcon again."

He didn't answer right away, likely because he had every intention of returning to Arcon. "I have an appointment with Larsen in two days to discuss an assault charge. Somebody reported what they saw at the party."

"Cancel it."

"No."

"Kellee. You don't know what he's capable of."

"You forget I've dealt with the fae. I know exactly what he's capable of. I'm keeping the appointment."

I remembered the heat in Larsen's gaze, the terrible knowledge that he could destroy a human life for entertainment. His kind had watched me do the same for them countless times.

167

"If he suspects you're on to him, he will kill you."

"I'm not that easy to kill. Will you be there?"

"I..." I scanned the empty room. "If I get you something solid to bring to Talen, will you cancel?"

"Kesh, you don't need to protect me. Doing the right thing...? It's what I do. It's my job. I'm not canceling."

"Dammit, Marshal. Your *right thing* will get you killed."

"I don't expect someone like you to understand."

Someone like me? As though I couldn't know what the right thing was? I laughed bitterly and hoped he heard it. "A slave-raised killer, you mean?"

"No, that's not what I meant."

"Forget it. It's amazing what I can hear without all your pretty distracting me." I plucked the comms off and dropped it into my pocket. I knew what he had meant. The fae had raised me to kill. How could I know what doing the right thing meant when I'd been doing the wrong thing since they first put a blade in my hand and told me to kill the child in the cell next to mine for a pat on the head?

But my moral compass wasn't so broken that I didn't know the marshal's sense of justice meant he would walk into an impossible fight. Larsen would eat him alive.

I returned to my room and picked up the broken fragment of glass. Dried fae blood flaked off and rained around my boots. I had to turn the situation on its head. While Larsen held my reins, nothing would change. It was time to see just how much I mattered to the warfae and why.

I sunk the blade into my wrist, embraced the pain, and tore open a vein.

CHAPTER 17

*B*lood loss made the world spin, or maybe it was magic, because everything around me was soft and bright and smelled fresh and too wonderful to be real. No, wait, that *was* magic. His.

I lifted a hand and tried to rub the fog from my eyes. Larsen was here, leaning against a table, upright and rigid like a blade forged in Faerie's deepest fires and sheathed in leather. Complete with wrist bracers, I noticed, as my eyes cleared. For the first time, I took the time to admire the points of his ears peeking out from his waterfall of black hair. The tight braids were gone. His hair hung loose over one shoulder. It wasn't all straight. Some ends licked up. I wondered if he hated that. He seemed the type to want everything as it should be.

Wait. I blinked lazily. Where was I? Dark wood panels wrapped the room up tight. The furniture, all wood, dictated each area. A desk, a table, chairs. But something was wrong here. The softness didn't fit. And then I realized there was no tek. None at all. What light there was streamed in through the windows. Black drapes stirred. Drapes that looked like his hair.

Wait, what? Had I been drugged?

No. Yes. Maybe. Why couldn't I think straight? I dropped my hand onto the pillow. Oh good, a bed. I was on a bed. A proper bed, not like the cot I'd been forced to sleep in. Maybe if I lay here a while, I'd get to the thing I needed to do eventually—whatever that thing was.

My fingers brushed the iron collar, and for a moment, I forgot the terrible thing I had done. I was back in Faerie, before that night when everything changed, before the first collar had been removed. Back when I had the illusion of freedom, but really, I had been no freer than the pitiful saru children still locked in their cells. Sometimes— actually, most times, an illusion was enough. Who needed reality when you had Faerie to answer your every desire, to tend to your every need? The only price was blood. And I'd paid with plenty of mine and that of my saru brothers and sisters. The boy, Aeon's blood. He hadn't bled like the others. But he had died all the same. *"Oh, how fragile mortals are."* The fae had laughed. *"Look at them fall to her."*

"Look at them fall," I muttered, reaching for the memory of Aeon's hand, holding on to it for a little while longer even as it cooled and stiffened.

And then Larsen was there, peering into my eyes, spoiling everything. "Go away," I told him and tried to brush the vision of the fae away.

One of his perfect eyebrows arched. "That was a foolish thing you did."

Killing the queen? I wondered. *But she had told me to.*

What did I do? What was I supposed to do? Something... something soon. Heat throbbed up my arm. I clawed at the bandage.

"Leave it," Larsen's voice ordered, distant now as he moved away.

I looked for him and found him walking away, and damn if he didn't know how fine he looked while just walking. I'd seen them fight. I'd fought ones like him. There wasn't an inch on that body that didn't have a purpose. He could run like the wind, and then stop and turn and cut his enemies down before they could draw breath to beg for mercy. They killed mercilessly. I had always admired that, always aspired to it.

I'm a bad person.

I blinked at the ceiling, my thoughts coming back to me. My arm. I'd cut myself, and here it had brought me, inside what had to be his personal chambers. Here I would discover things about him. Here he would have secrets. Secrets I would tell Kellee, who would tell the imprisoned Talen. And we'd know for sure who our insane fae was. Though I suspected... didn't I? I *knew*...

I turned my head. Metal rattled.

My fingers traced a line of iron links. I didn't need to look to know my triumph had been short-lived.

"Well, this is degrading," I mumbled.

"It is what it is," he dismissed.

Chain links dangled from my collar and trailed to where the chain connected to a latch in the wall. I tried to summon rage but couldn't. He was right. It was what it was. And it was nothing I hadn't dealt with before. Not since I was a naughty saru child tinkering with tek.

I dropped my head back down and wished I hadn't when his citrusy scent tingled on my tongue. He slept in this bed. How nice for him.

"Unlatch me now and I'll kill you fast instead of slow when the time comes."

"Kill me with what?" He smirked. "Bad thoughts?"

A snarl bubbled up. "Have I not earned the right to freedom? I bowed to you. I meant it."

"Worthless." He gestured. "Humans lie."

"So you keep saying, and yet here you are, living among them. You've been here so long, pretending to be human for so long, that maybe you think you are one?"

"I know what I am."

"An arrogant, selfish, sociopathic, narcissistic sluagh-bait?"

He chuckled, and the sound did horribly wonderful things to the feminine part of my brain that seemed to be more and more in control around him.

"You really can be entertaining."

"Fuck you." Not exactly my most intelligent of replies, but I was losing my patience. "You want me to entertain you? Unchain me."

His smirk grew, and so did my hatred. "I will," he said. "When I can trust you."

I wondered where my coat was. The comms—my only method of reaching Kellee—would be in the pocket. At least Larsen hadn't undressed me. I lay, fully clothed, on top of his sheets. Five years of freedom, a lifetime of killing, and I was reduced to a plaything tied to a bed.

Twisting on my side, I propped my head on a hand. "Am I your pet, then?"

His lips twitched and his eyes sparkled. "Perhaps."

No, that wasn't it. This wasn't a sexual thing. "A challenge? To yourself." He wet his lips and looked down. Yes. Something in those words rang true. "You want to see if you can resist the Faerie in me?"

He looked up, his smile still dancing in the corner of his mouth. No, not that, then.

I touched my collar. "This is for you as well as me, right?" He didn't want to make it easy for himself. The collar stopped him from turning me into a mindless human puppet, so he wanted me coherent. He wanted me to fight. I had seen evidence of that already. "You're curious." Yes, his eyes focused, unblinking. "Your queen adored me. Your people adored me. They cheered my name. Wraithmaker." I drew out my name, giving it dramatic emphasis. "But you weren't there. You don't understand, but you want to. You've missed so much by being here, sacrificed so much." Yes, his smile faded, and a new intensity settled on his face. "What did they see in me? What did Mab see in me—"

"Why did you do it?" he asked.

I knew what he meant. They all wanted to know why I'd killed their queen. "Because I am saru, and no matter how high up you lift me, I will always be saru. Because you taught me to slaughter, because it's all I'm good at, because I was so close to her that it was almost too easy."

"No." He came forward and stopped a stride away from the bed. "Lies. But I will find out the truth."

I narrowed my eyes at him. "Give me my whip. Unchain me. And I'll tell you the truth."

He dismissed my request with a dry laugh and headed for the door. "I will unchain you, saru, when I am ready." He shut the door behind him.

I tugged on the chain, knowing it was useless. I got my fingers under the collar and pulled, but it didn't give. All right. So, this wasn't necessarily bad.

As the chain only allowed me a few steps from the bed, I sat on the edge and diligently studied my surroundings. There had to be something here that would tell me more about Larsen.

Books sat snugly on wooden shelves. The last time I had seen a book with paper pages, it had been on Faerie. Only the fae had access to enough wood to be so frivolous as to paint paper pages with words. The spines of Larsen's books were all marked with swirling fae text. He must have either smuggled them into Halow or bought them at an underground auction. The sale of fae goods had been outlawed centuries ago, but someone like Larsen would have connections. Unusual pieces were scattered around the room. A lamp that looked as though it had been grown, not made, and even the rug had a suspiciously natural appearance, like living grass.

If anyone ever had any doubt about Larsen's identity, it was all here, in this room. All I had to do was find a key piece of evidence that would reveal his true identity.

≈

HE LEFT me long enough for the wound beneath the bandage to start itching and my bladder to ache. I was dozing when he strode in. His human illusion rippled carelessly off him before the door swung closed. He crossed the room, heading straight for his desk. Pressing his palms to the desktop, he bowed his head and sighed. His shoulders trembled.

I'd been about to demand that he release me so I could at least relieve myself, but now I stayed silent and *watched* his struggle. After a few moments, he lifted his head, breathed in and held that breath.

Something had shaken him. If I knew what that thing was, I might have a weapon to use.

He moved around his desk and melted into the chair behind it. His glare flicked up and widened at the sight of me. He'd forgotten he wasn't alone. A shadow crossed his face, and then with a flick of his fingers, the chain attached to my collar vanished.

I reached through the air where it had been, expecting to find the cool metal. When I looked back, he was smiling. Had the chain been an illusion all along?

Channeling the anger down deep, I visited his bathroom. The luxurious suite was double the size of my container home and furnished with the fae's typical elegance. A panoramic window revealed Calicto's domes from hundreds of feet high. I wouldn't be leaping from this one.

I stripped off the bandage, finding the wound healed but for a jagged, raw red line. After dry-showering, I rummaged around his cupboards and found a silken robe. It hung off my shoulders and licked around my ankles. The smell of lemons scented the air. A shudder ran through me as the cool silk slid across my skin. Damn him. He wasn't even with me and his touch still manipulated me.

All I had to do was find something unique to him. Something Kellee could use. Once we had a name, I would know for certain what I needed to do.

My hand lingered on the door handle. There was a way... In his current state he was vulnerable and alone. He had already revealed an attraction to the forbidden fruit that was me.

Fighting, I could do. But seducing? That had never been in my skill set. All fae were masters of desire. Humans were, and always would be, their pets. The way I was around him? It wasn't something I could consciously control. Something in human DNA sought the attention of the fae. Master. Slave. It was written into our programming from the time they first seeded humanity on Earth.

And I was saru. Born into their service. I'd fought for their appraisal, killed for their adoration, and risen in their ranks, but all that meant was I'd worn all the right clothes, opened all the right veins, and said all the right things while I bowed low.

I wasn't sure I had it in me to manipulate Larsen sexually. But he sure had it in him to manipulate me. I was a fly pretending to be the spider, and all I had to capture him with was his own web of lies.

I breathed in, steeled my iron-like saru heart and soul, and opened the door.

He hadn't moved from the chair. With his head resting back and his eyes closed, I wondered if he was sleeping, but he couldn't be. He would never let his guard down around me.

"Tell me about her," he said, his voice sudden and clear. Not sleeping, just resting his eyes. He kept them closed, dark lashes resting against his smooth skin.

He meant the queen. If I told him, if we found some common ground, he might open up.

"She was kind." His lips tightened, and I added, "Until she wasn't."

His chest slowly rose and fell, the leather straps breathing with him. Tantalizing glimpses of his warfae marks peeked out from under his collar. It was too easy, too enticing to imagine sliding those buckles open. But if I uncovered the extent of his markings, I'd know how high in the ranks he had risen, and I'd know the kind of fae I was dealing with. Were his marks from the wars, from killing humans or from slaughtering the likes of Kellee's people. I wanted—*needed* to know.

"Most believed her fair." I ran my finger along the edge of his desk, marveling at its warm, glossy polish. So very different from the metal and glass found in the rest of Calicto and most of Halow. "She was, according to fae law."

"She was the law," he said, his tone mild and unreadable.

I looked up. His eyes were still closed. Had he known Mab?

He opened his eyes and blinked, but a glassy sheen remained. Dark pupils expanded, soaking up the colors of his irises. I had only ever seen him utterly focused. Now he looked at me as though he didn't quite see me.

"When was the last time you saw her?" I skimmed my fingers along the desktop as I moved around to his side. He watched with the lazy appreciation of someone lost in thought.

"Long ago." He pulled his gaze away and whispered, "She told me the war would end soon." He rubbed his fingers over the bridge of his nose and massaged above his eye. "This pain? It will end. Soon. Some days are worse than others." A small laugh escaped him. "Not that there are ever days or nights, just endless false light. The air here is thin, cycled through a million bodies a thousand times a day. The food tastes like ash. And I am..." He swallowed. "I am—" He cut himself off and tossed a careless smile my way. "But I have you. Her killer." The glassiness washed away. "I am unsure whether I should hate you—as you hate me—or..."

His focus softened and roamed over me, snagging where the gown had slipped, exposing fragments of the marks climbing my thighs. "You have killed more of your kind than many fae soldiers. Do you think that makes you worth more than them?" he asked with a smile, but this time it was the dangerous one—a prelude to an attack.

My pulse raced, chest tight. "Mab did."

He reached out and flicked my gown open, exposing my leg below the knee and the patterns inked into my skin. Goosebumps scattered across my flesh. He saw. He saw and heard everything. Heard my heart race. Felt my shivers. He read and absorbed all the signs of human desire.

He touched my knee, settling his warm fingers over an elaborate, sweeping tattoo. "Does your kind despise you as they should?" His hand followed the mark higher, easing the gown back farther. I felt the beat of my heart everywhere, felt desire pulse low.

"If they knew, they would."

That answer brightened his eyes. He leaned forward in the chair and chased the mark higher, across my thigh. Where the ink thickened, his touch became heavier. His hands weren't as smooth as I'd imagined. He had worked them once, likely around the hilt of a sword.

He shifted to his feet, scooped his hands around my waist and lifted me onto the table. My thoughts raced, panic battling with need. I planted my hands on either side of me to steady myself, keeping my touch off him, despite the temptation. With his gaze fixed on mine, he eased my thighs open and pushed between them.

Bowing his head, he brushed his cheek against mine and whispered, "A monster among your kind and a monster among ours. It must be a lonely life, Wraithmaker."

Just words. Don't believe them. Don't let them in. But they did ease in through my defenses to toy with my heart. He was alone, like me. I didn't know why he had shut himself away or forced himself to live this life, but I understood the ache of loneliness.

I touched the hard line of his jaw. A muscle fluttered

beneath my fingers. From restraint or anger, I couldn't know, and the heat he summoned in my veins pulsed harder. He had been alone for longer than I'd been alive. Yes, I needed answers. Yes, I needed to know what was really happening inside Arcon. But in that moment, he was the closest thing to Faerie I had experienced in five years. For him, I was the closest thing to the home he had been shut away from for a lifetime and more. I hated what they had done to me, but that only made this need more savage. I could own him back. He hated me, hated how I was human, how I'd killed his queen, but he *needed me...* just like I needed him.

Slowly, methodically, he unwound the gown's belt, his breath brushing across the curve of my neck.

I hooked my fingers into the buckles holding his jacket closed and flicked them open one at a time. When the garment hung loose, I pushed it back, relishing the muscular curve of his shoulders. He tore it free, tossed it away, and captured my face in his hands. A fresh madness sharpening his glare, and his mouth. This wasn't about me. He wanted Faerie, but I'd do. I wanted answers and didn't care how I got them. I lunged in, sank my hand into his loose hair, twisted my fingers and yanked him into a kiss. He tasted wrong, like everything mothers warned their children about, like the old fairy tales; he tasted like sweet poison, the kind that would slay you slowly while you begged for more. His magic tainted the air, igniting my taste buds, and set my thoughts spinning, and I didn't care that he was about to drag me down into his fantasy, turning my reality inside out. It would be worth it. His mouth worked with mine, tongue taking, teeth nipping. He pushed and I pushed back, my grip in his hair tightening, reaping shudders from his body.

His hands fell. One sweeping around my hip, the other falling to my neck where he paused. The collar. If he removed it, he would taste all of me, but I'd also be free and have my magic to hand.

Do it, I silently demanded. Enslaved, this was nothing. But if he could take me while I was *free* and taste Faerie's magic in me? His body trembled against mine, muscles tight with restraint. He tore his mouth away and lifted his head, teeth gritted.

Do it. Take it off.

I rode my hands up his chest, lifting the shirt, revealing deep black ink. His marks interwove and danced and swirled like none I'd seen before. Entranced, I shoved the shirt higher and ran my tongue over the bramble-like maze that hooked and curled across his upper abs, leading me astray. I would have continued, would have fallen into the trap of tasting him, if the scar hadn't caught my eye. The fae didn't scar. But something had happened to him, something that had opened his chest right over his heart. Scar tissue distorted the flesh around the cut, and stitched down its middle, delicate metal threads glimmered.

Tek.

I froze. The *thump-thump* of his heart beat almost too loudly.

Larsen's touch fell away. He stepped back, putting space between us, instantly chilling my skin. He tugged his shirt down, covering the scar, and picked up his jacket. He stood still, holding the garment, his face turned away in... *shame?*

I wiped the sweet and salty taste of him from my mouth.

He had tek stitched into his chest, holding an old wound together. Tek that should kill him, but somehow...

He pressed his hand to his chest, his usually controlled face racked with pain.

"This was..." He waved at me, my gown askew, lips and body flushed with heat. "This is nothing." He wouldn't meet my eye. "I can't afford this distraction."

He pulled his jacket on and regarded the door across the room. His escape. But he didn't move, and I watched his expression crumble before he turned his back to me. Because out there wasn't an escape. This place was his sanctuary in an entire system that wanted him dead—had maybe tried to kill him from the inside out. The tek was inside him, combining with and living off fae magic. Like my whip lived. Like Sota lived.

Larsen had a human-made heart.

"You will fix me," he said firmly while dragging his gaze upward.

And finally, I understood why I was here.

The fractures I'd seen on his face had vanished, replaced by a sharp determination. "You can fix *this*."

"I..."

"You have her magic. Mab's magic. You create life where there is none. You weave magic and tek together. You're a tek-whisperer. I am dying, and you will fix me, Wraithmaker. Mab sent you to fix me. She gave you her gift of magic *for me*. You will serve your purpose. You will serve me as you served her. Remove the tek from around my heart."

"And if I don't?" My voice trembled under the weight of what I'd seen.

"Then I'll turn Arcon on itself and open the door to all of Faerie." He lifted his chin in defiance.

I already knew Arcon had complete control of Halow's security, including the barrier between our systems. He

181

could cripple the entire Halow system at the touch of a button or the sweep of his hand. It was a miracle he hadn't already.

"How did this happen to you?" I asked.

"Just agree," he snarled. "Unless you don't want to save your people? Unless you think opening the door will make the fae forgive you?" He paused, watching for my reaction. I didn't move. Didn't dare to. "Whatever you want, whatever your dreams, I can make them real." When I didn't answer, he came forward. "We're both monsters among our kind." He clutched my face, crushing it painfully tight. "Don't you want all your sins to be forgiven and to be loved by Faerie once more?"

CHAPTER 18

*A*fter Larsen brought me fresh clothes and my coat, he left to continue his charade as human. I contacted Kellee using the comms and told the marshal about the scar, the heart, the markings, Larsen's threat. I told him everything except for Larsen's offer to remove my crime of murdering a queen.

Kellee left me alone with my thoughts while he contacted Talen. I dressed, threw on my coat and wandered Larsen's private quarters. His books drew my eye. I plucked a large tome from the shelf and set it down on the desk with a heavy *thwump*. Gold leaf embossed beautifully intricate writing. But the content of the text wasn't pretty. The history of human evolution. The original humans were seeded on Earth and grown to serve the fae. But the fae underestimated their experiment and the time the new civilization would need to evolve. With their short life spans, humans rushed to evolve and learn and create all on their own. In the absence of magic, humans created tek—huge interconnected metal machines with brains.

By the time the fae returned to check on their experiment, late in the twenty-first century, humans had surrounded themselves with technological advancements that repelled the fae.

I flicked the pages and ran my fingers over the sweeping words.

The fae didn't take kindly to their pets creating what they saw as weapons and attempted to wipe humans from the Earthen system. That was when the fae learned their experiment had evolved beyond the whims of their creators. The resulting war lasted a thousand years. Billions died. Fae and human. Tek evolved and got smarter, launching humans to the stars and beyond to the neighboring Halow system.

The book described human advancement as a fae-engineered virus that stubbornly resisted the fae's best efforts to destroy it.

The final battle saw enormous human-built space-faring battlecruisers encroach on Faerie. The full force of the Fae Courts fought back. The summoning blasted human forces out of Faerie, creating an area of dead space littered with wrecked ships and ravaged worlds on both sides. Queen Mab, leader of the Fae, penned a truce, and a defensive net was strung across Halow and Fae borders, sealing one from the other indefinitely.

Over the years, the defense net thickened, backed up by human tek. Tek Arcon now maintained.

No human had seen a fae for at least a thousand years since the war. For all but the few at the highest echelons of government, they had slipped into the realm of myth and legend.

But one had survived in Halow. The fae with the metal heart.

When Kellee's voice came back through the comms, the news was worse than I'd imagined.

"His name is Eledan," Kellee said.

My heart sank. The world grew smaller and colder, the truth contracting around me. Now I knew why he appeared to be so powerful. "He's Mab's son."

"Supposedly killed in the war, before even my time." The marshal sighed. "Eledan has been missing and presumed dead for over a thousand years."

"Not dead." I swallowed. "Just hiding among humans, building Arcon and buying time. If he returned to Faerie with a tek heart, they *would* kill him. Royal or not." *He just wants to go home.*

No, don't fall for it.

It didn't matter why. He was insane, driven mad by tek exposure, and he was dangerous because of it. Whatever he might have been a thousand years ago—Mab's son, prince of the Fae Courts—he wasn't that now.

"Talen is suspicious," Kellee said, softer now, his words whispering through the comms and into my ear.

"Is he secure?" The last thing we needed was another dangerous fae on the loose.

"Yes." He didn't sound sure. "He had questions about you."

"None of that matters," I mumbled, thoughts churning.

A fae prince could disable the defense net and open the door to Faerie. Humans had forgotten what it meant to war with the fae. The fae had not. They thrived on the hunt. Lived by it. Even sought it out. And Mab—the only one who'd had the presence of mind to arrange a truce—was gone. Her son, Eledan's brother, Oberon, ruled in Faerie now—the same king who reared saru to hunt and kill and entertain their fae overlords. Oberon loved nothing more than bloodshed. Nothing crafted a king and his reign quite like war.

Billions of human lives hinged on my ability to fix Eledan's heart. And if I did, would he keep his word?

"Kesh?"

"Yes, I'm still here..." I closed the book.

"Can you fix him?" Kellee asked.

I lowered myself into Eledan's chair, listening to the old wood creak. "I don't know. The tek is there for a reason, either to keep him alive or to kill him slowly, and he's been resisting it all this time. I doubt it will be a simple case of just removing it or he would have done it himself." My magic would secure his life during such a tricky operation. "Did Talen say anything about the heart?"

"No, but I recall a legend, of sorts, from the warfiles during my training. The missing prince led a charge against a line of tactical drones. His unit broke through, suffering massive losses, but he went on to kill hundreds of soldiers before a colossus machine took him down. The colossus tore his heart out. They paraded his body through Aluna's streets. The city and much of the planet is gone now. Mab's retaliation was swift." Kellee's odd, slightly detached tone had me wondering if the marshal had been there despite him saying it was before his time. "It seems like Eledan survived the impossible."

"He's a powerful illusionary. It's nothing for him to fool a mob." Eledan could probably also live without his heart, for a while, but someone must have helped him or condemned him by replacing his fae heart with tek. An unsuspecting human who was likely killed once the job was done.

For me to operate on his heart, he would need to trust me. We weren't there yet, but now I knew who he was and exactly what he wanted. The power was in my hands. Once he trusted me, I'd open him up, cut out his heart and kill him.

"Kellee, don't come here tomorrow."

"Kesh—"

"Please. I... I'm afraid he'll hurt you. If he suspects we know each other—"

"He won't suspect a thing. Trust me."

"Why risk it? You can't do anything. Putting yourself at risk like this is foolish—"

"I have to come."

"No, you don't." His silence grated on me. "Why?"

"I want to see you."

I closed my eyes, ignoring the flutter of silly human hope his words stirred inside. "Kellee, pl—"

"No. I need to know you're all right. When I saw the collar he put on you..." An exasperated sigh interrupted. "Look, it's... I have to do this. His kind killed everyone I knew. They took away my home, my family. They stole everything from me. I won't let him take you. I know what he is. I need to know you're... you're alive, that you're real. That it's really Kesh I'm talking with. Do you understand?"

"I am real. I'm not some trick. He's not screwing with you. Right now, he doesn't even know you exist. Stay away and stay secret. I can't protect you if you come here, Kellee, and I need you on the outside."

"You don't need to protect me. You're more at risk than I am. You killed his mother. I have to come. I'm not discussing it."

I shook my head, wishing the fool didn't make me

smile. "Are all your people this stubborn?"

"They were." I heard the smirk and then the comms cut off.

"Be careful," I whispered into the silence.

~

LARSEN—ELEDAN arrived early the next morning, demanding I follow him. He spun his Larsen disguise between one step and the next as we left his apartment. Down through Arcon we walked, taking elevators and escalators. These excursions of his were deliberate. He needed to be *seen* to reinforce his act.

Larsen's office was everything his Eledan apartment was not. Glass and steel shone, their surfaces polished and angles sharp. Now that I had seen both sides of the fae, the contrast was shocking.

"Someone reported my behavior at the Arcon anniversary party to the marshal's office," Eledan said, seating himself behind a curved glass desk. "They're sending a marshal over to question us." Numerous screens descended above the desk, creating a curtain of monitors. His hands swept across the keys overlaid on the glass-top desk. "You will answer his questions," he said without looking up from his work, "and make sure to satisfy the marshal without raising suspicion."

There was a threat under those words, though he kept all signs of it off his charming Istvan Larsen face.

His biotek-masked eyes flicked to me. "Do I need to warn you about what you can and cannot say?" he asked.

"No."

"Close your coat collar."

I flicked up the coat's collar and sealed it closed, hiding

the iron one.

"Have you thought about my offer?"

"You mean whether to save one fae or potentially kill all the humans in Halow? That offer?"

"Or, in exchange for helping me, we have the fae return and tell them it was you who allowed them to enter Halow once more." He arched an eyebrow. "They will love you all over again."

The love of one race at the cost of the lives of another? "I won't condemn an entire system just to appease my guilt. Besides," I breathed in, "the Court will never forgive me."

"You would be surprised. Not everyone appreciated Mab's peacemaking techniques. Some are likely relieved you removed the queen and her treaty with her."

"Some like Oberon?" I watched him for any reaction to his brother's name, but his human expressions were too well schooled.

He leaned back in the chair and peered *through* his screens at me. "You have to admit, you killing Mab saved Oberon the trouble." Eledan's mask briefly slipped, and the full weight of his fae-glare rested on me—searching for what? "Frustrating, don't you think," he added, "for the first-born son, the next in line to the throne, to be in waiting forever?"

I returned his stare with a level one of my own. "Oberon has waited a few thousand years. What is another few hundred to a fae like him?"

He took the words, considered them and returned to his work. "A great many."

Eledan would know a great deal about waiting. A thousand years among his enemy. Did he even remember who he really was? What did that kind of stress do to a fae mind? "How many human lifetimes have you pretended to live?" I asked, keeping my voice quiet, easing it around his illusionary armor.

His hands stilled. He looked at me side-on.

"Larsen is just the latest. You've been here a long time..." I wasn't supposed to know how long.

His face softened as his thoughts wandered to the past.

"Did you come to know families?" I asked, sensing a weakness. "Were you ever invited to become part of one?"

Something new flared in his eyes. I wasn't sure what, especially with the biotek lenses dulling his faeness. But a thousand years? How many human lives had he touched?

"There were... times," he admitted.

Had he come to love them like he used to make them love him? Had he ever fallen into his own trap? A thousand years was a long time to be alone.

What if I was looking at this all wrong? What if he hadn't let the fae into Halow because he knew his kind would ravage what they found? What if he was *protecting* Halow? He had said he *should have* opened the door, but he hadn't. He'd held back, living his Larsen life among tek. A thousand years among the enemy would test even the most devout hater.

An alert chimed on one of the screens, drawing his attention away from me. "The marshal will be here in a few minutes," he said. "Make sure he leaves appeased or his subsequent death will stain your hands with more blood, Wraithmaker."

I curled my fingers into my palms, digging my nails in.

An empty threat? Eledan *had* killed Crater, but I didn't yet know why. Dammit. Kellee had better be good at pretending, because he was about to stand toe to toe with a professional illusionist.

CHAPTER 19

*M*arshal Kellee held out his hand. "Mister Larsen." He smiled the neutral lawman smile that said, *I'm your friend until I'm not.*

Eledan smiled back, his smile equally false. "Marshal Kellee." They shook, both of them lying with their body language, if not their words.

Kellee turned to me. "And you are...?"

"Kesh Lasota." I forgot to offer my hand, distracted by Eledan's simmering presence. The fae settled against his desk, gripping the edges on either side of him, knuckles briefly paling. A line of tension ran down his back, and a muscle twitched in his cheek. His strain was obvious, but the marshal didn't notice because the idiot was looking at me.

Something was wrong. Larsen should have been relaxed. He had been relaxed before Kellee arrived. He was in his territory, wrapped up in his comforting lies. This was supposed to be easy—answer the marshal's questions and send him on his way—but Larsen was looking at him without blinking, in the way all fae did when they were about to attack.

Kellee continued to stare at me.

"What?" I snapped.

The marshal's pretty face darkened. "I asked if you were well, Miss?"

"Me? Yes. I'm fine." I laughed like a lunatic. "We're all fine, *Marshal*."

"I feel like... we've met," Kellee mused, backing up to get a better look at me. "You seem familiar," he added, grabbing a chair. "Do you mind?" he asked Larsen. Before the fae had a chance to reply, Kellee sat down and leaned back, utterly at ease.

What was he doing? We weren't supposed to give Larsen any reason to suspect us, and the second thing he said was that he thought we'd met before? Had he lost his mind?

"No," I denied. "I don't think we've met." The heat of Larsen's gaze fell on me. I fought not to meet his glare. "I'd remember a marshal."

Kellee's shiny metal star winked.

This was insane. Larsen was not happy, and Kellee either wasn't picking up on the crackling tension or he didn't care. He had told me to trust him. He had said everything would be okay. This was *not* okay.

"So," Kellee began, "you know why I'm here, Mister Larsen."

"I do. The unfortunate report of an assault at the anniversary gathering. Who reported it?"

Don't tell him. Whoever it was might not wake up again.

Kellee opened his hands. "I'm not at liberty to say. But you understand I have to follow up on reports, even regarding esteemed individuals like yourself." Kellee

192

looked around him, likely reading all the modern elements of Larsen's surroundings. "Nice office. Not like mine. The department gives us cubicles. I much prefer being in the field."

"Of course, a man like you would naturally prefer not to be cornered." Larsen's smile was sharp enough to cut glass.

At least the marshal didn't have his sharp teeth on show. Yet.

"Did you have questions?" I asked before Kellee dug himself into a deeper hole.

"Yes." Kellee regarded me, his expression softening. "You were the victim of this assault?"

"No."

"No? The report said—"

"I'm not a victim of anything. What happened was a misunderstanding. We er... Mister Larsen and I were just... We had too much cyn. You know how it is."

"Not really. Please explain what happened, in your own words."

I glared at Kellee, wishing he could read my mind so he'd get out of Larsen's office now. "We argued, sure. But we made up."

Kellee's dark eyebrow arched and his green eyes sharpened. "What's your relationship to Mister Larsen?"

"Sister," Eledan answered for me.

"Sister?" Kellee's tone might as well have said, *karushit.* "Huh." He breathed in and leaned back. "Mister Larsen, I assume you won't mind if Miss Lasota and I talk alone?"

"Why would you need to talk alone?" Eledan asked.

"Because I'm a marshal, you're accused of assault, and Miss Lasota is the victim."

Dammit Kellee, just let it go already.

Eledan straightened and stepped toward Kellee, putting himself slightly in front of me. I gave Kellee a quick shake of my head. The marshal's determined glare narrowed. The fool wouldn't back down. Did he *want* Eledan to attack? If he kept pushing, the fae surely would.

I stood and reached for Eledan's arm. The undercurrent of illusionary magic prickled my fingers. "Istvan, it's all right."

But Eledan ignored me. He folded his arms and tilted his head, blatantly scrutinizing the marshal. Kellee peered up at the young CEO.

A citrusy bite tingled on my tongue.

"*Vakaru.*" The word dripped from Eledan's lips like a curse or a threat. I had never heard it before, but Kellee had.

The marshal's upper lip pulled back, revealing lengthening canine teeth in a smile crafted of pure malice.

Fae magic flared, and Eledan lunged. Kellee—a blur—kicked off the floor, knocking his chair backward with inhuman speed. Eledan's hand clawed at the air where Kellee had been sitting, and the marshal landed a punch to Eledan's cheek, nearly dropping the fae to the floor.

I stepped in. "Kellee!"

But he flung out a hand—"Stay back, Messenger!"—and sunk his hand into Eledan's hair, twisting him off the floor. The fae's illusion collapsed, revealing the warfae in all his black-haired, leather-wrapped alien glory. A growl bubbled up from Eledan as he turned his head to fix the full weight of his glare on the marshal. His eyes burned, crackling with the full force of his magic. Kellee wasn't leaving this room alive.

"*Vakaru el nislet,*" Eledan growled.

"Fuck you, fae." Kellee locked his hand around the

warfae's throat and drove him backward, slamming Eledan into the desk.

Eledan wasn't fighting. Why wasn't he fighting? He smiled at the marshal, and that smile was a terrible portent. He was *toying* with Kellee.

I had to do something. But with no weapon and my magic contained, the pair of them grossly outmatched me.

Five black knives appeared in Kellee's hand and punched into Eledan's chin. The fae jerked his head back, yanking free.

Not knives. Claws.

Citrus spritzed the air, so pungent it burned the back of my throat, and Kellee launched away from Eledan, coat whirling. Air shimmered, Eledan's illusions coming to life and surrounding Kellee. The lawman roared and turned away, shoulders heaving.

Shudders racked him.

Eledan straightened. He brushed a hand down his jacket, straightening it, and wiped his chin, smearing blood across his cheek.

"Interesting," he said, eyeing his spilled blood and then the shivering marshal. "Do you know what he is?" Eledan asked, addressing me.

A fucking idiot. "No."

"No, you shouldn't. We wiped his kind out long before the saru were conceived."

I wet my lips and swallowed, finding my throat dry. Kellee stood rigid, his back to me, his long coat rippling, amplifying his trembling. "What's wrong with him?"

"Besides the obvious, I showed him something from his past. Something he didn't want to see," Eledan said, blasé. He retrieved a towel from inside his desk drawer and wiped the blood from his chin and neck. Not a mark remained. "I believed they were all dead."

"We are," Kellee said, grinding the words out from between his teeth.

Eledan rolled his eyes in a very human expression of dismissal. "The Vakaru were bred as soldiers and designed to feed off violence, making them crave the kill. They were Oberon's pet project, and they served us well, until one of their kind started harboring rebellious ideas. They have a pack mentality. Once one turns, they all turn. It sealed their fate."

After wiping his hand clean and dumping the bloody towel on the desktop, Eledan crossed the room to stand dangerously close in front of Kellee. But the marshal didn't lash out. He lifted his head, I assumed to look into Eledan's eyes, though I couldn't see Kellee's face.

Standing so close, it was clear which of them was designed for combat. Kellee's presence was broader, even draped in his marshal's coat. Eledan's taller, slimmer frame was meant for stamina, for weeks spent on the hunt, for illusion and trickery. Kellee was designed to deliver a punch to the face, which he had done spectacularly to Eledan, for all the good it had done him.

The fae rubbed his jaw. "What shall I do with him?"

He was asking me? *Let him go!* I approached, giving them both wide berth, and stopped in front of Kellee. With his lips parted, Kellee's sharp teeth were obvious and lethal—but his slack expression revealed Eledan's hold on his mind. The fae was likely surrounding Kellee with illusions. Painful ones, from the haunted look crossing the marshal's face.

I sighed. If only the fool had listened to me and stayed away. "Let him go."

Eledan laughed. "I thought you might say that."

A blade dropped from Eledan's right bracer into his hand. I caught the shimmer of metal too late to stop him from slashing open Kellee's neck.

"No!"

The marshal staggered, reflexes holding him up. His hand went to his throat, fingers sinking into the gush of blood. Blood soaked his shirt and poured down the front of his coat, obscuring his marshal's badge. Panic stuttered my thoughts. I grabbed Kellee's arm. He caught the back of the chair, but his grip slipped and his knees buckled. We dropped together.

"Oh, Kellee, no..." I knelt beside him, reaching for the gaping wound pumping out too much blood. His eyes rolled back. I was losing him.

His wet fingers touched my face. "*Messenger*," he mouthed, his voice drowning in blood.

No! He was the last of his kind. A good man. He had saved me from Eledan's assassins. He was only trying to do the right thing. He didn't deserve to die this way.

I shot to my feet and slammed my palms into Eledan's chest, splattering blood across his fine leathers and shoving the fae backward. "Remove this collar. NOW!"

"So you can use Mab's magic to heal a vakaru?" Eledan scoffed. "No. I'm putting him out of his misery. Life as a vakaru, alone and hungry, is no life at all."

"That's not your choice to make!"

"Yes, it is. His life belongs to the fae."

Rage and fear overrode all reason. I snatched Eledan's blade from his hand and pressed it to my neck, feeling the sting of the blade cut. "Heal him or lose your only chance at being fixed."

Eledan reached for the blade. I jerked back, nicking my

skin. "If he dies, I will never help you. Do you understand? You'll have that metal heart in your chest forever."

Eledan snarled at the pale, listless marshal. "You would put the entire system—several billion lives—at risk, for one worthless *vakaru?*"

I poured all my indignation at being enslaved, all my resolve, all my rage and frustration into my glare and dragged the blade across my skin, opening it up. Fiery pain fizzled. Blood dribbled over the iron collar. Kellee wasn't worthless to me, but Eledan was right: I wouldn't go through with this. I lied and cut myself because it was the only weapon I had left. *Believe it, you fae fuck.* "Heal him!"

Eledan's amusement turned dry. Reluctance making his movements too damn slow, he knelt beside Kellee, pushed his hand into the blood soaking the marshal's neck and looked the marshal in the eye.

My heart thumped too loudly. I blinked the blur of fury in my vision away.

Eledan sighed. "It will take more than I can give."

No, those were not the words I wanted to hear. "Heal him, you have more fae magic here. Use it."

Eledan frowned over his shoulder. "The additional magic is not for a vakaru—"

"Do it!"

He studied the marshal's glassy, unresponsive expression and then leaned in and heaved the marshal onto his shoulder. With a sudden flood of magic, illusion wrapped around them both and they were gone.

I turned on the spot and, checking I was alone, lowered the blade. A sob broke free, but the others I swallowed down, adding them to the pit of rage simmering inside. I'd won that battle and Kellee would live. Eledan wouldn't risk losing me. Not until he had the metal heart out of his chest.

Striding to Eledan's desk, I stabbed the blade into the desktop. It pierced the glass. Cracks scattered across its perfect surface. When I had Eledan under my knife, I'd be sure to carve out his heart. And his soul.

I eyed the office door, realizing Eledan had left me unsupervised and unchained. I was free to roam Arcon.

~

"HEY, SINDY."

"Oh!" The woman I'd met at the anniversary party peered through her translucent screen and blinked. Large hoop earrings framed her smiling face. "You have er..." She waggled her finger near her neck. "A little sauce or something there."

It was blood, but I didn't have time to argue semantics. Eledan might be back at any moment. I scooted around her desk and tapped a few keys, bringing up a 3D image of Arcon's layout. "There." I pointed at the sealed-off lower sections. "How do I get down there?" Eledan had avoided those levels during our numerous tours. That had to be where he was hiding his source of magic.

"Storage?" She frowned. "There's nothing down there."

"Uh-huh." That's what Eledan wanted them to believe. "So how do I get there? None of these corridors or elevators go down that far."

"What?" She laughed dismissively. "Of course they do." She pressed a few more keys that zoomed in on our view of the map. "Right there. See. That stairwell will take you right to it." She pointed out a section of corridor that ended without any way to descend farther below Arcon.

Illusion.

"Your perfume is nice. What brand is it?" she asked.

Eau de Eledan's magic. I smiled at the woman's innocent question and the dreamy look on her face.

Around us, the entire floor of administration staff chatted into their ear mics while eagerly tapping away, doing Arcon's bidding. I hadn't paid them much attention before, but now that I didn't have Eledan beside me, I saw them for exactly what they were. This department didn't actually do anything. They all played the part, but the actions were automatic. They all had Sindy's glassy look. Worker drones. Human, but utterly clueless.

Eledan had them all under his spell. Arcon wasn't just a business that created and maintained defense and surveillance. It *was* a machine and the human staff was another mask. He probably only needed a handful of people to run Arcon, but he had to keep up appearances, keep up the illusion.

"Are you okay?" Sindy asked.

She had no idea her working life was a lie. Did she go home at night feeling refreshed, as though she had accomplished something important during her days at Arcon, when really, all she did was follow a script Eledan had put inside her head? "Do you like working here?" I asked her, ignoring the rush of goosebumps scattering across my skin.

"Oh, I love it. Istvan is a *fabulous* boss." She laughed self-consciously. "You already know that. How's the training going?"

"Fine. Everything is just fine." I placed my hand over hers and held her still. Her silly smile fractured. "You should quit. I don't know what this place is, but it's not what you think."

She yanked her hand back. "I think you should go now."

She wouldn't or couldn't see the truth. "Sure."

I drifted down the corridors. There had to be almost a thousand employees working at Arcon, not counting the satellite offices. And Eledan had the entire staff under his spell. How far did his reach go?

I touched the iron collar under my coat collar and swallowed, feeling it bob.

I activated my comms and whispered, *"Kellee...?"*

The marshal didn't reply.

It had only been a few hours since Eledan had taken him. Now, I wandered Arcon's maze of corridors and offices, searching for a way *down*. The magic was down there. Kellee probably was too.

What Eledan was doing, casting an illusion over an entire workforce, should have been impossible. For any other fae, it would have been. But he was Mab's son. A prince. He had access to the kind of power I had only dreamed of. His power was royal and ancient, the same as his mother's. But Mab hadn't sent me here like he thought. Her only order had been to kill her. But there had been other orders, things I had deliberately forgotten, choices that had been made for me.

I'd brought me here to Calicto, nobody else. Mab hadn't possessed the means to control that.

I massaged my temple. Yes, those memories were real. Eledan couldn't change my past. He couldn't get inside my head and mess with my mind.

My pace quickened. I wasn't like these doe-eyed people.

"Kellee... please answer me."

I stopped and found myself outside Sota's clear-walled

room. Pressing my hands to the glass, I willed Sota to fix his lens on me, but the drone didn't move. Sota could cut through illusion. He wasn't susceptible like humans were. He would have told me what was real. I missed him.

All I had to do was kill Eledan. The people working at Arcon would be free. Sota would be free. The company would collapse, freeing its hold on the Halow system. But what about the defense net? Without Arcon behind it, would it open? There had to be fail-safes in place. The human governments would have insisted. There had to be more stopping the fae than just me.

Pressure pushed against my skin, rippling my coat with unseen movement.

I turned my head.

Eledan's magic pushed down, rippling the space he carved through. The walls he passed bowed slightly, reality distorting around him. He wore soft gray leather pants and a partially armored gray jacket, unbuckled to reveal a loose white shirt. I blinked. He was blatantly fae, but nobody looked up, nobody cared. He wasn't pretending for me anymore.

"You've been busy." He opened the door to Sota's room and gestured for me to enter.

What was happening here? All around, through the glass walls, people went about their business. There had to be a hundred witnesses, and yet not a single soul looked up. In fact, they seemed to be going out of their way to *avoid* looking. Some switched their paths mid-stride, veering away. Others turned their chairs away.

"That's what happens when you leave your prisoner alone," I mumbled, his power crackling across my skin.

"Knife." He held out his hand.

Damn, I'd hoped he had forgotten that. I hesitated,

but he had Kellee, and withholding the knife wouldn't achieve anything. I handed the knife over.

He slipped it into a leather sheath and hooked it to his belt. "You are beginning to understand the weight of the decision on your shoulders."

I was beginning to understand that nothing was as it seemed. I had assumed he was weak. I had been wrong. I had assumed much of Arcon was real, but I had been wrong about that too. The people were his puppets. Was I? "I want to know one thing."

He nodded, his gaze sweeping over me, seeing too much.

"Are you saving this system or condemning it?"

He lifted his chin.

"You've had your hands on the defense net for years. Why haven't you let them in?"

He sat on the edge of the steel table next to Sota. "You believe I care what happens to the people here?"

"I think, over the years, you've learned to care. You didn't have much choice." Saying it out loud brought home exactly how insane it sounded. The fae didn't care for humans. And a prince? He cared less than most.

He laughed. The smooth, luscious sound tried to influence my mind and body. I swallowed, holding myself under control, feeling a terrible sense of foreboding pressing in.

"Your human naivety is adorable. I thought they bred those ridiculous notions out of saru."

I clenched my hands. Something was wrong. The air was too tight, the magic too sweet. "You can't breed out compassion."

"No? I've heard the stories of you mercilessly slaughtering your kin. Where was your humanity then, Wraithmaker?"

I clenched my jaw until my teeth ached.

"I thought so," he replied, smug as always. "You like the pretty idea of being human, but you are no more human than I am. You are saru. It must have been easy to forget that while playing at being a messenger for... what was it? Five years. A blink in a fae lifetime, and you believe you understand *me*? You actually believe I feel something for humans?"

Clearly not, but at least I had my answer. His motives were purely selfish. "So why the delay?"

He shrugged. "It isn't the right time."

"What are you waiting for?"

"You."

Icy dread clamped around my heart. Me? But he couldn't have known I'd come to Calicto. He couldn't have planned for that. He had been in Halow a thousand years. I was only twenty-six. It wasn't possible. Unless...

I reached for a nearby chair as the world necessary tipped, taking my memories of the queen's murder with it. "You knew I was going to kill Mab..."

"You don't think she plucked you out of the arena to actually serve by her side?"

I had. I had strived to be the best. I had longed for them to notice me. And they had.

"She had warriors, a thousand years old, trained in the art of battle. A saru is nothing compared to them."

"I don't—"

"Why would the Queen of Faerie pick a saru as her personal guard? You're not stupid, Kesh. But you are blinded by your love for her and for Faerie."

No, she had picked me because... because I was the best. I had killed all the others to prove I was like them. She had picked me to reward my devotion and the blood

I'd spilled. She had loved me as I loved her. She had respected my advice, and she had confided in me. She was mine and I was hers. *I was hers.* I would always be hers... She had told me so.

I flinched, the memories turning jagged and sharp.

I was hers.

I would always be hers.

I had made sure of that.

"You're lying." The words were weak, clutching at hope.

He dipped his chin and peered through his lashes. "You know I can't."

"But she gave me her magic. She said it was a gift."

"It was. For me."

I gripped the back of the chair, all my strength draining away. "But I'm the Wraithmaker," I whispered. *I had earned my name. Earned her respect.*

He touched my shoulder, suddenly beside me. I hadn't seen him move, and now he was so close, filling my view of everything. "We gave you that name. We built you up. We made you what you are. From the moment the saru breeding bitch squeezed you out, bawling into this world, you belonged to Faerie. Everything you know, everything you are, we gave to you. My mother, the Queen of Faerie, put you in her bed and gave you the blade to kill her."

"Why?" I whispered, ignoring the cold tears that fell.

"How is it possible you came to be here, in this room with me, without all of Faerie knowing I still lived? It had to be you—someone who wouldn't be noticed, a tek-whisperer, a ghost, a nobody girl with a queen's magic tied around her heart." He pressed his hand to my chest and pulled. All at once, an integral part of me arched toward him. Power—mine—surged from my heart and poured outward into his hand. His lips parted, eyes widening. I couldn't move, couldn't breathe. Screams shattered my mind but never left my lips. Prince Eledan leaned close. His mouth brushed mine, and his gaze burned. "Your life was never about you. You are just the messenger, and you are here for me."

More and more he pulled, draining the touch of the divine out of my veins. The queen's love had filled me, made me into something, and now he was taking it all away, emptying me out and leaving me hollow. And I couldn't stop him.

It was a lie.

All of it.

My entire life.

I had always known. But it had been easier to dream of more. To make it mean something. Anything.

His fingers brushed the collar. It clicked, fell open and clattered to the floor somewhere far away. "I've waited a long time for this," he whispered.

My eyelids fluttered down as the last strings of Mab's gift left me. Her magic had been all that held me up. I collapsed into Eledan's arms. He stole permission and licked his tongue over the corner of my mouth. "They call me the Dreamweaver, little saru. I will show you why."

No, no, no, no... My vision fluttered, the edges of my world tearing apart. My heart stuttered, his hand still pressed close, still taking, still pulling more than just magic.

He lightly brushed his fingertips down my face, closing my eyes. "Sleep. Dream. When you wake, the worlds will be better for having the fae in them."

He hadn't needed me—Kesh Lasota—at all. All he had wanted was my magic, his mother's magic. It would make him whole again, make him the prince she had lost so long ago. She had died to give me the gift that would bring him back to Faerie. He would be the prince who would herald in a new age by poisoning Halow from the inside out, starting with Arcon at the system's heart.

As I fell into nothing and nowhere, I wondered if anything I had lived had been real.

If I was just the messenger and I had served my purpose, what was left of me now?

PART II

"Come away, O human child!
To the waters and the wild
With a faery, hand in hand,
For the world's more full of weeping than you
can understand."

W.B. Yeats - Old Earthen, 1892

CHAPTER 20

When dreams were layered one on top of another on top of another, reality became the nightmare. I lived a thousand lives, loved a hundred souls and lost them all. With every day that passed, the dreams buried me deeper. I dreamed of carving out Eledan's heart. I dreamed of thrusting a sword through Mab's chest. I dreamed of a prince seated on a throne of bones. I dreamed of wishes and nightmares and all the things that mattered, until they didn't. I dreamed until there was nothing left to dream, until the fantasies had emptied out my mind, leaving it barren and ravaged.

"Reach out to her. She's calling your name."

"I can't."

I knew those voices, but from where, I couldn't recall.

All around there was darkness, and I heard him laugh. The sound of his laughter stirred me to life, and the dreams began again. Over and over and over, they turned me inside out and upside down.

I heard myself weeping like the saru who had begged me for their lives moments before I'd cut their throats. I'd killed them for praise, and their blood on my hands was worthless.

Dreams became nightmares that tore me apart. The ghosts I'd made came back to haunt me. I was the worst ghost of all. Kesh Lasota didn't exist. I didn't know who I was.

A hand waved in front of my face.

A man blinked at me. His eyes were green. Pretty.

"I don't think she sees us," he said.

He wasn't real, so I didn't answer.

He straightened and propped his hands on his hips. He seemed frustrated, but I couldn't imagine why. Then he gestured at someone standing to the side, almost swallowed inside the darkness threatening to wash over me again. "You try."

A second male came forward. Although his stride was casual, he moved like a killer. Each step was a statement, each footfall placed to pivot and launch if he needed to. He wore their leather clothes, adorned with too many ties and straps. Silvery hair veiled half his face.

Fae.

My teeth chattered together, adrenaline racing through my veins.

He stopped, his violet eyes darting over me.

He wasn't *him*, the one who had made me dream. The Dreamweaver. But he was one of them. My top lip twitched.

I heard laughter. It sounded terrible, like nails on glass.

The first man turned and shot me a concerned glance.

The laughter had come from me.

"What did you do?" the man asked.

"Nothing." The fae backed away, sinking into the shadows. He lurked there, waiting. I kept my eye on that one.

"Kesh?"

Kesh, Kesh, Kesh... There's no Kesh here. I giggled and lifted my hand. So pale and thin, it didn't look like my hand. But it must be mine. I waved it. Yes, definitely mine. *He* had taken my hands from me. I couldn't remember when. But they were back now. This dream was confusing. Was I supposed to do something? And I knew these males, didn't I? Or were they dreams too?

"I think she sees us." The man ran his hand through his shaggy hair. He had claws, though they weren't out now. I remembered those claws piercing *his* throat. Was this man my friend? He looked a lot like a man who had died in many of my dreams. His blood had painted me. So much blood.

I looked at my hands, seeing blood there. I blinked. Gone. Not the hands. They were still there. I laughed again or maybe cried. It was all the same.

The fae male hissed, and I shot him a silent glare.

"Maybe you should leave," the man suggested. *Vakaru.* That's right. He was like me, maybe. Created to serve the fae.

"I am not going anywhere," the fae replied stiffly.

The man sighed. I often dreamed of that one. I'd lived a few lifetimes with him inside my head. In one, we'd had a family. The Dreamweaver had killed them. In another, I'd killed them. In so many dreams, the Dreamweaver had cut him open again and again. And there was something about a fish in a glass bowl, but I couldn't remember.

I pressed the balls of my hands to my eyes. I wanted to go away again. It was cold here and dark, and these two... I didn't want them here. Their being here was wrong. It was all wrong. If they were here, and I was here, then something terrible had happened and I didn't want to know it.

"You killed her."

I opened my eyes and found the violet-eyed fae crouched in front of me.

"Do you remember that?" he asked.

My face crumpled and fell away. Beneath it, I was a ghost.

"I'm not real." The words tumbled. "Not real, not real. Everything is a lie."

Violet-eyes moved away. "It's hopeless. He always broke them. Every time. They used to throw his used ones in the pit for the *sluagh*. It's all they were good for."

I was broken?

"Stop," the man growled.

"You don't want to hear it, but it's the truth. She's too far gone. He breaks human minds. It's what he does, and he's been doing it for thousands of years. We can't save her."

Save from what?

"You should have left her there," he added, driving the words in like spikes into a steel coffin. "This is... this is cruel."

"I couldn't leave her," the man snapped, making me jump. I hugged my knees closer. "She saved my life."

"And it cost her hers."

The man pushed the fae's comments away with a growl.

I liked this dream. I didn't have to do much. Just watch them fight. The Dreamweaver would probably take them away soon, but I could enjoy them for now. The man, he was pretty looking. Dark hair, too long. But it would be nice to run my hands through it. And his green eyes, there was an intensity to them that I hadn't seen before. Rage lurked inside, making his eyes piercing. He was a dangerous one. But the fae, he was the opposite. Ridiculously long hair—pin straight because they never could stand a single strand out of place. Its ends were a bit ragged. This one had let himself go compared to other fae, but I liked his rough edges. He was wary too, holding back, deferring to the man. A curious pairing.

"She hears us," the man said, coming forward.

"But she doesn't believe any of it," the fae dismissed.

"Do you remember me?" the man asked me.

I closed my eyes and buried my face against my knees. The Dreamweaver would take him from me, and I didn't want him to go. If I hid, maybe *he* wouldn't come.

"Kesh, please. I want to help you. Just... just let me know you're in there."

I peeked over my knees. "He'll find you."

"No. He can't find us here. You're safe."

I whipped my head from side to side and touched my temple. "Up here." Tears filled my eyes, making him all blurry. "He's up here."

"No, Kesh..." His hand touched mine. "He's not."

I stared at the contact, panic clutching my heart. He felt real. But I had been here before, and every time *he* came to take it all away.

A suffocating pressure pushed down. I smelled the fresh scent of lemons. I looked up, straight into the eyes of the Dreamweaver, and screamed.

~

THEY CAME AGAIN, the pair of them. Violet-eyes and the pretty one. I couldn't talk to them. If I did, *he* would come. I shut down, made myself small, and hid. If I didn't talk, he didn't come, and so I listened and watched and studied.

We appeared to be in a cavern. Many corners harbored shadows. The Dreamweaver might be in any of them, so I avoided staring too long into their darkness.

I wanted to believe the pair were real. I wanted it so much that my heart ached. Tears fell when they weren't looking, and when they left me, I rocked back and forth, pushing the bad thoughts away.

But when I closed my eyes, the dreams came. I danced in the rain. I danced with the Dreamweaver. And then I carved out his heart.

~

MY GUT HEAVED, throwing up nothing, but it woke me from the nightmare. My arm stung. I reached for the pain, noticing the black tattoos, and found Marshal Kellee kneeling on the bed, looking at me with hopeful eyes, an empty syringe in his hand.

"Kellee?" I croaked.

"Kesh...?" His eyes frantically searched mine. His lips parted. "Do you...?"

Wait, wait... This was a lie. I shot from the bed, but my legs turned to jelly beneath me, and I collapsed, dropping to my knees. *He* was coming—it was coming. The truth was barreling forward, about to roll right over me. I clutched my hands to my head to squeeze out the horror of knowing. "Oh Kellee..."

His arms came around me, pulling me against his chest. I locked my fists into his shirt and twisted my grip, tearing the fabric. His strength and warmth were too much, too real. "Please, make it stop..."

His chin brushed the top of my head. "It's all right. We have you."

He smelled masculine, like soap and something woody that made me think of earth and the outdoors on a world far away. He smelled real. But if I opened my eyes, I'd be clutching the Dreamweaver.

I couldn't stand this.

I pushed him away, my eyes squeezed closed. "No, no... don't."

"Kesh, please. It's me."

"NO, NO, IT'S NOT!"

An arm hooked around my neck and yanked me up and off Kellee. Another arm hooked around my waist, pulling me back against a lean, hard body. I writhed and kicked and bucked, but every twist tightened the hold.

"Open your eyes," Violet-eyes said. Talen. It had always been Talen beside Kellee. The fae and the marshal. The pair. But Talen being free didn't make sense. Nothing made sense anymore. I was surrounded by lies. I was the biggest lie of all.

I sobbed and sucked in the air the useless noise had cost me. I would open my eyes. I would be in the Dreamweaver's arms. But it was okay. I knew that now. I fluttered my eyes open and blinked at Kellee.

He rubbed his jaw where my heel had caught him. "Hey."

I blinked, breathing hard through my nose. Another blink. Still Kellee. "Hey."

He lifted the syringe. "It looks as though this helped," he said to Talen.

Talen, who had me trapped in his arms. Talen, who was too much like Eledan. Saliva pooled in my mouth. "Put. Me. Down."

"Your muscles suffered a great deal of atrophy—"

"Put her down, Talen," Kellee ordered.

The fae let me go. I hobbled away from them and fell against the wall. The wall was good. The wall was real. Okay, they were still here. Kellee had given me a drug to ground me. I was here. This was the now. But for how long...?

I swallowed, still feeling sick, but I was upright and thinking. I looked down at myself, at the oversized white shirt someone had dressed me in. One of theirs, probably. My legs poked out, knees and ankles jutting. The fae marks were so dark against my skin that they appeared to glow.

"How long?" I rasped.

Talen glanced at Kellee. A sure sign the answer would hurt.

"How long?" I asked again.

"Nine months," Kellee replied.

Laughter threatened, tugging at my mouth. Nine months of dreaming. Nine months of being *his* to toy with as he pleased. The drug they had given me could only last so long. Every time I closed my eyes, he would be there. Every time I lay down to sleep, he would be waiting.

I looked at them. Kellee's concern was easier to read, but worry also pinched Talen's brow. They had brought me back. Why? Dozens of questions surfaced, but I didn't ask them. Not yet.

"I just... Can I have some time alone?"

Talen tensed. "I don't think that's wise."

"I don't care what you think, *fae*," I snarled.

He flinched, and I might have regretted the words if I'd had the energy. I owed him and Kellee a debt, but the chittering insanity in my head wouldn't shut up.

"Go," Kellee ordered.

Talen's mouth set into a line. "If her awareness slips—"

"Get out!" I screamed.

He left, long hair swishing like a tail.

"I didn't mean..." I reached out a hand, and Kellee took it, leading me back to the bed. "I'm sorry. It's just... He's..."

"He understands."

I didn't think he did, but I didn't have room in my head to feel sorry for him. I sat on the edge of the bed, cupped my hands on my thighs and sighed. "I have a million questions, but I'm not sure I can handle the answers right now."

"There's only one thing you need to know. You are safe here."

He was wrong, but I smiled anyway. "The last time I saw you..." I winced, trying to find the real memory. My mind was a soup of dreams. "I think... he cut you?"

"He would have killed me. You saved me. Do you remember?"

I did and nodded. I also remembered stabbing him over and over while the Dreamweaver laughed. I swallowed the acid in my throat and looked away. The memories were slippery and difficult to hold on to. But the dreams, the dreams were so real. So real I could reach out and take one.

"It will take time," Kellee was saying.

The bed moved as he stood. I didn't want to look up. It would be easier if I didn't care about anything here. Easier for when he came and took it all away.

"Kellee?"

I didn't know if Kellee looked. I wasn't even sure if he was still in the room.

"Thank you."

The door clicked closed, sealing me alone with the madness clawing at the insides of my skull.

Blood welled in my hands. I plucked my nails free of my palms. That pain was real. And this room was real, and Kellee was real, and I was real. Reality hurt.

~

THEY WERE KEEPING me in chambers carved into rock. Occasionally, I'd hear something clunk somewhere far off, like a heavy door closing, but there were no other voices, besides the ones in my head. I dry-showered alone, watching my thin arms tremble and the black marks sink deeper into my skin—skin that hung off my bones, distorting the once beautiful swirls.

I had been so proud of those marks. Now I wanted to sink my nails under my skin and peel them off. Sinking my long nails into my palms instead alleviated those urges.

As I exited the shower room, I discovered that one of the males had left some clothes folded at the end of the bed. Simple gray jogging pants and a black long-sleeved top. I returned to the bathroom and looked in the mirror for the first time.

I was skin and bone and nothing else. I poked at my face, below my right eye. The skin barely sprang back. I hadn't been this emaciated since I'd been punished for fiercely defying an order as a child. I'd learned how to behave after that. How to please my fae masters.

My eyes were sunken, my cheeks too. I was all edges and angles, and not in the striking fae way.

"Shit," I hissed. It sounded good. Felt good too, forming the word around my tongue and pushing it against the top of my mouth. "Shit, shit, shit." Then my head spun, and I had to grip the rail to keep from falling over.

I probably should have lain back down, but I couldn't.

I had lain and wasted away for nine months, lost to the dreams. I would have died like that if it hadn't been for Kellee and Talen.

I scratched my arms, leaving red marks behind. Pain. It was real—or as real as I could tell.

I left the room and drifted wraith-like down a cold corridor. Lights buzzed above, flicking on as I passed under them and blinking off again behind me. Emerging around a bend, a cavern opened ahead. Normal household things were huddled around the edges. A chiller, chairs, couch, a few tables, two cots. A glass cage sat dead center in the middle of the cavern. Its door hung open, chained in place so it couldn't fall closed.

Talen sat on the edge of a bed on the opposite side of the room. He looked up through the cage's transparent panes.

Kellee wasn't here. My empty saru heart fluttered like that silly bird trapped in its cage.

Talen seemed to sense my apprehension. He looked down at the book in his hand. "Kellee will be back soon."

Why wasn't he in the cage? Why wasn't he locked up like he should have been?

His violet eyes flicked up. "I won't hurt you."

I swallowed, knowing he heard the click in my throat. I needed a weapon. My hand dropped to my hip, but my whip was long gone. Wouldn't matter anyway. Without my magic, it was just a metal whip. My fingers brushed the grazes on my neck. I heard—recalled the clatter of the collar hitting the ground. Recalled *his* hand pushed against my chest. Recalled the life leaving me.

My breath caught, throat closing.

"Are you hungry?" Talen asked.

I blinked. The memory shattered.

He had moved to where the couches formed a circle. Behind them a line of cupboards had been pushed together, forming a kitchen area. I bumped against the wall, unaware I'd been backing up. And now I had nowhere to go, but Talen wasn't looking. He took a bowl from inside a cupboard, poured something into it and set it on an old heating hob.

"Why...?" I croaked out.

"Why am I not in the cage?" He leaned back against a cupboard and folded his arms. "You will have to ask Kellee that."

Vague fae karushit. They were all the same. I breathed in through my nose and lifted my head. I was in no condition to fight back. He could snap me like a twig. But I would at least keep my head up and pretend I had strength enough to fight him.

"This is your prison," I said, stating the obvious.

"Was."

"Freedom must be nice for you." I started forward, one foot in front of the other. *Not backing down.* One foot, then the other. Nothing bad happened. Again. One foot, then the other, then the first again.

"Perhaps it would be, under better circumstances."

"What do you mean?" I reached for the nearest couch. So close.

He looked down but didn't hide the full range of emotion on his face. Pain. Shame. Fear.

What in all Halow had happened while I was *gone*? I opened my mouth to ask and all the expressions on his face fled. He knew what I was going to ask and was already shaking his head. "Wait for Kellee... Right."

I had only made it as far as the first couch. I wasn't sure my legs would carry me much farther.

Talen scooped up the bowl and set it down on the table at the center of all the couches. Without saying a word, he returned to his cot and picked up his book.

It was a trick.

He would often do this to me.

Offer kindness and then rip it away.

But the soup smelled good, and I was so hungry my stomach might eat itself at any moment. I pawed my way around the couch and lowered myself into their mismatched cushions. Keeping one eye on the fae, I picked up the bowl and ate, unable to contain the groan when the soup touched my tongue.

Talen's little smile didn't go unnoticed.

While eating, I studied my surroundings. The pair had been here a while. But why? If Talen was free to leave, why hadn't he? And why would Kellee hang out here when he had that glorious apartment all to himself? What was keeping the sworn enemies together?

I scraped the dregs from the bottom of the bowl and fell back into the couch cushions, feeling more normal for the first time since I'd come back around to myself.

The quiet was thick but not uncomfortable. Occasionally, Talen would turn the book's pages, and curiously, I found that papery scrape comforting. Only a fae would read old physical books.

"You said some things while I was... not all here."

He looked up.

"You said, 'He always breaks them.'"

"Yes." Talen nodded.

"You know him?"

He hesitated, sensing he was on dangerous ground. "I know of Eledan. Kellee refused to believe me when I told him the prince wasn't dead."

"Wait." I shook my head. "That's not what happened. *I* told Kellee, and he came to *you* with questions."

Talen blinked. "You remember incorrectly."

"No, I remember perfectly. I saw the extent of Eledan's warfae markings first and warned Kellee about him. I thought Kellee might decide not to visit if I told him. The fool came anyway and then... Well, I guess you know what happened next."

He rolled his lips together, carefully placed a bookmark between the pages of his book and set it down beside his bed, next to a neat stack of paperbacks. The movements were slow, deliberate, buying him time to think.

"Talen's right." Kellee emerged from another doorway, carrying a bag of what I assumed were supplies. "He told me who the fae was right after we found you and got you away from Arcon. You and I didn't speak, Kesh, not until that meeting."

I laughed because how could he have forgotten our many conversations over the comms? Had they meant so little to him? His voice had been my lifeline then and during... the dreams. Always his voice. "The comms."

The marshal emptied out his bag, avoiding my glare.

"Remember, we talked over the comms I made at your apartment. You told me about your job, told me a lot of things, and I..." I stopped and snapped my mouth shut. They were both looking at me, gazes filled with pity. "Don't..." I heaved my withered body to standing. "I don't... I can't hear this. I don't want to hear it..."

"The comms didn't work, Kesh. The last time I spoke to you on the comms was when you went through Arcon's scanners without me. I lost the signal right after. I didn't see or hear from you again until the meeting with Larsen."

"But we..."

The nights I'd fallen asleep listening to his voice, needing to hear him, to know I wasn't alone.

I had been alone all along.

It had been an illusion.

Something inside me broke open, and a long, drawn-out wail left my lips. I crumpled to my knees and no longer cared about anything. Kellee had been my lifeline during those days and nights, my one hope, and it had all been a lie.

A hand touched my back. I shook it off. "DON'T TOUCH ME. DON'T FUCKING TOUCH ME." I scrambled to my feet. The two men watched me warily. Kellee was closest, but Talen stood behind him, ready, waiting—waiting for me to snap. "Don't. Please don't." I blinked at Kellee. I didn't even know him, did I? "We talked. For hours, we talked."

He swallowed. "It didn't happen."

"You said—you said you needed to know I was real. That's why you came to the meeting. I told you not to come and you came anyway."

"I came because of an assault report—"

"You were never at the party, were you?" I already knew the answer.

He looked alarmed and then just sad. "I don't know about any party."

Then, the last time we had really spoken, he had learned I was the Wraithmaker. The entertainer gladiator. The fae's pet killer. And to someone like Kellee, I was abhorrent. "You left me with him because I'm the Wraithmaker, didn't you?"

He shifted back a step and opened his mouth to speak, but nothing came out.

"Then why come at all?" I asked. "Why come to the

meeting?"

"Because I suspected he was fae and I knew, if he saw me, saw that I'm vakaru, he would reveal himself. I didn't expect him to be so... powerful."

I twitched, words breaking on my tongue. How could I know for sure what was real? "I think I want to go home now." My container was a mess, but I could go to The Boot. I'd have a drink and see Hulia. It was something, anything. I wanted to go back to that life, not this one I now found myself in.

Talen turned away and stalked back to his book.

Kellee watched him go, a muscle twitching in his cheek. When he next met my gaze, he sighed. "You can't. I had hoped to tell you when you'd had time to adjust..."

"Tell me what?" A thudding started in my head, burying Kellee's voice.

"The fae came." His voice cracked. "There's nothing left." He tried to say more, but words failed him. Turning back to his bag, he continued emptying it out. "We don't have homes to go to."

Eledan had opened the door. He had let his kind in.

"The people?" I whispered, thinking about The Boot, and Hulia, and the sinks. And all those people on Calicto. So many lives.

Kellee shook his head.

The darkness rushed in, and I heard the Dreamweaver's intoxicating laugh. This time, I laughed with him.

CHAPTER 21

*A*sting dragged my consciousness back from oblivion. For a long time, I didn't move from the couch the males had lowered me into and stared at the empty glass cage in the middle of the cavern.

Hours or days may have passed in silence, when I finally said, "Show me."

Kellee wordlessly escorted me toward the prison's dock. We passed through empty chambers, past abandoned guard posts and static scanners. When we boarded his little stolen shuttle and backed away from the prison, I watched through the screen as the dock grew smaller and disappeared into the cliff-like rock face.

"Anything larger than a four-seater and the fae ships will notice," I heard Kellee say. He may have said more, but my thoughts had gotten lost in the stretch of black before us.

"Their tactics have changed since my people fought them," he added.

I half listened and let the pleasant drone of his voice smooth my frayed nerves.

"I guess you already know their ships are organic?" he asked but clearly didn't expect an answer as he continued. "They've *evolved*."

I nodded. It was hardly surprising. If they could grow it, the fae could manipulate it. Kellee and I were both products of the fae's genetic engineering, and Faerie was full of weird and wonderful creations—all built to serve the fae.

He talked more about how the ships had avoided Halow's deep-space early warning systems. How much of it was Arcon's doing, nobody outside the fae knew for sure, but when the fae came, the people in Halow had been defenseless.

Kellee slowed the small vessel as we approached an area of sparkling debris. When he pulled the shuttle to a stop, I checked the location screens, but something didn't add up. Where was Juno? Flotsam drifted, glinting against the endless black of space. I pushed to my feet and leaned closer. What was I seeing? And then, the vast mass of the wreckage caught the light from a distant star. The devastation glowed, light flaring off countless shiny surfaces. Juno was gone. Nothing larger than our shuttle remained. The wreckage of the once beautiful station spun and turned, twisted and broken. Steel clawed at the dark. Glass shone like a dusting of stars.

That's not glass.

I gasped, pulled back, and covered my mouth.

"It's not your fault," Kellee said. Somehow, his voice penetrated the noisy denials.

Tears skipped down my cheeks.

I couldn't look but couldn't look away.

The dust was... *bodies*. Thousands. Scattered among the

wreckage, frozen and twisted. Adults. Children. So, so many.

If I had stopped Eledan, if I hadn't wavered, if I hadn't let his fae charm undermine everything I knew about them. I should have killed him the first chance I had. My stupid demands—to save Sota—were ridiculous. I *knew* what he was. I knew what he was capable of.

This was completely on me.

"How many?" I whispered.

"Does it matter?"

"Yes."

"On Point Juno, maybe..." He wet his lips. "Thirty thousand."

Thirty thousand lives.

Scattered among the stars.

"In Halow, I don't think anyone knows the death count for sure," he went on. "They laid waste to any human civilization nearest the debris zone, firing from planetary orbits. Their warships are..." He drifted off. "This would have happened anyway. He always had Arcon. He was always going to disable the defense net. They have been preparing for centuries. You couldn't have stopped it—"

I pressed my trembling hand to the screen, covering at least a hundred bodies in the distance. "Millions of lives?"

"Yes."

Genocide.

The fae would wipe humans out. We were theirs to do with as they pleased, and they had grown tired of our games. I looked at Kellee, the last of his kind, and saw the barely hidden distress behind his brave attempt to remain detached. He had seen all this before.

I gently lowered myself into the flight chair. "Where is he?"

Kellee engaged the shuttle's engines and turned us away from the wreckage. Juno would forever be a graveyard. "The fae were delighted to have their prince return. And with humanity gift wrapped too. I have no idea where he is. Probably in one of the warships at the front line."

Gift. *It was. For me.*

"Do you know if he went back to Faerie?" I asked, listening to the hollowness in my voice and wondering if I'd ever be full again.

"Reports are sketchy. Communications barely function. Some say he's back in Faerie, some say he hasn't been seen anywhere and might still be in Halow. I haven't seen him since you threatened to kill yourself to keep me alive."

"I was bluffing." The words startled me. I didn't remember thinking them, but there they were, out and real.

He tensed, hands pausing over the shuttle controls. "It was a good ruse."

You left me with him, Marshal. You left me with a monster.

I closed my eyes and shook my head. These thoughts weren't helping. I was alive, and I was here, thanks to Kellee. Alive was always better than dead. It wasn't over. I could still carve out Eledan's heart.

"How did you escape?" I asked, opening my eyes.

He flicked the autopilot on and turned his chair toward me. "He healed me and left me alone somewhere in Arcon's hundreds of rooms. I cut through the restraints and walked right on out. Nobody tried to stop me."

Probably because Eledan had been preoccupied, draining me of magic, and he hadn't had time to weave new instructions into his puppet-staff.

I glanced at Kellee's hands. There was no sign of the

claws he had used to cut himself free. He had left me there a second time. "But you came back?"

Kellee rubbed his jaw and ran the same hand down his neck. I hadn't seen it before, but now I caught a glimpse of a fresh scar there. Eledan had slashed his throat wide open. He shouldn't even be here. He should be dead like the millions of others. "After what I saw, after you... tricked him into saving my life..." He bowed his head and took a few moments before looking up. "I couldn't leave you there."

Again. Leave me there again. Leave me to the whims of a fae who fucked with my mind for nine whole months.

"You took Talen with you?" I asked, shaking the thoughts away. It didn't matter. None of this mattered. I knew what I had to do now.

Kellee leaned forward, resting his elbows on his knees. He rubbed his hands together. "I freed him in exchange for his help in getting you away from Arcon."

"Why is he still with you?"

Kellee looked me in the eye. "He knows who you are. Figured it out the second he saw you. I suspect he wants something from you. Besides, I doubt he has anywhere to go."

Talen didn't know me. He believed he did, just like Kellee believed. "He could go home, to Faerie?"

"The fae exiled him for rebelling. He won't—can't go back to Faerie."

"How convenient."

Kellee caught the derision in my words and glowered. "Centuries ago, I hunted him down in the debris zone. He was scavenging ancient tek and abandoned ships to stay alive. If he could go home, he would have long before then."

There was more to it, something he wasn't telling me, but we both had secrets and now was not the time to interrogate him. If he wanted to befriend his enemy, that was his mistake. "And you're not concerned that he might want revenge for the years you kept him imprisoned?"

"It's possible." Kellee leaned back and shifted in the chair, sinking down a few inches. He propped his boots on the flight controls and cast his gaze out of the shuttle screen. "Keeps things interesting." The marshal smiled. "He's not a fighter." He lifted his hand and turned it in the light. His nails sharpened to points and grew out into claws. "He knows I am."

I admired the five half-moon-shaped claws, feeling the bite of instinctual fear. The marshal was useful. Eledan had surprised him, like the fae had surprised me, but Kellee had experience fighting the fae. And he had a score to settle.

I needed Marshal Kellee.

"You can bind him," Kellee suggested, raising an eyebrow as though the thought had just occurred to him. He flicked his hand, banishing the claws. "He's already offered once."

Talen had. He had submitted to me the first time we had met but only to get himself out of the cage. "You heard that?"

"Not much gets by me." Kellee's eyes turned shrewd. "He offered to be yours. Agree and he can't hurt you. Ever."

"Maybe," I mused. Part of me liked the idea. Liked it enough to almost silence the concerns. But why would a fae willingly submit to a saru? They wouldn't. I'd already had my beliefs turned upside down. I wasn't sure I could ever trust Talen, even if he was bound to me.

"He's useful," Kellee added, echoing my thoughts. The marshal twisted, angling himself once again toward me. He leaned forward, bringing himself closer. "There are pockets of resistance out there. I've contacted a few. Right now, the human population is trying to stay alive, but when the dust settles, they'll fight back. They're humans. It's what they do. We can help."

"We?"

"Me, Talen, and you..."

Perhaps, once, I may have believed it. But I was a ghost, wasn't I? "What can I do?"

Kellee's stare darkened. "I can't imagine what he did to you. But I know what you were like before. We only met a few times, but you were something, Kesh. You had a spark. You know the fae and how their system works. You wanted to get your friend back and you wouldn't have stopped until you found him. You were brave enough to go up against Eledan, even knowing what he was."

In the end, my so-called bravery hadn't mattered. "You have Talen."

"He's fae. The people won't listen to him."

"*You* look human."

"Until they see me fight."

"What are you asking of me, Marshal?"

"I just... I've seen the fae ruin worlds. I can't sit back and watch it happen again. We can do something." Enthusiasm and hope brightened his green eyes. "Not yet, I know that. But... will you think on it?"

I looked into the marshal's hope-filled gaze and searched inside myself for the spark he'd mentioned, for any sign that I cared enough to help. But all I found was the yawning emptiness that threatened to pull me down and bury me.

"He took everything," I said. "He stole it all. My past, my mind, my purpose. The only thing I know for sure is that I don't save people, Kellee. I kill them."

The marshal turned his chair to face the screen and lifted his hand, propping his fingers against his temple, half hiding his face. The words hurt him, but whatever hope he had was wasted on me. He closed his eyes and kept them closed for a second or two too long. I had disappointed him, and I couldn't find it in myself to care.

CHAPTER 22

"Get up."

I blinked lazily up at the marshal. His grimace spoke volumes.

I had fallen into the dreams. It was easier there. Nothing made any sense in reality. And it hurt. Everywhere I looked it hurt. Dreams didn't hurt. Compared to the new world, dreams were old friends that didn't die, unlike real ones.

Kellee grabbed my wrist and hauled me off the couch. My knees hit the floor. Pain sparked. "Hey!"

"Kellee!" Talen's lashing reprimand startled Kellee and me. The marshal let go and whirled away, sinking his hands through his hair and holding them there. He left the chamber. The slam of the door shook my bones.

"What did I do?" I asked Talen.

He turned his attention to the book in his hand and turned a page. "It's what you didn't do."

When Kellee returned some time later, he wore a loose sweatshirt that was damp enough for the fabric to cling to his chest in places. He tossed a coiled leather whip to the floor. "Pick it up."

Who was he to order me? "Why?"

"Pick it up."

I glanced at Talen, but while the fae had stilled, he kept his eyes on the book. I wouldn't be getting help from him.

Planting my bare feet on the floor, I eyed the whip and then Kellee. "I don't want to."

Kellee came at me, aggression driving his strides. He snatched the whip off the floor and shoved it against my chest. When he let go, the whip fell into my lap.

"Come with me." He glared through me, daring me to defy him.

"I said, I don't want to."

He pressed his lips together, making them white. "You know what I don't want to be doing? Babysitting your lazy ass. Now get up!"

A low warning growl sounded, but it wasn't Kellee's. Talen's eyes blazed over the rim of his book.

"Shut it, fae," Kellee snapped.

"She's not ready." Talen set his book down and rose to his feet. I remembered Kellee's words about the fae not being a fighter, but he looked as though he might give it a try.

What was going on here?

Talen stepped forward and Kellee's entire body stilled. His green eyes hardened, and the man worked his jaw, likely making room for those sharp teeth. *Oh no.*

I picked up the whip. "I have it. Okay. I have the damn thing. Now what?"

"Good." Kellee turned, ignored Talen's watchful glare, and left the chamber, leaving the door open.

"You don't have to go," Talen said.

"What is he asking exactly?"

Talen swept a hand toward the door, inviting me to follow the marshal. I expected him to follow and spent so much time looking behind me for the fae that I didn't realize where I was heading until I stood in an open space. Padding cushioned the floors and walls. I wasn't even sure I wanted to know what this room had been used for. Kellee stood at its center. He beckoned me forward. I stopped a few steps from him, not daring to get any closer.

"Try to strike me with the whip." He jumped on the balls of his feet and curled his fingers, urging me on. "Come on, Messenger."

You're just the messenger.

I flinched.

"Look at me," he ordered. I did. His damp hair curled a little at its ends, licking at his cheek, jaw, and over his right eye. His lips were tight, revealing the tips of sharp teeth. "Hit me."

I dropped the tail end of the whip and tested the weight of the grip in my hand. I'd learned to use a whip with one just like it. I'd stolen it from Dagnu. He had dealt me exactly fifteen lashes when he discovered it in my cell. It had been worth it. With every lash, I knew I had won. Where had Kellee gotten this one? Did he know whips just like it were used on saru?

I flicked the tail, letting it lick across the dusty padded floor.

"Wraithmaker," Kellee growled. There was nothing nice on his face. None of the patience or compassion I'd seen in him. His beast lurked there now.

I flicked the whip, working its length upward, and snapped it back down with an audible crack. But Kellee had vanished from where he'd stood. I spun, feeling the room tip. This was too much. My footing stumbled, the room whirling.

Kellee's warm fingers encircled my wrist and pulled, tilting me upright. But he pushed at the last second, almost toppling me over my own feet. His hand found my lower back and steadied me. I twisted, trying to fix him in my sights so I could at least see him coming, but all I saw was a blur. Another shove and I fell forward with a cry. Then he was there. Right up close. His hand spread over my heart, and his eyes burned into mine.

The whip fell from my fingers.

It wasn't Kellee.

Eledan smiled.

A scream surged up my throat. It echoed in my ears and in my head.

"It's not real." Eledan's lips moved, but the voice was Kellee's. It didn't matter. I was already falling. "Fight, Kesh. Look at me. See me."

I shook my head, dropped to my knees, and curled into a ball.

"I told you." Talen's smooth voice held all the smug confidence of the fae. Hearing it broke my heart into a thousand pieces, creating countless jagged shards, and I felt the edge of every single one. I felt them burn, each one igniting a spark of fury.

My fingers closed around the whip.

"It will take years. We don't have that long."

Years? He knew everything, didn't he? Knew it all. Like they all did.

"Dammit, Talen, I don't need to hear—"

The whip felt right in my hand. It felt like a part of me, an extension of my will. I snapped it around me and cracked the tail inches from Talen's face. The fae hissed and hunched low, adopting a fighting stance. Kellee had said Talen didn't know how to fight. The fae knew how to react, at least.

I was on my knees, moving automatically, circling and thrashing the whip in a protective barrier. Talen ducked, but I hadn't been going for his head. The whip snarled around his wrist. I pulled him off balance and flicked the whip around his neck. I would snap that smooth neck of his—

His elbow jabbed me in the gut. Air whooshed out of me, doubling me over. I fell forward, into him. The fae twisted and threw me onto my back. I hit the floor and the frenzy ended. The whole attack couldn't have lasted more than two seconds.

The sound of my hurried breathing grew louder, as did the pounding of my heart. I turned my head a little and saw the two males. Kellee smiled. Talen rubbed at the raw marks around his neck and eyed me warily.

"It worked," Kellee said, triumphantly. He slapped Talen on the back hard enough for the fae to flinch. "She just needed to kick the shit out of you, not me."

CHAPTER 23

Every day, I fought them. And every day I saw less of Eledan. Muscle formed where it had wasted away. I jogged the prison circuit with Talen—who held back for my benefit—and did my best to wrap my whip around Kellee. At first, the pair were careful, afraid I might break. And in the beginning, I did. But as the weeks wore on, the laughter in my head faded.

My body healed faster than my mind, until I almost looked like Kesh Lasota again. On the inside, I was a mess. I continued to need Kellee's daily injections to stop me from falling back into a stupor, and at times, the dreams called to me, whispering in my ear in different voices the way Eledan had. But I had enough control to function. To think. To consider how I might get close to Eledan—close enough to carve him open.

To distract my thoughts, Kellee brought me disused tek from around the prison. Parts and pieces with which I crafted new comms. We tried them from one end of the prison to the other, through miles of rock. And this time, they worked.

Slowly, carefully, I became almost whole again.

"All right, today, I want to try something new," Kellee was saying as he walked away, bare feet padding across the mats. He raised his hands and pulled his hair back into a stubby ponytail. While he sauntered away, thinking I was still warming up, I figured it would take three long strides to reach him, and if I launched my attack from the right, I might have time to get the whip in before he could fully turn. He always turned to his right. I knew he was fast. Too damn fast to beat in a straight fight. I had to cheat.

He was still talking when I sprang off my back foot, swung the whip, and veered in from the right. He twisted, right shoulder first, exactly like I knew he would, giving me a few extra microseconds. The whip sailed overhead. Kellee saw and twisted into a crouch, but he kept on going, dropping into a roll I hadn't expected. The marshal was too low. I tried to adjust, to skip away, but he caught my ankle. I was going down, but I could salvage it. Dropping my shoulder, I fell into the unfolding disaster, corrected the flailing whip, and lashed out. I hit the mats on my back with an *oomph*.

The whip cracked. Kellee hissed.

His knee came down, pinning my wrist and whip to the floor.

"Good," he admitted. Blood welled from the cut marking his cheek.

I arched an eyebrow. Did he think the Wraithmaker would give up so easily? Sinking my hand into the pocket of my jogging pants, I pulled out three tiny silver balls and tossed them into the air. I'd used similar tricks in the arena, horrifying my fae audience by bringing forbidden tek into the game.

He frowned and watched the balls hang suspended a

few inches from his face. When he looked down questioningly, I winked and turned my face away. The balls exploded, filling the chamber with brilliant light. Kellee recoiled, spluttering a curse. I rolled away, hopped upright, leisurely wrapped my whip around his neck, and gently tightened it so there was no misunderstanding about who was in charge.

He blinked rapidly, shook his head and grumbled, "This had better not be permanent."

I crouched and watched him blink me into focus. This close, the all-green in his eyes wasn't green at all. The outer edge of his irises was blue, fading to green and then to the black of his pinprick pupils. "Submit."

He chuckled. "Not happening."

I hadn't beaten him. I'd barely ruffled his feathers. His teeth weren't out, neither were his claws. If he brought all his weapons, he could cut the whip with one swipe. This scuffle that had left me breathless was little more than a fun tumble for him. What would it truly be like to face the real Marshal Kellee? I barely knew what he was capable of, but I knew enough to guess how his people must have been a magnificent force in battle.

I thumbed the blood from his cheek. He froze. His eyes still weren't fully focused, but he saw enough to catch my hand, preventing me from licking my thumb clean.

"Don't."

I stalled.

His pupils widened, focusing, drinking me in, and then he closed his hand around mine and brought my thumb to his mouth. He wasn't about to—

His tongue swept up the side of my thumb.

I watched, entranced by the strangeness of having a man's tongue lick across my skin. He moved my thumb closer and closed his lips around it, gently sucking it clean. He probably heard my heart and definitely heard my rapid breathing. But he couldn't know how his intimate touch sent need fluttering inside me. The moment narrowed to just him and me kneeling on the mats, my thumb in his mouth and where we might go from here.

Kellee eased my thumb free, grazing it across the edge of a sharp canine-tooth, and turned my hand palm up. His hazel-flecked green eyes flicked up, checking for permission, and then he brought my middle finger to his lips and rested the most delicate kiss on the tip. I hadn't known he could do *delicate* until that moment. He tipped my hand down, settling a snowflake kiss on my palm, and then brought my arm up a little and hesitated, his mouth hot where it hovered over the thin skin of my wrist.

His own breathing came short and fast. Each flutter against my arm summoned telltale goosebumps. He slowly, gently rested a single kiss atop the beating vein and sighed as though that one small kiss had cost him too much.

He lifted his head, and his eyes appeared to shine with longing, his smile tantalizing. Oh, he knew exactly what he was doing to me.

I wanted to curl my hand around his neck and draw him to me to taste that teasing, smart mouth of his. From the heated look in his eyes, he wanted me to. But I wouldn't stop there. I would sink my hands into his hair and pull him close like I had in my dreams before the Dreamweaver stole him from me. Every. Time. But this would be real. He was on his knees, and in this one moment, he was *mine*. Maybe this was a dream? It felt like a dream, like we were the only two people left in all the worlds.

I ran my fingertips across his bottom lip, marveling at

the maddening softness. He breathed too hard, moments away from taking what he wanted. Our tussle hadn't taxed him, but holding himself back did. He liked it though, liked that this anticipation hurt, liked that I had control.

Kellee was gentle now, but his barely restrained tension told me he wouldn't be once I gave him permission. This promise of more stretched thin, almost to the breaking point. And I would gladly take him, take all of him. But a wrongness chimed inside my mind and the ache of loss grew in the place of desire. I couldn't do this.

I lowered my hand and turned my face away. I cared too much to hurt him.

Kellee pulled away and climbed to his feet. "The fae took the essence of *cadaloup* leaves and inserted its strands into our DNA." His voice sounded colder and clipped. "Making vakaru blood poisonous. A drop can paralyze. Any more ravages the nervous systems, killing in three minutes."

The moment we had shared slipped away like a dream on waking. "Does it work on the fae?"

"It disorientates them."

I got to my feet and straightened my clothes, focusing on those simple movements instead of watching Kellee shut down behind facts and warfare.

"A messenger is here," Talen said.

I reached for my whip and whirled. Talen stood a few steps inside the room, his violet eyes flicking to the whip, reading the warning. He could have been here the entire time and I hadn't heard a thing. My pulse raced. *Stealth and stamina.* I couldn't afford to forget what he was.

"From?" Kellee asked, ignoring me as he passed by and headed toward the exit beside Talen.

I followed, whip in hand.

"Calicto." Talen eyed me as I passed him, his expression unreadable. Had he seen the moment with Kellee? If he had, did he care? I didn't understand this fae, or why he was still here, and I certainly didn't trust him.

"There are people left on Calicto?" I asked Kellee.

"A few," the marshal replied, striding ahead.

A new shuttle had docked next to Kellee's rover, this one just as small, but it looked as though it had been strung together with little more than glue and tape. A young woman waited inside the airlock. A shock of red hair cut shorter at one side framed a pale, round face dashed with freckles. She spotted the three of us through the airlock window, her gaze lingering on Kellee.

"It's Natalie. Let her in," Kellee said.

Talen obliged, opening the airlock.

Air hissed as the door retracted, and out stepped Natalie. "Marshal," she acknowledged.

"Natalie." He held out his hand.

Natalie's blue eyes read me and Talen in an instant. Whatever she thought of us, she kept it all hidden behind an icy stoic mask. She shook Kellee's hand, adding a familiar squeeze before letting go. "Is there somewhere we can go and speak in private?"

Kellee nodded. "Sure." To Talen and me, he said, "I'll meet you by the cage."

Talen struggled to repress his snarl at the marshal's dismissal. He wasn't the only one. I watched Kellee escort Natalie along the dock and into the prison. Before disappearing inside, he touched her shoulder and leaned in, speaking too quietly for me to hear.

"What did he say?" I asked Talen once the door had closed behind the pair.

"That he has missed her."

A stab of jealousy struck low, but I quickly dismissed it. He wasn't alone. And that was good. He would need a friend for what was to come.

I left Talen behind and changed out of my sweats and into clean pants and a turtleneck top, making sure to cover all incriminating fae marks. Just because Kellee knew her, it didn't mean she wouldn't lose her mind over seeing warfae marks on a stranger.

Leaving the chamber, I considered how this prison had been my sanctuary. As cold and hard a place as it was, I had come to consider it safe. It was Kellee's and Talen's refuge and mine. I'd gotten used to it being me, the marshal and the fae. Natalie's presence jeopardized that. She brought reality in from the outside worlds, and I wasn't sure if I was ready.

Talen was already in the kitchen area, cooking. He liked to dabble in the kitchen and had cooked up some excellent feasts with the dull prison supplies available. He had changed out of his instantly recognizable fae leathers and into more human dark trousers and a dark purple dress shirt. He made no attempt to hide the pointed tips of his ears and had braided some of his silvery hair at both sides, deliberately displaying his faeness. The rest of his hair fell loose down his back, all the way to his ass. A toned ass that the black pants neatly shaped. I caught my gaze lingering and veered away, wandering the chamber instead. Kellee's intimate kisses had fired up my blood, reminding me what it felt like to be *touched* by a male. To be *longed* for. But all those needs and wants were tangled up with Eledan's mindfuck and my own human weaknesses.

I came to Talen's cot and stopped at his stack of books. "You may take a look if you wish."

He didn't look up from his sizzling pans, but his fae senses knew exactly where I stood in the room.

Up close, I could see the books were all old human titles. I had assumed he was reading fae books.

"How did you get these?" I picked up the book he had been favoring lately and opened it where he had left his bookmark.

"Kellee brought them."

Kellee had brought him books in prison? My first impulse was to ask why, but I managed to keep the question to myself. Kellee had likely pitied the fae. I already knew the marshal had visited Talen often. Gifts just showed that Kellee had a heart, even when it came to his enemy.

I flipped the book over. The cover was dark and faded, but I could make out the title. I wasn't familiar with the language, but I took a guess at sounding it out. "Drak-uule?"

"Kellee thought it... amusing."

"Why?" There it was. I couldn't help it. Kellee and Talen's relationship didn't fit with what I knew about them. They should be at each other's throats, not living together in relative harmony.

"You'll have to ask Kellee."

"Ask Kellee, right." He always deferred to the marshal. I set the book back down and scanned the spines. I had never read a physical book before.

"Would you like to read one?"

I glanced across the room, expecting him to be watching, but he concentrated on cooking and retrieved some plates from a cupboard. Talen wasn't like any fae I had met before. The families had slaves—saru—to run their houses. How did he know how to cook? He could fight, I'd seen evidence of that when he had defended himself, but he preferred to run and read and watch.

"They're written in an archaic language," he said. "I can teach you to read it if you like."

I picked up a small paperback, its cover torn and text faded. The picture on the front depicted an Earthen bird with black wings. Carrying it to Talen, I showed him the title. He nodded. "I think you'll enjoy that one." And went back to his bubbling sauces.

"Thank you." And I meant it. The old relics were precious, yet he trusted me with one. I was curious enough to spend time with the fae to decipher the words.

"Let's eat," Kellee said as he and Natalie entered. "We don't have water, but we have a concoction of syrup and barley Talen mixed together from the stores." Kellee brought with him his smiles and jovial persona.

"This is some place you have here," Natalie remarked, her gaze falling to the massive glass cage. "Shit, all this prison for one prisoner? Who did they keep in there?"

Talen set her plate down in front of her, rattling it against the tabletop. He caught my eye, and we shared a moment. I wasn't sure what kind of moment, but a mutual something. Distrust, maybe. He didn't like her. I had to agree.

"This isn't poisoned, is it, fae?" she asked, making it sound lighthearted, but there was a sharpened jab in there too.

Talen wasn't laughing. "If I wanted to kill you, human, I wouldn't waste good poison when I could merely break your neck"—he flicked his fingers—"like that."

Natalie paled.

"Talen," Kellee growled.

Inappropriate laughter almost burst free. I cleared my

throat and caught Talen's eye. The fae's mouth ticked up at one corner, only known to me.

"Ignore him," Kellee suggested. "He doesn't get out much."

"Uh-huh." Natalie tasted her meal, side-eyeing Talen. "Damn, fae, this is good food. We don't have much in the mines, and what we do have tastes like salt. Everything tastes like salt down in the shafts. Even the air."

"How long can you hold out?" Kellee asked. He sat close beside her and tucked into his dish.

Talen and I chose to stand at the counter and eat. I had one eye on our guest and one on Talen, who trusted her about as much as I did.

"A few months with our existing supplies. Scavenging has gotten harder now that we've exhausted the first dome. But it could be worse, right? At least the fae haven't noticed us."

"And your air?" Kellee asked.

"The mines were always closed-circuits. The filters will work as long as the geothermal pumps are running." She fell silent while eating, and then added, eyes brightening, "There's one thing we have that'll make you jealous."

"Go on." Kellee smiled and it reached his eyes. He knew this woman well. There were none of the guarded sideways glances he gave me.

"We have so much water we have to drain it out of the shafts or drown in it." She laughed. "The fucking irony, right? We're millionaires and now nobody gives a shit because there's nobody left to care." Her laughter twisted into a harder, bitter sound and slowly died. Echoes of it around the chamber soon followed.

I poked at my food with my fork, no longer hungry.

The silence grew, each of them lost in their own

thoughts. I hadn't been there when it happened, when the fae came. I hadn't seen the first wave or heard the screams or fled for my life. I had been dreaming the whole time, trapped in another world entirely.

Talen had set his plate down, virtually untouched. He was watching me, I realized. As Kellee and Natalie chatted, I tried on a small smile to reassure the fae I wasn't about to let the dreams pull me under. But nothing about any of this was reassuring. He studied my face while his expression revealed all the sadness I'd seen in him when he had begged me to free him. He had known about the Dreamweaver, known how badly Eledan ravaged his victims. And in his keen eyes and the press of his lips, he *understood* it all.

"What was your message?" I asked Natalie, deliberately breaking away from Talen's gaze.

She slowly finished her mouthful and glanced at Kellee, I assumed for permission to tell me. But he was finishing his food and didn't see. Instead of answering, she pushed the last bites of food around her plate. "You seem familiar, but I can't place from where, and Kellee here... Well, he says you're just a survivor like the rest of us, but..." Breathing in, she pushed her plate away and brushed her hands together, wiping them clean. "Your pet fae is a quiet one."

Talen could look after himself, but that didn't stop the shards of my heart from twisting at the sound of her derisive tone.

"Natalie—"

"No," she cut Kellee off, fury shortening her words. "Our world is slowly dying and you're here, what? Playing house?"

"You know I've been trying to rally the cells." Kellee pushed his plate away. "Communication isn't easy—"

"It's not fucking good enough, Marshal. I had to come out here myself to see what you're doing. Turns out, fuck all. You said you were working on something. So, where is it? Huh?" Her accusations bounced around the chamber.

Kellee's gaze caught mine and nerves rattled through me. Wait. I remembered him asking me to help, telling me to think on it. Was *I* his something?

Natalie stood and moved to the outside of the cage. "And the worst of it is, I have to go back and tell them you don't have anything. That their marshal—the man they've pinned their hopes on—lied."

"I didn't lie." He spoke too softly, his tone already defeated. "It's not ready."

"There are kids in the mines. Kids whose parents acted fast enough and knew the mines were the only place that could survive a fae warship assault. When the domes shattered, we heard it. All of Calicto trembled like the whole planet was breaking apart, and the glass screamed." She pressed her hand to the glass cage and added softly, "Or the people did."

Did Kellee have a plan? Surely, the woman couldn't be pinning her hopes and the hopes of her people on me?

"When we found the well, I thought..." Her hand closed into a fist. "You said it would change everything."

What well? I tried to catch Kellee's eye, but he had bowed his head. Why hadn't he told me any of this?

"We're all going to die down there," Natalie whispered.

"You won't." The words were mine. Alarmingly. But they felt right, as though I really could do something to back them up.

"Right." She laughed and turned. "You and your pet fae

will do what exactly? We can't get anything larger than a shuttle off Calicto without the fae noticing, and even that's a risk. There are almost a thousand people hiding in the mines. Are you going to save them?"

"Yes."

"With what? Your whip?" She flicked a hand at the whip coiled at my hip and then pulled her hand back. Confusion clouded her face. "Wait... I know you." Her eyes widened. "You killed him!"

Killed who? "You're going to have to narrow it down."

That was the wrong thing to say. Natalie lunged at me. Kellee shouted a warning to her or me, I wasn't sure which. A silvery blur of hair appeared between the girl and me, and everything stopped. Talen had gently rested his hand on her face, as though the pair might be about to kiss. But Natalie stood limp and dazed, pupils so large her eyes looked black.

"Talen!" Kellee thundered in. "Let her go."

Talen didn't move. I stepped out, moving around so I could see his face. His eyes, like Natalie's, were filled with blackness. The soft, careful, wary Talen who had lent me a book to read was long gone. In his place stood the killer species I knew so well. There was the fae who would have the three systems bow down to him and his kind. There was the fae who would make humans dance for him until they died on their feet. I had known he was in there some-where, but seeing the truth filled my broken heart with fear.

"Talen..." He looked at me, through me, just like they all did—as though I were nothing, just dirt to be scraped off his boot.

"*Talen,*" the marshal warned. "TAKE YOUR HAND OFF HER."

Talen's transformation had me gripped, but I suspected Kellee's claws and teeth were out and ready. I reached out slowly, carefully, but didn't touch Talen. Whatever he was doing to Natalie, he would likely do to me too. "Talen, tell me about your favorite book?"

He blinked, and the blackness subsided. Violet blazed through. He looked at Natalie swaying on her feet and plucked his hand free. The messenger gasped and stumbled back into Kellee's arms. She looked around her, panicked, until she set her eyes on Kellee. "What the...?"

Talen turned away, barely registering that anything out of the ordinary had happened. What *had* happened?

Kellee wrapped his arms around the trembling, dazed Natalie and took her out of the chamber, leaving me alone with Talen. Fluttering fear tried to pull me away. I knew he was dangerous. They were all dangerous. But somewhere in all the times we had jogged the prison circuit together, in the moments I'd caught him watching me and when I'd watched him, I'd allowed myself to believe he was different.

Talen came back with a book in his hand. He held it out. "This is my favorite," he said, oblivious to the pain he had caused Natalie.

I looked down, forgetting for a moment what I'd asked him. Right. His favorite book. It had worked, bringing him out of his trance, but now that I had seen something of the monster inside, I wasn't sure I could ever look at him again without seeing *fae*.

"She had been about to attack you," he explained.

I swallowed and looked up into his normal eyes and saw something like hope in them.

I took a step away and the hope faded.

He was fae, and this prison was his for a reason. "What did you do to her?"

"She intended to hurt you."

"What did you do, Talen?"

He clutched the book against his chest and locked his sights on my scowl. "I was protecting you."

I backed up another step, and he noticed but didn't move. I could never trust him or believe his words. Kellee had once told me that words were all the weapons Talen had left. That was before the marshal had freed him. Now he had plenty of weapons at his disposal.

"What did you do?" I asked again.

"I tempered her emotions."

He had made her feel something else. Dread undermined everything I had built up. Right now, he could be manipulating me. I was human, saru, and he could twist me around his little finger without me knowing.

"When we first met, here... in this room." My voice trembled. I swallowed and hoped when I next spoke, I sounded stronger, because what I was about to do would have consequences for us both. "You said if I let you out, you would serve me. *Do this one thing and I will be yours.*"

"Those words are mine. Yes." A muscle in his jaw ticked.

"Talen, I can't ever trust you. Do you understand?" He stared back, immovable, emotionless. "What you did to that woman, I'm guessing you've hurt people like her many times... You're fae. It's in your nature to twist lesser beings to your whims." Of course he had. He was hundreds of years old. The Talen standing in front of me was a product of Faerie, and in Faerie, everything was seductive and beautiful so that you bled your life away while begging for more.

"Yes," he hissed. "It is my nature, and I have hurt many." He narrowed his eyes and looked at me side-on. There was the threat again. It had always been there, buried under his quiet pauses and watchful glances. Talen was more dangerous than Kellee. He was the snake in the grass, the killer you never saw coming.

"You can't help what you are." I steeled myself for what was to come. "But I can help you. Do you know what I'm asking?"

He nodded once and dropped to one knee. He didn't have to do this. I wasn't forcing him. He could leave, take one of the shuttles and go. He was a creature made to manipulate, made to rule all other species, but now he offered himself to me. He *wanted* this because he knew there was no other way forward for us.

He closed his right hand into a fist and pressed it over his heart, just as I had done with Eledan. The saru had been ruled by the fae for thousands of years, but now a fae knelt to a saru. It shouldn't happen, not in this multiverse, but it *was* happening.

"Do you submit?" I asked.

"I do." He bowed his head. "I am yours. I will always be yours."

Magic flooded the room, rich with the scents of jasmine and honeysuckle, old scents from an ancient world. His words held a power I hadn't expected, but I felt them, felt their touch wrap around me, lick across my human skin and sink inside. Pleasure spilled through me, arching my back and briefly silencing all thought, all fear. It rolled on and on, sinking to my human core and knotting tight.

I staggered, reeling from the embrace. The threads of the binding tightened, combining with my humanity. Heat

256

strummed through me, heat and power and desire, until in one sudden compounded moment, it snapped. The chamber came back into startling focus. Tingles danced across my skin and tiny sparks traced my tattoos, leaving needle-like shivers behind.

I blinked, breathless. Somehow, I'd stayed on my feet, which seemed like an enormous triumph. Kneeling, Talen looked up, almost composed. Almost. The hand pressed over his heart trembled, and his breaths came in short and sharp between parted lips. If he had felt half of what I'd just gone through, then he did well to stay as composed as he was. What we had shared, I'd never felt anything like it before. No saru had.

I nodded, afraid my voice would betray how racked I was.

He bowed his head, collected himself, stood, and returned to his cot where he woodenly lay down, closed his eyes and sighed.

Now I could trust that Talen would never hurt me.

CHAPTER 24

Talen and Kellee argued about returning to Calicto. Kellee refused to take him, probably because Natalie now watched the fae as though waiting for the first chance to attack. And I wasn't allowed to go because I *wasn't ready*. It was *too risky*. There was no point in all of us getting caught in one shuttle should the fae come looking. That last one, I reluctantly admitted, was a good point.

So Kellee left with Natalie and my improved comms in his pocket, promising to return in a few days.

"I know you killed Crater," Natalie said under her breath, passing me on her way to the shuttles.

I smiled at the absurdity of her claim. It was so long ago and a lie. She had me all wrong. I hadn't killed one activist miner. I was the Wraithmaker. I had hunted my fellow saru for sport and then helped annihilate a civilization. When she glanced back, I flashed her a smile worthy of a mass murderer.

"You're making it worse," Talen remarked under his breath. He stood beside me, calm and collected.

"I don't think it can get much worse. Do you?"

The prison felt colder without Kellee. During the next few days, I jogged alone, avoiding Talen the same way he avoided me. On one of my circuits, I found a storage room and poked around inside, digging out spare tek parts.

Talen observed me collecting the equipment on the floor in the main chamber without comment, until his curiosity got the better of him and he crouched beside me on the floor. In front of us was a spread of what looked like scrap metal, but to me, it was a hundred possibilities.

Talen watched me work, and rather than find his focus on me uncomfortable, I welcomed it. Knowing he couldn't hurt me allowed me to relax in his company, something I had never been able to do among the fae, not even in the palace when the queen had favored me.

"What's that one?" Talen asked, pointing to a compact silver box.

"A sub-band communications device." I picked up the box and turned it over. "It'll send out a low-range frequency the fae won't think to look for." Picking up a second box, I weighed them both in either hand. "It will talk to its partner, over several hundred thousand miles. Kellee mentioned his communications problems, so..." I shrugged. "I fixed it. I just need two good power sources for them to work."

"And that?" Talen pointed to a string of metal links, all hooked in a line.

"That"—I tugged on one end and the links magneti-cally followed one another, slithering across the floor like a metal snake—"will be a new whip. I can't charge it with fae magic, but it will still make an effective weapon."

His fae eyes brightened as he ran his gaze along the whip. "How did you come to wield it so well?"

"Necessity."

He looked up and likely imagined all the things a saru had to do to survive. His ideas probably only came half as close to the reality.

"They—the chief saru trainers—weed out the weak ones early on. They employ many methods, but the first is leaving newly harvested saru inside the delivery crate." I searched his eyes, wondering if he had seen the vast crates the children were harvested into. I doubted it. But like always, his expression remained neutral, although the glisten in his gaze betrayed a little of the emotion he otherwise hid well from view. "They told us only ten would be spared. Twenty-one of us were harvested from our village. Ten left the crate. I strangled one with his belt and kicked another in the face until she stopped moving."

Talen looked away, thinking I wouldn't see him flinch. "How do you not despise me for what I am?"

Everything would be so much easier if I did. "Saru don't despise the fae. We can't afford to. Our villages, our homes, our food, it all belongs to Faerie. We understand that. We don't hate you, we love you. Without the fae, there are no saru." I ran my hand along the whip's metal links. The words had been bred into me, into saru life. A large part of me believed them and always would, but I had also harbored a forbidden seed of doubt. I still did, buried under all the lies. A seed Aeon had planted, before I'd killed him.

"I can help you charge the whip," Talen said, suddenly enthused. "Not directly, the tek will repel me, but through you." He looked up, lips pressed into a determined line. "Through our bond."

"You would share your magic with a saru?"

261

"Yes. It costs me nothing and…" Whatever he had been about to add, he stopped himself. "It can help you."

A flutter of excitement brought a smile to my lips. Ever since Eledan had taken his mother's magic, I'd felt as though a piece of me had been stripped away. The thought of having that back, or at least something like it… "Will it hurt you? I don't want—"

"No." His lips curved. "I can show you if you like." He lifted his hand. Liquid golden swirls spiraled around his fingers. The humanity in me immediately reacted, spilling *want* and *need* through my veins. The desire wasn't something I could stop, but its sudden appearance reminded me how Talen wasn't without his weapons.

I pulled back and shut down. "No, I don't think so."

He frowned, puzzled. "I won't hurt you."

"I know." I touched my hand to my chest and felt the fearful flutter against my ribs. "He… He took Mab's magic from me. From inside…" I remembered the terrible pulling and how every second had dragged like hours as he'd drained me. "I don't want to have it only for it to be taken away again."

"I assumed as much." Talen lowered his hand and considered my words during one of his thoughtful silences. His gaze roamed over the tek scattered around us. "What you do, it's a talent, Kesh. You should be proud."

"Proud?" I did what I did to survive. Why would I be proud of necessity? I wasn't proud of killing my fellow saru and I wasn't proud of what I had become or what necessity had made me. No, that was a lie… I had survived. I was proud of that.

"I have lived a very long time and all of this…" He gestured at my tek experiments. "I don't understand human tek. I resist it, endure its endless gnawing on my senses, but that is all. But you shape it and control it. You create where nothing was there before. Tek is your magic. It's... fascinating. You're fascinating." He said it matter-of-factly but his words burrowed in, breaking open some long-neglected part of me that craved the praise of my fae masters.

I wasn't sure what to say, or even if I could reply. Only one fae had praised me before, and to hear such words from Talen? It felt... peculiar. Like I couldn't possibly deserve it or that I'd stolen the praise from someone worthier. Saru weren't meant to be praised.

You are a nothing girl. A ghost.

His voice whispered poison into my ear.

I turned my face away, clinging to the pride Talen had given me, even as it slipped through my fingers. *Just the messenger. You are what we made you.*

I was falling, the dreams clamoring for me. "Talen?"

I reached for the table or something, anything real. But I couldn't see. I was slipping, chasing the dreams, reality folding in around me. A wood-paneled room. The oak throne was empty because Eledan stood behind me, his fluttering breaths on my neck, his words poisoning my confidence.

Couldn't listen. Couldn't let the dreams capture me.

A sharp pain stung my arm. I looked down, distracted, and when I looked up, I was back in the prison chamber, right where I had been all along, sitting on the floor, surrounded by tek, and Talen was there, setting down the empty syringe.

I hadn't won my battle with the dreams.

Not yet.

I was clinging to the edge, so close to letting go, and I

always would be until I killed Eledan. And I would kill the prince. I had to. It was the only way I'd survive.

Heat raced through my veins, the dangerous kind. I coiled the metal whip in my lap and looked up. "Do it," I told the fae.

He didn't hesitate, didn't give me time to change my mind. His hand settled on my chest, and the smell of jasmine and something I had originally assumed was honeysuckle, but now I knew that to be wrong. The scent was from a night-flowering lily, the kind found only on Faerie and rare enough that it bloomed only once in a saru lifetime. Its sweetness was fleeting, just a flash and then gone. Talen's magic swelled inside, filling me out where Eledan's theft had left me empty. In my hand, the whip glowed a faint golden light. Strength poured into my body. The kind of strength a saru should never know. Mab had given me her gift for her son, but this was for me. All mine.

It was glorious.

And then the power died off, leaving me shivering. Talen withdrew his hand.

I caught his wrist, barely aware of how I was gripping him. "Why did you stop?"

"Too much too soon could damage you."

I pulled his hand back and pressed it against my chest. "Damage away. I'm ready."

"Kesh." He tried to pull away. I arched an eyebrow. There was trying, and then there was his half-hearted tug.

"I'm serious," I said. "I haven't felt this good in forever. Hit me with it again." He hesitated, stalling for excuses. I leaned in. "You want to. Don't tell me you don't. It feels good for you too, right?"

His flash of a smile was a devilish thing. He spread his

fingers, pushing against my breasts. I wanted his mouth on me and could see it clearly, see him peering up the length of my naked body. The second that image struck, the flood of battling fear and desire almost derailed me, until his magic bloomed again, and I drank it in. The whip crackled to life, buzzing brightly with the same thrilling energy that zipped down my spine and pulled a gasp from my lips. It was everything the human body ached for, everything Faerie offered us, all our dreams and desires in one.

Talen yanked his hand away.

I swayed and reached for it again, but the fae stood up and stalked off, shoulders hard and strides clipped. "No more," was all he said.

Breathless, I shuddered, careful not to groan out the little ripples of pleasure still sailing through me. Hot damn, I wanted more of that. But I had apparently over-stepped some kind of boundary. I wasn't used to magic-sharing. Such intimacy was forbidden to saru. And when the queen had given me the gift, it hadn't been like *that*.

Heat warmed my face, and a familiar shame weighed on my back. I'd taken something I didn't deserve. Something illicit. I wasn't allowed to touch the fae. They were out of bounds, above me.

I shouldn't have forced Talen.

The golden glow around the whip flickered and died out.

Perhaps the whole magic-bond-sharing thing hadn't been such a great idea.

An alarm sounded, and Talen altered his course toward the exit. "The shuttle has returned."

I jogged to the dock alongside Talen. He kept his gaze ahead until the last doorway, where his stride wavered and he allowed a small smile to touch his lips. It was enough to know he'd forgiven me. I followed him into the dock area, wondering when his opinion of me had started meaning something.

Kellee's shuttled docked, and the airlock hissed open, revealing its occupant. Not Kellee.

Machine dust covered Natalie's freckles. Tear tracks had cleaned lines through the dirt. She bit into her cracked bottom lip. "There was an accident."

CHAPTER 25

A fae warcruiser drifted above Calicto's atmosphere. The sleek claw-shaped vessel blotted out the light from Halow's sun, casting its shadow over the small planet. Our shuttle was a speck of machine dust in comparison.

"It can't see us?" I asked.

Natalie shook her head. "We're too small for it to bother with us. But they shot two passenger cruisers out of orbit when we tried to evacuate." Her lips pressed into a grim line.

Below us, as Natalie piloted the shuttle in low over Calicto's surface, the biodomes glittered like upside-down crystal bowls. Two were cracked wide open, the sectors inside exposed to Calicto's poisonous atmosphere. One remained intact, and at its center, the Arcon pyramid stood defiant. I fought back the memories and dreams trying to muscle in on my consciousness.

Natalie flew through uninhabited valleys and across the shattered skyline. There were no signs of life.

The mines sprawled several miles from the domes. Self-contained with their workings all underground, the small, single-story patchwork of buildings could easily be missed from orbit, and fae scanners may not be able to penetrate the substrate to scan deeper for life signs. Or they simply didn't care about the few remaining survivors.

As we circled in, it was clear something had taken a chunk out of the miners' complex, opening some of the tunnels and shafts to Calicto's atmosphere.

Natalie docked the shuttle and opened the shuttle doors.

"I'll be back soon," I told Talen. We had agreed he wasn't to leave the shuttle. His reception among the remaining human population wouldn't likely be a good one.

He flicked his hood up, hiding his distinctive ears and hair, and nodded grimly. "Three hours." His tone made it clear this wasn't negotiable.

"They're in the Nymn sector," Natalie said, opening the second airlock and stepping inside.

She hadn't said much on the trip back to Calicto— clearly uncomfortable around Talen—but she had explained that a section of the mines had imploded. Pressurized fail-safes had locked down, sealing anyone alive on the other side. Kellee had last been seen in Nymn.

What she believed I could do, I wasn't sure, but I hadn't thought much beyond getting here and rescuing Kellee. I still had the comms, and I pressed the small circular unit into place behind my ear.

We passed down narrow mine shafts, boots splashing in puddles, and through chambers like the ones in the prison, only much smaller. A few people passed us, some wearing masks, others coated in dust.

"You're the messenger, right?" Natalie asked.

"I was one," I replied.

"No, *the* messenger. The one who that fae nut sack framed for Crater's murder?"

Kellee must have told her the truth. What else had he told her? How I'd been out of my mind and lost to the dreams while her people fought for survival? "I was her."

She screwed up her nose. "Was it you or not? Because he said you're something special and we need special right now."

"It was me—it is me," I corrected. "I'll do what I can." *Special?* Dammit, Kellee. He should never have built me up. What in the fresh Faerie hells had he been thinking?

"Guess the bounty means shit now, huh?" Natalie mused, gripping a guardrail and splashing ahead.

I'd forgotten about the fortune on my head. "Well, since the *fae nut sack* was the one paying the bounty, the only reward would probably have been a quick trip to a hole in the ground." If lucky.

We marched on, weaving between rubble and around cracks in the floor.

"You know why he had Crater killed, right?" Natalie asked, tossing the question over her shoulder.

"No idea." Eledan had never told me.

"Crater and his team were drilling into uncharted ground—because they're idiots and never knew when to keep their heads down and do as they're told." Her voice echoed ahead, joining the mumbling of other voices. "He had some grand idea to lead a rebellion. They were looking for water to fund his crusade."

"What did they find?"

"The well." Natalie's eyes crinkled above her mask. "The mother lode of magic—off the fucking charts—with Arcon's foundations drilled right into it. Crater reported it. Next day, him, his drilling team, and the marshal he reported to were dead."

A reservoir of magic below Arcon? *The* magic Eledan had been harvesting? The magic he had used to heal Kellee? This was significant. Eledan wouldn't abandon a find like that. Was that why the warcruiser was sitting in orbit? "Is it still there, untapped?"

She snorted. "You don't think Arcon surviving in the middle of all this devastation was luck, do you? The Arcon buildings are all intact—no people, we checked. I guess the magic it's sitting on is too."

A source of natural fae magic outside of Faerie? I eyed the jagged cracks in the tunnel walls with concern. The magic was nearby, and the fae lingered in orbit... This didn't feel right. "Who else knows about this?"

"Only a few of us. But Kellee said you would want to know."

"He was right."

A line of men and women cleared debris from the tunnel ahead. Their murmurs grew louder as we drew nearer.

I couldn't shake the image of the hulking warcruiser sitting in orbit. Waiting. For what? "Natalie, are you sure this was an accident?"

"Well, there ain't no fae down here, and we've got early warning systems in place. No landing craft or missiles came from the cruiser if that's what you're getting at. Maybe it was an accident, maybe not, but right now we're more concerned with getting people out. Here." We stopped where a central junction stretched in five directions. Two of the tunnels were blocked. "This is as far as we can get. Kellee said you were good with tek." She waved at a blocked tunnel. "So... do your thing."

People stopped digging. Grim, dust-coated faces watched me. Some looked hopeful, others barely looked as though they were mentally in the same place as the rest of us.

I tapped the comms to activate it. "Kellee?" The signal hissed in my ear. "Kellee, can you hear me?" Nothing. I shook my head. "I need to get closer to the section behind the rubble. Is there another chamber nearby? It doesn't have to be connected."

"The rec room," a young woman said, maybe half my age. "When it's quiet, you can hear the drilling through the walls."

Natalie led me along more tortuous tunnels, passing more pale faces and blank stares. These people... they couldn't survive long down here. Their quiet desperation worked niggling concerns into the back of my thoughts. But with the cruiser in orbit, they had no means of escape. They were trapped. And their withered expressions said they knew they were just waiting out the days until the fae came or their filters gave up.

My comms crackled, and a voice tripped into my ear. Just fragments of words. But I knew it. I stopped outside the rec room. "Kellee?"

"Kesh..."

Natalie whirled. "You hear him?"

I waved her question away and closed my eyes, listening hard. "Kellee, move around. I need you to find a better spot. I almost have you."

"Are you sure it's him you hear, little saru?"

I snapped my eyes open at the sound of Eledan's smooth, silky question and spun, looking for the Dreamweaver. He wasn't here. Of course he wasn't here. He couldn't be here.

"What?" Natalie asked, eyes widening as she caught my panicked expression.

"I..." Just Natalie and I stood in the corridor. Eledan was a hundred thousand miles away on a warcruiser. He wasn't here, playing games in an abandoned mine.

"Did you hear him or not?" Natalie huffed.

"Shh!" I snapped. "Just... just be quiet. Let me listen."

"I'm not so far away that I can't hear your heart fluttering, little bird."

No. This was not the time to fall into madness. He wasn't here, even if the touch of his words teased through my hair behind my ear. It wasn't real.

"Kellee? Please..." It had been lies before—the nights and nights we had talked—but I needed him to hear me now. I needed this to be real, not just for me, but for the hopeless people here.

"Kesh!" Kellee's voice boomed.

"Yes! I hear you. I hear you—"

"Get off Calicto!"

My eyes snapped open.

Eledan wrapped his arm around Natalie's neck. His long black hair swept forward, over his shoulder and her. He whispered sweet words into her ear, words that held her still and emptied out her mind. Her eyes lost focus. A lurid smile alighted on her lips. Eledan smothered her face with his other hand and yanked.

I heard the sickening crack and watched her collapse.

Not real, not real, not real.

Eledan stepped over her crumpled body.

No, there were hundreds of people here. He couldn't be real. They would have seen him.

"Hello, Wraithmaker." He lifted his gaze, looking through delicate eyelashes. "I neglected to thank you for the message you brought me." Liquescent green power rippled around his fingers. The power of illusion.

A shout sounded behind me, tugging on my awareness and bringing me back from the dream. The teenager who had helped earlier fell to her knees beside Natalie's body. "What happened?" Her fingers went to her neck, though it was clear from the unnatural angle of the body that Natalie was dead. "You..." She looked up. "Did you do this?" Her hand flew to her mouth.

She thought I'd killed Natalie? "No, no, I..." She couldn't see the prince because he was in my head.

Eledan arched an eyebrow and came closer. "Killing is all you're good for." I watched his lips form the words, lips that were quick to snarl, quick to whisper promises. "And you never did like that one. She was a touch too close to your marshal for your liking."

No, it was a lie.

Eledan's lips mimicked a sad frown. "Oh, I can almost hear those thoughts in your pretty head desperately trying to rationalize what you've done."

The woman was screaming. Others would come. If this wasn't real, then had I killed Natalie? I had killed Kellee's friend.

Eledan approached, so clearly fae, wrapped in fitted leathers. Leathers painted with his kill marks. The same marks tainted his skin. He was right there, just a few strides from me. So real. So close that the people should see him.

"You can't see him?" I asked, but my voice was too soft and the screams too loud.

Eledan circled around me. The air tightened with the scent of citrus. He threaded his fingers through my hair, brushing it back from my face. "When did you last inject yourself with the vakaru's clever nectus oil? It has been too long, no?"

I blinked up at Eledan. He couldn't know about that, unless none of this was real. And so, if none of this was real, it didn't matter what I did or said, or what happened next, because I was asleep somewhere, lost to the madness. *Please, let me be sleeping.*

Eledan's deft fingers plucked the comms from behind my ear. He studied the small device. "All those nights you spoke with me, revealing your weaknesses, your secrets. You begged him to stay with you, to keep you real. And all the while you were begging *me*. I know all your little secrets, Messenger." He leaned in, his gaze filling mine, pulling me down. "I know your desires. A little saru who only really wants to be loved. You poor creature. My kind can never love something like you, and you kill your own kind, so..." He dropped the comms and brushed his fingers across my mouth. "I knew if I created a disaster, plucked on the strings of human compassion, your marshal would bring you back to Calicto."

The rock fall had been his doing? So, this was real. All of this was real. And he was wrapped in illusion. "What do you want, *Dreamweaver*?"

He took my hand in his—the touch so gentle I could pretend it meant something—and pressed it to his chest. "Mother's gift was not enough."

His heartbeat drummed against my palm, and inside, tek ticked. Mab's magic hadn't cured him. He still had his human-made metal heart.

Shouts erupted around me, but all I could see was his terrible beauty, his piercing eyes, his razor-sharp smile. I saw it all, and I saw the truth behind it. The fae weren't beautiful. They were monsters. They might have raised me and I might have spent my entire life begging them to let me love them, but that life was over. That nothing girl was gone.

I stretched onto my tiptoes and brushed my lips against his. "I'll remove your heart, *Prince*."

With his hand on mine, our wrists pressed together, I felt the shape of the dagger hidden inside his bracer. His mouth brushed against mine, his breath cool on my tongue. I remembered his taste, his poison.

With my left hand, I snatched the blade free—the same dagger he had slashed across Kellee's neck—and thrust it forward. The blade punched into his chest. Magic burst, and his illusion collapsed. He roared and tore away, stumbling over Natalie's body and into the crowd of stunned onlookers.

"They see you now," I whispered.

Blood dribbled down his chest and dripped around him. I had missed his heart, but that didn't matter. I had never seen anything so satisfying. I wanted more.

Eledan's face twisted into a snarl. He snagged the gazes of the two people nearest him and barked, *"You. Humans. Stop her. Don't kill her."* He swayed and looked down, noticing the blood coating his hands.

The two onlookers—drenched in his magic—charged. I spun away from the first, sinking an elbow into his neck to drop him, and kicked the legs out from under the second.

"I see you now," I called to him. "I see you, and I will ruin you like I promised I would."

Shouts rolled in from behind me. More people were coming.

"Stay back!" I barked, hoping they listened. He would kill them.

Eledan straightened and pulled his top lip back in a snarl. "You're nothing, Messenger."

I eyed his chest and twisted the dagger in the air. Blood coated my hand and ran down my arm. "Come close and I will carve out your heart for you. Isn't that what you want?"

His gaze skipped behind me, and whatever he saw gave him pause. He didn't want me dead, and the situation was rapidly spiraling out of his control. This wasn't the place for us to dance. We both knew it.

He turned and ran.

"Don't," I warned those who started after him. They saw the blood on the dagger, saw the raw intensity on my face, and hung back. "You won't catch him." But I would.

Their faces turned to me. Anger and fear blazed in the eyes of the young and old. They weren't soldiers. Eledan would toss them aside the way his kind did with saru. But I wasn't just saru. I wasn't just a messenger. I had one more trick up my sleeve.

I breathed in, denying the itch of insanity its hold, and addressed them all. "There's a fae among you. The Dreamweaver." Gasps broke the quiet. "Stay together. If anyone starts acting out of character, restrain them. Nobody goes anywhere alone."

Fearful shouts rose up. "We have to run." "Can't fight him." "He'll kill us!"

He might. "No!" I barked. "Stay calm. Stay close. I will stop him." His blood, stark against the steel of the stolen dagger, sold my argument for me. I lifted it, let them get a good look at the dagger, at me. It was real, so damn real. And there would be more fae blood spilled. A river of it. "I'm your messenger, and I promise I will end all of this."

The crowd huddled closer, Natalie's body between

them and me. Beside her lay the discarded comms unit. I picked it up, ignoring the wary but hopeful glances flicking over me.

"Kesh, he's here!" Kellee said. "You need to get off Calicto—"

"No. I need to kill a prince, and you, Marshal, are going to help me."

CHAPTER 26

"That fae prick is somewhere in the mines. He won't stray far from the unmapped section where the well is." The marshal—bloody and racked with too many emotions for me to decipher—paced back and forth in a room that had once been a monitoring station. Some of the cameras still worked, relaying live images from the inhabited sections of the mine. Talen monitored the screens, his hood up to conceal his faeness, while Kellee seethed behind him.

It took a day to dig out Kellee and the rest of the survivors, during which time I walked all the tunnels and shafts, leaving no corner unexplored. I had found no traces of Eledan.

"I knew..." Kellee muttered. "I knew something was wrong. That section of mine should never have collapsed."

"It's done." I watched the screens, searching for anything suspicious among the displaced miners while keeping Kellee in the corner of my eye. "He wants me, and to get to me he'll use anything he thinks I care about." I didn't look up, but I sensed Kellee abruptly stop pacing.

"So, whatever you care about, we use it as bait," Kellee suggested, apparently volunteering. He just didn't know it.

Eledan had ensured, during the long nights of loneliness when he had pretended to soothe me to sleep, that I cared for the marshal. I despised how easily he had suckered me. The thought alone twisted my insides. But that didn't change the fact I did care for Kellee, even though I hardly knew him.

Talen looked my way, reading my expression without me having to say the words.

Kellee noticed our shared glances. "What is it?"

"Marshal Kellee." Talen turned the chair to face Kellee. "*You* are her weakness. He uses you against her. Why do you think it was your name she called out while we worked to bring her back from the madness?"

"I..." the marshal stammered. He looked at me, and then quickly darted his gaze away.

I leaned back against the monitoring consoles and folded my arms. "He went to a lot of effort to use you, or my knowledge of you, against me."

Kellee laughed, actually *laughed*. It was so unexpected I couldn't hide my surprise. "You know that wasn't real," Kellee scoffed.

My feelings were a joke now? "It was to me."

"Whatever it was or wasn't," Talen interrupted, "he will use you or Kesh's awareness of you to pull her back in. We need to set up the trap on our terms."

Kellee dropped into a chair and hunched forward, sinking his fingers into his hair. He stayed that way—shoulders locked—long enough for me to worry. His friend had died, and he hadn't once mentioned her. I'd seen him angry, seen him barely restrained, but this was different. He was hurting, and I couldn't help him. It was made worse by the fact I had watched Eledan kill Natalie and hadn't lifted a finger to stop him.

"He needs the tek removed." I sighed and rubbed at the ache building at my temples. "The fae won't accept him if they know he has human tek around his heart. That's why he's here and why he's desperate. He's the returning prince. He's supposed to be their hero. As Mab's son, he's in line for the crown, but the tek taints all that. He'll do anything to have me remove it. I've already shown him that I'm willing to kill myself to protect you... He will use you, Kellee."

Kellee lifted his head, dragging his hands down his face. His eyes were brighter, glassier, but he had packaged away the hurt. "All right. We trap him. How?"

"Iron. There's a ton of iron-based equipment just lying around. If there's a furnace somewhere or another heat source, I want two collars forged."

"Two?" Talen asked, likely wondering if the second was for him.

"It will nullify much of his magic, but he'll still be able to warp perception. He can't get inside my head and twist my own thoughts if I'm wearing a collar—he can't make me dream. If I'm going to face him again, I'll need that protection. The second collar is for him. He'll capture you, Kellee, thinking it was his idea. He'll tell me I have to give myself up for you and then demand I remove the tek."

Talen nodded. "How do we get Kellee away from him?"

"That's where you come in." I smiled at the fae, knowing the grin wasn't entirely friendly. "He doesn't know you're here. While I'm pretending to operate on him, you'll find and release Kellee."

"You're going to kill Eledan, right?" Kellee asked.

"Yes."

Kellee gave me a pointed look, not entirely believing me. He was right to be suspicious. I would kill Eledan. I'd made him a promise, and I was going to keep it.

"To get a collar on him," Talen added, "you'll have to get close."

"Getting close has never been a problem. And inside Arcon, we'll be surrounded by metal. He won't notice the iron until it's too late."

They fell silent, probably considering all the things that might go wrong.

"So, we're going to Arcon?" Talen asked.

Kellee sucked in a breath. "Arcon? Are you sure?"

He was really asking if I was ready, and I wasn't. I never would be. But the time was now. "It has to be Arcon. Natalie said—" Kellee flinched. "She said it was empty. I think he's there. It's familiar territory for him. I don't want him anywhere near the people here. With this *well* Crater found, he could have people dancing to his tune. They've been through enough. Arcon is far enough away to keep them safe."

"And the cruiser in orbit?" the marshal asked. "If it's his?"

"I don't think Eledan wants any of the fae knowing what's going on down here. Once we've dealt with him, we can figure out what to do about the cruiser." I held Kellee's weary gaze. "I'm going to get everyone off Calicto—for Natalie." *For you.*

He nodded tightly, tearing his gaze from mine. He couldn't know I had watched his friend die. But I knew, and the guilt was eroding my focus. I, at least, had an opportunity to honor her memory.

Kellee strode to the door.

"Kellee?" I started after him.

"I just need time—"

"Let him go," Talen said, turning back toward the screens.

He was already gone anyway. The door swung shut behind him with a final *clunk*.

I spent the next few hours studying maps of the mines and the nearest biodome, where Arcon's abandoned complex waited. Eledan would be inside, waiting for me.

Talen called me to the monitors, and we watched the downtrodden people of the once-shining Calicto say their farewells to Natalie. Kellee was with them.

"He knew her well," Talen remarked. In the screen's glow, his eyes shone a little brighter.

Did Talen care, I wondered. Did he care about any of this? Or was he just going through the motions because he had nowhere else to go?

"Kellee will attack Eledan," the fae said, leaning back in his chair. "The first chance he gets."

I folded my arms and stayed quiet. There was no need to reply. We both knew it was inevitable. "Eledan would expect nothing less from the last surviving vakaru." I dug into my pocket and handed Talen a comms. "That's why it's up to you to get Kellee out."

Talen took the little comms unit in his hand. He would have to wear it to communicate with Kellee after he was captured. The thought of wearing the device didn't sit well with him. He was tek-resistant, but it would still hurt him.

"He freed you," I said. "Now you get to repay the favor."

He lowered his hood and pressed the comms behind his pointed ear. "You care a great deal for Kellee."

"I do," I admitted, almost wishing I didn't. "I can't make the feelings go away just because they're based on a lie. What about you?" I leaned a hip against the console as the fae looked up at me questioningly. "You like him too."

"I've known him a long time. There's comfort in familiarity."

A fae far away from Faerie was hardly a fae at all. I saw some of Eledan's need to go home in Talen's cloud of loneliness. When all this was over, if we survived, I might ask him why he couldn't go back.

"I would like to give you more of my magic, but I fear he'll notice."

That hadn't gone so well last time. I squirmed at the thought of having his hand on me, pouring the delightfully maddening fae magic back into my veins. "I appreciate the offer, but I need to think clearly and you..." I circled my hand in the air between us. "You're distracting."

He stood, reminding me how damn tall he was now that he was suddenly very close, and touched my chin with two fingertips. "If I may?" he asked, his politeness startling.

For a terrifying heartbeat, I thought he meant to kiss me on the lips, and panic took a hold of my instincts, but in a blink, he planted a chaste kiss on my forehead and drew back, looking down into my eyes. "Don't die, Kesh Lasota. I've become quite fond of you."

Will he look at me like that when he knows the truth?

"I'll do my best." A smile found its way onto my lips. Only a small one, but it was real. And I could use all the *real* I could get.

～

I ENTERED A LONG, low-ceilinged space, stepping into sweltering heat. Molten metal hissed and bubbled in a cauldron-like vat. Of the four forges, only one was lit, spewing out orange flames.

Kellee stood with a man I assumed was the metalworker. He had his back to me, but I'd recognize the solid cut of his shoulders and short, messy ponytail anywhere. His friend saw me first, nodded my way, then left us alone.

The marshal had summoned me here, using the comms, and now that I had moved closer, I saw why. Two circles of metal lay on a table beside the forge. Each had a hinge and latch. They weren't the crude, heavy collars saru wore. The metalworker had added a gentle ripple allowing them to sit comfortably on the collarbone—or as comfortably as iron against skin would ever be.

Kellee killed the switch to the forge, and the fire spluttered out, plunging the room into a settling quiet. Equipment ticked as it cooled. I ran my fingers along the nearest circlet. Ignoring their purpose, they were almost beautiful.

"What do you think?" Kellee crossed his arms. "They're still heavy, but any less iron and his magic could seep through."

"They're perfect."

Pride shone in his eyes.

"You made them?" I asked.

"Right over there." He gestured at a row of anvils, one with a hammer resting on top. "The metal is stronger if forged and quenched, not poured. Eledan could break poured metal."

Looking at the marshal's late-twenties exterior, it was easy to forget how old he really was behind all that sass. These handmade forging techniques were an art, one rarely found in Halow, and it showed in the twin circlets.

"You really are full of surprises, Marshal."

He picked up a circlet and let it fall open. "May I?"

I lifted my chin. I had been collared as a child and again under Eledan, but this was different. I'd chosen this.

Kellee stepped closer and hesitated. Doubt crossed his face. His people had probably been collared long before the saru were conceived. He had similar memories to mine.

I touched his arm. "I trust you."

His gaze lifted from the circlet, and I knew from the pain in his eyes that he had worn collars and bore all the scars that came with them. The pieces of my heart ached for him.

I nodded and closed my eyes. Kellee's heated presence burned so close I could feel him. Cool iron kissed my neck and then, with a click, the collar was on. Fluttering my eyes open, I fell into Kellee's gaze.

"I've lost everyone," he whispered. His hand pushed into my hair, tilting my head back. "I can't lose you." His mouth sought mine, brushing painfully close, the promise of a kiss stoking desire. A tiny voice told me this was wrong, a mistake, but I shoved the doubts far away and pulled Kellee down, kissing him like I'd wanted to since I'd seen his out-of-place prettiness in the sinks. I was distantly aware that we'd shoved the table back, but I was even more aware of Kellee's hand diving around my waist and down my back so he could pull me into him. The press of his thigh against mine, my leg caught between his, and his growing hardness digging into my hip—I soaked up every touch, groaning a small, treacherous sound as I threw my head back and let his mouth burn down my jaw and my neck. I wanted more. I wanted all of him, wanted the attack, knowing he wouldn't be gentle.

Kellee's warm hands found my face and held me still.

"We finish this..." he growled, the beast sharpening the trick of hazel and greens in his eyes.

Nearby voices drifted through the sounds of our panting, making me aware that we were pushed up against a table in a public place. I lunged in and nipped at his mouth, darting my tongue in, teasing him quickly and delighting in the warning growl that trembled through his body.

He pushed away, swallowed and drew in a deep breath.

Running my tongue over my top teeth, I smiled crookedly as his gaze tracked the suggestion.

If the two miners hadn't wandered into the room, he might have taken me up on my offer to run my tongue over him. Instead, he chuckled and picked up the second circlet. Handing it out, he nodded. "Later."

A stab of guilt struck fast and deep. "Later." I forced a smile through the pain, knowing there likely wouldn't be a later, not for us, and took the second circlet.

CHAPTER 27

*K*ellee ventured into Arcon ahead of me. With instructions from me, Talen had already split off to seek a good vantage point among the abandoned buildings inside Arcon's shadow. The three of us were linked by comms. I sought out the same seat by the window in the eatery opposite Arcon's main entrance. The silence was thick. Nothing moved, no wind stirred the air, no crowds chattered. I didn't hear any of the typical metallic Calicto sounds. The place was a metal corpse and so very different from the bustling brightness of nine months ago.

I slept through the death of a world.

This silence awaited the rest of the human systems if the fae weren't stopped. I couldn't stop them all—just one.

I'd found a long coat in the mines, torn and covered in dust, but it had a few pockets I could use, and it concealed my new magnetic whip.

Now that I was alone, I wished I'd taken Talen's offer of magic, but it wouldn't be enough to stop Eledan and would only reveal the fact I had a fae at my disposal. It would have spooked Eledan, and I needed him to feel in control.

"I'm in and I've got company approaching," Kellee said through the comms.

"Understood." I touched the thin iron circlet clasped around my neck. As protection went, it was better than nothing. Eledan couldn't pull me into any dreams with him, but that didn't stop me from swallowing too much saliva as it pooled in my mouth or stop my heart from racing. I had to do this.

"Hello, Messenger." Eledan's sweet voice spilled from Kellee's comms and coiled around my confidence, chipping off the edges. I closed my eyes and listened to the pause, listened to the moment before it all began—and ended. There was no going back.

"I have something of yours," the fae prince said.

Kellee. He would be okay. The marshal knew what he was dealing with now. This wasn't like before. He would have been careful. Eledan was mine.

"Something you'll want back." There was laughter in the Dreamweaver's voice, laughter I had relished in. I shoved those memories away.

"What?" I whispered. "What gift do you have for me, Prince?"

The marshal was stubborn and brash, but he wouldn't risk this for blind revenge. He was too clever for that.

"K-Kesh?" a woman's voice stammered.

It took me a moment to unwrap the past few months and find the memory of that voice.

"Don't come, Kesh!" she screamed. "Don—"

A resounding crack cut her off.

No!

I shot to my feet, burst from the eatery and dashed

across the abandoned street and up Arcon's steps. "Hulia, hold on!"

Eledan's laughter filled my head, and when I shoved through Arcon's cracked doors, the liquid laughter rolled through the abandoned foyer and echoed far into the empty building.

CHAPTER 28

Tree roots as thick as my arm had grown along Arcon's glass corridors, sending spider-web cracks through the glass walls. I jogged the floors and climbed the stairwell, knowing exactly where he had her.

Was Kellee there too? I couldn't risk calling to the marshal, and I would find out soon enough anyway.

Sota's data held information on Hulia. After everything that had happened, I'd forgotten about Kesh Lasota's old friends, her old life, but Eledan hadn't.

I flung open the meeting room door and walked in, head up, shoulders back. The prince sat on his oak throne, only now the throne had speared its roots through the floors and walls. Atop his braided black hair, he had fashioned himself an oak crown. And Hulia lay sprawled on the long oak table, writhing. She clawed at her clothes, twisting off fabric strips in her fists. Her back arched, and her eyes rolled back.

"Stop it," I snapped.

Eledan leisurely rose from his throne. "But her mind is such a delightful place to be. She is *nama*, did you know?"

Hulia let out a pleasure-laden groan.

"Eledan, stop."

The corner of his mouth twitched. "Nama were one of our first creations. We made them out of the spirit of the wild meadows. Can't you tell?" He beamed at her, so pleased as she twisted and clawed at herself. "We made them sing for us. Won't you sing, dear Hulia?"

She screamed, so loud and so shrill, that I thought it might shatter my skull.

I lunged for Eledan. He whirled away, caught my wrist and yanked me hard against him. Bucking, I tried to unravel myself from his grip, but he clamped his arms around me tighter.

"We made them dance for us," he purred, then flung me away and turned on the spot, hips rocking to the music in his head.

"You're insane," I hissed. I had known, but I hadn't really seen it, not like this.

"Oh, they danced for years and years, until we grew bored, and so we made them pleasure us." He snatched Hulia from the edge of the table, hauling her into his arms, and kissed her like he had kissed me, like he'd been starved of what she was giving him. Hulia lifted her legs and hooked them around his waist, grinding against him. She fell back, letting him cradle her as he trailed his mouth and tongue down her neck to the rise of her breasts. Her eyes were clouded over with what looked like frost. And I knew she was dreaming—dreaming like I had. Had I behaved like that? Clawing at myself, drenched with madness and need? Somewhere in all the terrible memories, in all that fantasy he had poured into my head, I knew I had.

"I'll do it," I blurted. "Just let her go."

Eledan turned his head. Hulia clawed at his shoulder

and sank her hands into his hair. He pushed her off and regarded me with a new hunger. "You will?"

As though I had a choice. "Let her go, okay? Let her go, and I'll fix your heart, just like you wanted."

"Hmm..." He clicked his tongue. "If only it were that easy to trust the worthless word of a saru." Lifting his hand, he clicked his finger and thumb together. "Ah-ha! Sota, bring him in."

Kellee marched into the room, his hands held at shoulder height. Behind him, Sota hovered. The drone had his weapons drawn and sights locked on the back of Kellee's skull.

Oh, Sota... no.

Kellee...

Sota wouldn't miss.

The marshal's face remained firmly neutral, as though this was nothing more than an inconvenience. It was a good act, but one neither I nor Eledan bought.

"Well." Eledan clapped his hands together once. "Sota, if the marshal moves without a direct order from me, kill him." Eledan pointed at me. "If she harms me, kill Hulia and then kill him."

"Received," Sota's neutral voice confirmed.

I clenched my jaw. "Even without the tek, the fae won't ever take you back. You're an embarrassment. The tek exposure has twisted your mind."

"Mmm..." Eledan tore open his jacket, his movements jerky with frustration. He pulled his shirt over his head, revealing the pattern of marks running over his abs and up his chest. And there, just to the left, the ugly tek scar and its metal veins clawed at the fae's otherwise perfect body.

He sprang, too fast for me to counter, and pulled me by

295

the wrist to the table with him. I tried to yank free, only for his fingers to tighten around my arm.

"Come now, Messenger," he hissed through his bared teeth. "You won't risk your friends' lives, will you?"

I shoved against his chest, against him. "Let go."

The blow came out of nowhere. His hand struck my face so damn hard I didn't feel it until I'd hit the tabletop and almost dropped to my knees. Hulia's giggles sounded alongside the marshal's low growls.

Pain thumped through my head, blurring my vision.

And then his steely grip was on my arm again, yanking me upright. He shook me. "Come on, saru. Admit how much you want to touch me. Admit how you've desired my kind since that human body of yours aged enough to know what true desire means."

He peeled back my coat collar and wet his lips. Upon seeing the circlet, he raised an eyebrow, but said nothing. "Do not lie. I've seen your dreams. I've featured in so many of them. I do believe there was one where both I and the marshal featured prominently in various *positions*. You have a talent with that tongue, saru." He winked.

I looked away, face burning, and his cool hand settled against my stinging cheek, forcing me to look him in the eye.

"Sota," Eledan said, his eyes locked on mine. "Shoot the marshal in his left shoulder."

Sota's motors whirred. The drone fired. Kellee cried out. I heard him fall, heard him panting. He couldn't stop this. And Talen, if he was close, couldn't stop this either. Sota was too fast. He would kill everyone in this room in a single second if Eledan ordered it.

Eledan didn't even look to see if the marshal had fallen. He brushed a knuckle down my face, catching real tears.

"That's for dreaming of him. Now fix my fucking heart, saru."

He took his dagger back from where I'd hidden it inside the coat and handed it over, handle first. "Careful now. It's your friends' lives at risk."

Bracing both hands on either side of him against the table, he breathed in, presenting his chest, and waited for me to make the cuts. I mentally reached for Sota's link but found it dead. I couldn't communicate with Talen or Kellee without Eledan knowing, and even if I could, I could only tell them not to move, not to provoke Eledan. I hadn't counted on Sota being here.

I spread my left hand against Eledan's feverish skin and applied the dagger's tip to the first metal suture. It popped apart, wrenching a hiss from between Eledan's teeth.

The sound of Sota's whirring motors filled the room.

"Kesh!" Kellee warned.

I hesitated and pulled the blade back. "Change the drone's order."

Eledan glared down his nose at me.

"This will hurt, and you ordered Sota to kill Kellee if I hurt you."

A brilliant grin crawled across his lips. "Then don't hurt me, Kesh."

One maddening, terrifying thought climbed over all the others: to stab the dagger in and cut out his heart, no matter the cost. Hulia and Kellee would die, but so would Eledan. It would be over. And I'd be *finished*.

My hand trembled.

"Kesh...?" Eledan purred.

At one time, I would have made that trade, but I couldn't. Not even to kill a fae I despised with my every living, breathing moment. There were lives at stake.

"Close your eyes," I told him.

His brow furrowed.

"I can't hurt you, but with you watching me... I can't do it like that. Just close your eyes."

He had to trust me with his heart. And despite holding Kellee and Hulia against me, he still wasn't sure whether I would kill him. He was right to hesitate, but his need outweighed the risks. He had no choice. Warily, his eyelashes fluttered closed.

I pressed the blade to another suture with my right hand, but with my left, I eased the second iron circlet from inside my coat. This one hung open on its hinge. I pushed the blade in deeper with my right hand as I brought my left hand around, angling the open circlet toward Eledan's neck. When it closed, he would lash out. He might order Sota to kill Kellee. But Hulia would be free of his dreamweaving. I couldn't save them all. I didn't save people. I killed them. Kellee was fast and strong. He might be able to deflect Sota—somehow. This was the best I could do.

Kellee, I'm so sorry...

I snapped the circlet around Eledan's neck. It clicked, locking into place. He opened his eyes, fae colors blazing.

Hulia screamed. Her eyes were clear and filled with terror.

"Saru bitch! Drone, kill Kellee!" Eledan roared.

CHAPTER 29

For one terrible, breathtaking second, nothing happened. Just like when Crater's face had exploded in front of me, time funneled into a singular point, crystallizing the citrus scent of magic, Sota's whirring motors, and the color of blood streaking Eledan's chest. Then it snapped, unleashing chaos. Eledan brought his forearm up and shoved me back. Pure, blazing fury possessed him. He locked his hands around the circlet and fought to yank it free. His power flexed outward, drawing tight, about to snap.

Hulia reared up on the table, her murderous glare fixed on Eledan's back.

I tossed Eledan's dagger over the fae's head. Hulia snatched it out of the air and sprang, landing on Eledan's back. The blade punched into his shoulder, up to her knuckles, and they both screamed.

I whirled and saw the blur that was Kellee duck and twist as Sota's single red light brightened. The marshal thrust his claws through Sota's under armor, hooked into the drone, and slammed it into the floor, smashing Sota wide open. Sparks flew.

Eledan's magic breathed out, crushingly tight, and shattered. The oak roots that had entwined the room crumbled, in great clouds of brown dust. The iron circlet had broken the prince's link to his magic.

He screamed, but not in pain. His scream of rage sounded like twisting metal, and the saru in me whimpered away. I dashed for Kellee. He tried to wave me off, but I wasn't saving the marshal. I gripped his shoulder, sinking my fingers into the gunshot wound and smearing his blood across my hand, and then spun back toward Eledan.

I flicked my whip open—heart racing—and cracked the weapon in the air.

Eledan had Hulia by the hair. He bowed forward, pulling her over his head, and tossed her away like she was nothing. The whip cracked, drawing his eye. He reached for the circlet around his neck. The whip's tip sailed in and wrapped around his neck, trapping his hands there. A dangerous thrill buzzed through me, lighting me up. *I have you now.* I jerked him forward, reeling him in. *Mine.* He pulled, bucking and snapping against the whip's hold, but the magnetic links tightened, choking off his air.

His eyes blazed, his teeth bare, but I had him.

Eledan dropped to his knees.

All those dreams, all those fantasies he had forced on me, twisted me up inside. This was the one he had never let me live, but I was living it now. I stepped in close like he had done to me so many times and reached my left hand around his trembling shoulder. He bucked and snapped his teeth at my neck, until I pulled the dagger free from where Hulia had left it. His gasp scattered twisted ripples of pleasure through me. *Wraithmaker*. They'd crafted me to kill for them. I was *made* for this. And as I looked down into his eyes, I realized nothing had ever felt as right as this single moment. I would kill for them. I had killed their queen, and now I would kill her son.

I pulled the tip of the dagger down his face and watched his sweet blood well in its wake. Flicking the blade off his chin, I brought the bloody dagger to my lips. I had vowed to taste fae blood again. His tasted like victory and revenge.

I set the tip against his shoulder and swept it down his chest in lazy *s* patterns. He tried to twist free, but the whip tightened. The resulting strained gasps delighted my ears.

"I promised I would carve out your heart."

His mouth moved, but the prince with the pretty words couldn't speak.

"I promised I would ruin you."

He tugged again, but his efforts were weak, trapped inside my whip's coils.

I stopped the point of the dagger above his heart where the scar ran. I wanted this. I wanted it so much I wondered if this too was insanity. If it was, I welcomed it.

"Can't..." he wheezed.

I eased the dagger into the scar tissue, slowly, reopening the old wound one careful millimeter at a time. "Can't I?"

"People..."

I ignored him and watched the blade peel back his skin. Tek gleamed beneath. Beautiful, functional, elegant tek encased his black fae heart. A cage like the one he had trapped me in. A cage like the one he had buried my mind in.

Kellee called my name. I pushed the sound away.

The dagger cut away his flesh, painting streams of blood down his chest. I flicked my gaze to his eyes and found them wide with fear. He hadn't believed I would hurt him. I had told Sota my secrets, secrets he had stolen. He had listened as I'd told the drone how I loved the fae, how I would do anything for them if they would take me back. And he had believed it.

His black heart thudded inside its metal cage. So small a thing. So fragile now that it was exposed.

I wiped the flat side of the blade across his gasping mouth and leaned in so close. "Did you truly believe my human lies, Dreamweaver?"

Tremors spilled through him.

"Did you believe your mother sent me to save her forgotten son, or was that the hope of an insane mind clawing at its own dreams?"

Confusion clouded his face. He tried to shake his head, shake the understanding away, but the truth had him. *I* had him.

"I am a messenger, Prince. But not for Mab."

Oh, what a beautiful thing it was to see his reality come crashing down around him. To see the blinding truth —the truth with its hand around his heart. I licked his blood from his lip. "You were right about one thing. The chances of us finding each other were impossible. I came to Calicto *for you*. I waited for you to make a mistake and reveal your whereabouts. And then I did what I was sent to do." I paused, making sure he was looking only at me and listening only to my words. "Oberon sends his regards. He told me to tell you, *You're in my way, brother.*"

"*You're... his?*" Eledan rasped.

"Goodbye, Dreamweaver. And thank you for making this message feel so damn good." I thrust the blade in, cutting around the cage, cutting into spurting arteries and veins, jerking the blade's edge through the wires and metal structure. Eledan's back arched, and his head jolted back. I dropped the whip and smeared Kellee's blood across the prince's poisonous mouth. His trembling turned into vicious convulsions.

I let go and watched him fall.

At my feet lay an empty shell—the carcass of the prince who had toyed with my mind, and in my hand his heart beat, safe inside its tek-built cage.

I looked up, blinking through cold, empty tears. Kellee stood to my right. The fear in his eyes betrayed him. He had heard it all. Every. Single. Word. I was Oberon's assassin. I had lied to him, lied to everyone, lied to myself. I had lived the nothing life of Kesh Lasota to keep the truth safe. And now, my work was done.

I stepped back from the prince's body.

Eledan's caged heart thudded, nestled and warm in my hand.

I tapped my comms. "Talen?"

"Kesh, are you all right?" Relief sent his words in a rush. I had told him to wait, no matter what happened. Wait until he heard from me. Would he still want to serve me knowing what Kellee knew? Would he still look at me like he had, as though he cared what happened to a saru?

"Hail the fae ship," I ordered, my voice like stone. My *real* voice.

Silence. I felt the heat of Kellee's stare scorching my skin.

"Do it," I told Talen.

"I don't understand."

"Use the magic stored in this building and mentally hail the fae vessel in orbit. Tell them I have their prince, and if they want him alive and *intact*, they must let the surviving population of Calicto escape." I could do this one thing and save Natalie's people.

"Kellee?" Talen asked, deferring to the marshal. He didn't trust my words. I couldn't blame him.

I looked up. Kellee's claws glinted. He had heard Talen through my comms. When he replied, he revealed long, dagger-sharp fangs. "Do as she says, Talen."

It was the only way to save the people. He knew it. He didn't like it, but he knew it had to be done.

"You're handing him over to them?" Kellee asked me, the beast inside him so close to the surface that perspiration beaded on his face.

I lifted my chin and looked the marshal in the eye. "My orders were to kill him. I wanted nothing more than to crush his heart. But I'm going against Oberon's wishes to save your people. When the fae arrive, as far as anyone is concerned, I am Kesh Lasota, the messenger saru who Eledan manipulated to retrieve his mother's magic. Do you understand, Kellee? They cannot know who I'm working for."

Disgust twisted Kellee's mouth downward. "Was it all Oberon's doing? He planned all of this?"

"You already know the answer."

He shook his head and backed up. "I thought I knew you." He flinched, all the memories hurting him. "I saved you from him. I helped you recover. I thought—"

"And I am grateful. Believe me or don't, but I do care for you."

"Believe you? I don't know who you are!"

I did care for him. Everything Eledan had done to me —the imprisonment, the dreams—wasn't a lie. Kellee and Talen deserved more. But I couldn't give it to them. But the people—I could save the people, just like Kellee had hoped I would.

I approached Kellee and held out the prince's caged heart. The marshal snarled at it, at me. "Take this and take shelter somewhere nearby. When I contact you, you will return it to me and I will make the trade."

"The marks..." He blinked, refocusing on me, seeing the truth standing in front of him. "They would never give a saru the fae marks that you wear. I should kill you. You're one of them."

It hurt to see the hatred in his eyes, hurt to have the words thrown at me. I was saru, I was human, I had been raised to kill or be killed. I was the Wraithmaker. Oberon had given me the marks for my services. Gifts from the fae prince who had grown tired of waiting to rule. But now was not the time to explain. "Kellee, I'm saving the people here. Help me."

A thunderous trembling shook Arcon's windows, and outside, a fae shuttle began its descent, sparking a plume of color through Calicto's atmosphere.

"I don't know what's real around you," he mumbled, face crumbling.

"Lies are all the weapons a human has in Faerie."

Fresh resolve shut down his expressions, banishing all emotion from his face. "And you wear them well, Messenger." He snatched the caged heart and dumped it into his pocket. "This isn't over."

I should kill him. He knew too much. He didn't mean a damn thing to me.

So then why did it hurt so much to see him turn his back on me and walk from the room? I wanted to call after him, to tell him everything we had shared, everything he had done for me mattered, tell him I wanted to be with him and Talen, but I never could be because none of this was my life. Kesh Lasota might as well have been a dream too. I belonged to Oberon.

"Kesh?" Hulia, trembling and dazed, staggered closer. "What just happened?"

I nodded after Kellee. "Follow him. He's a good man. He'll help you."

"I..." She scooted around Eledan's cold body and looked at me. "Thank you."

I would have liked to have her as a friend. "Go."

Alone with the cooling body of the prince, I moved to the windows and watched the fae shuttle land outside the dome, kicking up great clouds of dust.

I had done everything Oberon had asked of me. I would earn another mark from my beloved prince.

So why did I feel as though I wanted to tear out my heart to stop it from hurting? I had done nothing wrong. Eledan was dead—as Oberon wanted. After the exchange —a prince's heart for the humans of Calicto—the fae would try to put Eledan back together again. They may even succeed, only to find him utterly mad. And he would be forsaken—ruined—just as he had feared. I'd gotten my revenge and more. I was saving people. That was a good thing. Oberon had always planned to return to Halow and claim the system for Faerie. I'd merely been one weapon in his arsenal of manipulations. I was his blade, but I had another edge. I *had* saved people here.

A sound behind me. The fae were here. I turned and found fierce violet eyes staring into my soul.

"You left us no choice."

A sudden sting burned through my arm, and Talen's words followed me down and down and down into darkness.

I did not dream.

CHAPTER 30

I woke surrounded by glass and steel. My heart and my thoughts jolted to a halt. But neither of the two figures standing outside the cage were Eledan, and this was not Arcon's shimmery offices. Beyond the glass, floodlights illuminated a familiar rock-lined prison chamber.

The star pinned to the marshal's coat shone under the prison's lighting. It was the brightest point on him. The rest of him was shrouded in disgust. Hate. Disappointment. He probably felt all those things. I remembered the pain in his eyes when he told me he had lost everything, how he had said he couldn't lose me too. He was hurting, but he hid it beneath the hatred my betrayal had summoned.

Talen's silver hair was gathered in one thick braid and slung over his shoulder. He just looked disappointed and sad. I wasn't sure which one hurt the most to look at.

I closed my eyes. This could have ended so very differently. They were alive. That was a good thing. And so were many others—hopefully. "Did you make the exchange?"

"Yes," Kellee answered. "The fae escorted the Calicto refugees off the planet and shuttled them to various outposts. Your people kept their word."

The fae, *my* people.

The Calicto refugees would have died on that planet, one way or another. It would have been better if I had made the trade personally. Oberon would have forgiven me. Now? Now he would come looking...

Opening my eyes, I saw them still standing there, watching, judging, wondering if they had known me at all. "And Eledan?" I asked.

"The fae have him," Talen replied. "They're reporting he's alive and well."

Alive, maybe, but he wasn't well. If it wasn't for the people on Calicto, I would have carved out his heart and crushed it—magic and all. I still wanted to. I craved the taste of the mad prince's blood. But what I wanted didn't matter. It never had. I served a different prince. I would get my reward—once these two let me go.

"More fae are arriving daily. They're setting up Calicto as a base," Talen continued. "Using the magic Eledan found as proof Halow is theirs by divine right."

Eledan had wanted to keep that well for himself, which was probably why he had returned to Arcon after the invasion. Without his tek heart, he would have been unstoppable. Oberon had been wise to eliminate his brother by way of his mother's magic.

I swung my legs off the bed and rested my elbows on my knees, bowing my head. A book sat neatly beside the bed. The one with the black-winged bird on the cover. Talen's gift.

I didn't deserve it.

I got to my feet. My coat and whip were gone. All I

wore were my sweatpants and a tank top. The fae marks wrapped around my arms took on a new weight now that Talen and Kellee knew why I had so many.

I approached the glass. It was ironic how I looked out on Talen when, not so long ago, I had been the one looking in. Did he think it ironic too, or was it justice? I pressed my hand to the glass in front of him. He blinked but didn't smile, didn't do anything. Just *looked,* masking everything from his face. Kellee would have told him everything. The two of them were inseparable. But Talen knew what it was like. He would understand. He would have had saru in his household. He knew how I had lived, how I would do anything to survive, how I owed Oberon my life. My prince was my world. Had Talen always known I was made of lies?

His violet fae eyes searched my face, perhaps for hope. I almost wished I could give it to him.

"Thank you for the book," I said.

Talen nodded. Kellee growled and turned away. The marshal was easier to read.

"This is a mistake," I told them. Oberon would kill them for this. They should have left me on Calicto. They could have crafted lives somewhere. Now? "When I was a nobody, my mission was incomplete—"

"You were never a nobody," Kellee said. "That was a lie."

I hesitated. I'd lied, yes. But I had it in me to do much worse. "Eledan will tell his brother everything. He won't have a choice. This rock won't keep you safe."

"You used us." That was from Talen. It hurt all the more because he was so right. I couldn't deny it.

"Yes. I used you both as a means to an end."

He briefly looked away. "Was any of it real?"

I could tell them my feelings for them were real, that I knew I wouldn't be alive without them, that I owed them more than they could know and it pained me inside to hear the distrust in their voices and see the disgust on their faces. But what good would it do? Oberon would come, and soon, I would be my prince's shadow once more.

If Oberon knew about Talen and Kellee, he would order me to kill them. I couldn't. I couldn't choose between my prince and my friends. "No," I lied. "None of it was real. I do not care for you. I used you both. You mean nothing to me."

Talen made a low noise in the back of his throat and turned away from my cage. I bit my tongue, refusing to allow myself the luxury of telling them the truth.

Kellee dropped onto one of the couches and spread an arm across the back. His smirk held none of the warmth I had found in his smiles before. "Your prince will come for you, and we'll be waiting when he does."

He would get himself and Talen killed.

I curled my hand into a fist and thumped it against the glass. "You can't stop him. You can't stop *them*. They're here, and there is no going back. Kellee, you more than anyone know what they're capable of. Leave here—"

"You want me to run?" He chuckled. "I never run from a fight."

"And all your people are dead."

He sneered, revealing lengthening fangs. "We can stop them. Me, Talen, and you—Kesh Lasota. We *will* stop them. Because, despite all the lies, all the illusions and misdirection, you saved those people on Calicto. And you want to save more. But up until now, you couldn't. You've always been in a cage, always been someone's slave, but now you have a choice."

I opened my arms and stepped back from the glass. Nothing had changed. I was still in a cage or was it a gold-fish bowl and I was supposed to be Kellee's precious little fish.

"You can get close to them. You know how they work, how they think, and you're in the confidence of their new king. A king who only rose to power because *you* killed the queen."

"I loved the queen." At least, I believed I had, but sometimes even I fell for my own karushit lies. Kesh's life, I'd fallen for that one. Fallen for the people the pretend messenger held dear. Hulia, Merry, and others throughout the years.

"Your love is a lie," Talen said, his back to me as he crouched beside his cot and rifled through his books. "You don't know real love."

Kellee arched an eyebrow as if to say, *"Even the fae agrees you're a cold-hearted bitch."*

"You have a choice, Kesh Lasota," Kellee said, leaning forward. "You don't have to kill for them. You can save people with us. You are in a powerful position, and for the first time in your life, you can use that power against the fae. You've already killed a queen. What's a dead king to you?"

His heroic ideas were pretty, his hope blinding and so typical of the marshal's view of the worlds. "I don't save people, Kellee."

"Liar," he drawled.

What he was asking was impossible. All my life I had killed for the fae. Without them, I wasn't sure who or what I was.

"Lie to them as you did to us," Kellee continued, sensing my hesitation. "And they'll never see the blow coming."

I glared hard back at the vakaru and the honorable ideals shining in his green eyes. I had known a boy like him, a proud boy, a boy filled with defiance and heroism. Aeon had begged me to help him, and together he and I had plotted against our fae masters. He had trusted me, and when it mattered most, I had turned on him and killed my fellow saru to the sounds of a cheering crowd, earning my first marks in service to the crown. Deceit was all I knew and I was good at it. Did I have it in me to wield deceit against the crown instead of for it?

"And if you don't..." Kellee lifted a syringe, the liquid sloshing inside. "Eledan will be waiting in your dreams."

I slammed a palm against the glass, rattling my cage. "You would use his abuse against me?"

"Let's get one thing clear, Messenger." His eyes were cold, hard, and honest. "I cared for you. I believed in you. And you shattered my trust."

"That's your mistake!"

He waited, letting my words ring throughout the cavern. "And I can't afford to make that mistake again. I have no idea who you are, and until I do, I'll trust you as much as I would any enemy." His beast shadowed him, darkening his eyes and sharpening all his teeth to points. Here, now, he was the predator, the last of his species and I was his prey. "Do we have a deal, Wraithmaker?"

Kellee's cage or Faerie's?

I glanced at Talen and found him lying on his side in his bed, flicking through a book as though this were just a minor discussion. His eyes flicked up, and a fierce resolve burned there.

When I faced Kellee, I shrugged and backed away from the glass. He would use me like I had used him. That was fair.

"We have a deal, Marshal," I lied. As soon as I got free of the cage, I would return to my prince—my *king*—and in doing so, I would keep both Kellee and Talen safe. Because Kellee was right. I *could* save lives. Theirs.

～

Kesh's, Talen's & Kellee's journey continues in Messenger #2, coming July 2018.
Sign up to Pippa DaCosta's mailing list here for all the news, cover reveals and exclusive free ebooks.

～

Did you enjoy Shoot the Messenger? Please leave a review. Every review helps. Just a few words will do.
Thank you.

Edge of Forever (#6)

∽

The 1000 Revolution

#1: Betrayal

#2: Escape

#3: Trapped

#4: Trust

∽

New Adult Urban Fantasy

City Of Fae, London Fae #1

City of Shadows, London Fae #2

Made in the USA
Lexington, KY
05 December 2018